P9-DEK-520

THE WORLD'S CLASSICS

A RUSSIAN GENTLEMAN

SERGEI TIMOFEEVICH AKSAKOV was born in 1791 and brought up in the eastern Russian steppes, on family property inherited from his pioneering grandfather. Educated at the University of Kazan, he worked briefly as a civil-service translator in St Petersburg, but thereafter lived mainly in or near Moscow with his wife and sons Konstantin and Ivan (both to become writers well known for their espousal of the Slavophil cause). During these years Aksakov, who had a private income, was absorbed in various literary and theatrical enterprises, though for seven years he also held the office of press censor. He took up writing seriously late in life, under the influence of Gogol. In 1846 there appeared the first instalment of his *Family Chronicle*, known in English as 'A Russian Gentleman'. It was at once acclaimed as a masterpiece, and when published in volume form ten years later was accompanied by *Recollections* ('A Russian Schoolboy'). *The Childhood of the Bagrov Grandson* ('Years of Childhood') followed in 1858. While working on these partly fictionalized accounts of family history, Aksakov also wrote descriptive sketches of fishing and shooting, his favourite country pursuits, and his fine *Recollections of Gogol*. In an age of great writers, by his death in 1859 he was widely acknowledged as a master of Russian prose.

J. D. DUFF (1860–1940) was a classical Fellow of Trinity College, Cambridge, and is best known for his edition of Juvenal. His translations from Russian include, besides Aksakov's trilogy, Parts I and II of Herzen's *My Past and Thoughts* (*Childhood, Youth and Exile*, The World's Classics, 1981).

EDWARD CRANKSHAW, writer and journalist, has published many books on Russian subjects, of which the latest are *Tolstoy: the Making of a Novelist* and *The Shadow of the Winter Palace*, a study of Russia's drift to revolution.

THE WORLD'S CLASSICS

———

SERGEI AKSAKOV

A Russian Gentleman

———

Translated by
J. D. DUFF

With an introduction by
EDWARD CRANKSHAW

Oxford   New York
OXFORD UNIVERSITY PRESS
1982

Oxford University Press, Walton Street, Oxford OX2 6DP

London Glasgow New York Toronto
Delhi Bombay Calcutta Madras Karachi
Kuala Lumpur Singapore Hong Kong Tokyo
Nairobi Dar es Salaam Cape Town
Melbourne Auckland
and associates in
Beirut Berlin Ibadan Mexico City Nicosia

Introduction © Edward Crankshaw 1982

First published under the title Semeinaya khronika
(A Family Chronicle) 1846
This translation first published 1916
Reissued as a World's Classic paperback 1982

All rights reserved. No part of this publication may be reproduced,
stored in a retrieval system, or transmitted, in any form or by any means,
electronic, mechanical, photocopying, recording, or otherwise, without
the prior permission of Oxford University Press

This book is sold subject to the condition that it shall not, by way
of trade or otherwise, be lent, re-sold, hired out or otherwise circulated
without the publisher's prior consent in any form of binding or cover
other than that in which it is published and without a similar condition
including this condition being imposed on the subsequent purchaser

British Library Cataloguing in Publication Data

Aksakov, Sergei
A Russian gentleman.—(The World's classics)
1. Aksakov family
I. Title   II. Semeinaia khronika. English
947'.009'92   DK37.8.A3
ISBN 0-19-281573-3

Library of Congress Cataloging in Publication Data

Aksakov, S. T. (Sergei Timofeevich), 1791–1859.
A Russian gentleman. (The World's classics)
Translation of: Semeinaia khronika.
1. Aksakov, S. T. (Sergei Timofeevich), 1791–1859—Biography—Ancestry.
I. Duff, J. D. (James Duff), 1860–1940. II. Title.
PG3321.A5Z53513 1982   891.73'3   81–22327
ISBN 0-19-281573-3 (pbk.)   AACR2

Set by Western Printing Services Ltd
Printed in Great Britain by
Hazell Watson & Viney Limited
Aylesbury, Bucks

CONTENTS

CONTENTS

INTRODUCTION

SERGEI AKSAKOV was born in 1791 at Ufa, almost on the edge of European Russia, some seven hundred miles east of Moscow. His father was then an official of the provincial law-courts, but when the boy was five years old his grandfather died and his father gave up his government post and took over the running of the family property at Aksakovo deep in the district of Orenburg.

Stepan Mikhailovich Aksakov, the grandfather, the Russian Gentleman of the title of this volume, was indeed one of nature's gentlemen, a backwoods squire in the age of Catherine the Great, rough-hewn, majestical, who had sold his inherited lands in the neighbourhood of Simbirsk (the middle-Volga town into which both Lenin and Kerensky were to be born a hundred years later) and moved his family and his household, his flocks and herds and dead-stock, his serfs, everything he possessed, two hundred miles further east into the greater freedom of a still largely unsettled land of nomadic tribesmen—Bashkirs, Chuvashes, Mordvinians—where he had purchased twelve thousand almost virgin acres, an uncorrupted earthly paradise. There he set his peasants to work building huts for themselves, a fairly primitive manor-house for the master, a mill, barns, stables, byres, the beginnings of a church—all that was required for an almost wholly self-enclosed patriarchal existence.

It was to this remote and isolated community that the son brought his young wife and two children when the old man died. Nothing could have been more different from the life she had been used to. The daughter of a senior official in the provincial government, she had taken over the running of her father's house at Ufa when he was incapacitated by illness and turned it into a centre for the rudimentary cultural life of that remote outpost of Russian civilization. High-spirited, emotional, intelligent, in many ways sensible, she was yet unable to reconcile herself to the bucolic existence to which she was now called after six years of marriage. Strong and clamorous where her young husband was easy-going and undemanding, adored by her son and devouringly possessive of him, she was so un-comprehending of the quiet rhythm of country life that she made no attempt to enter into the small boy's passionate delight in the animals and birds, the sights and sounds and smells of that unspoilt countryside, the fishing and the shooting and the growing of crops in which her husband also found contentment. It was a wonderful land, teeming with game and with fish, its rivers so pure that if you threw a coin into a fifteen-foot-deep pool you would see it shining on the bottom until the winter ice came to cover it and the spring floods swept it away. Sofya Nikolaevna stood impatiently outside this world.

The small boy was allowed to enjoy it until he was nine years old, and then came desolation. He was sent off to boarding school in Kazan, an arduous two hundred and fifty miles from home, by a mother agonizing between her desire to shield a child of delicate health and unusual sensitiveness from the bruising of the world, and her fixed resolve to save that child from what in her eyes was the worst imaginable fate, an uncultivated existence among rural philistines. The child was more than desolated. He was made ill by homesickness, and after some months his mother fetched him home for one more year of happiness. Then another sortie into the brutal world. This time it worked. Sergei was well looked after, found comfort in his mentors, made friends, developed new and unexpected interests.

In 1804 the school at Kazan was converted by imperial decree into a university—that same university which the young Count Leo Tolstoy was to attend some forty years later, and later still describe in the third volume of *Childhood, Boyhood and Youth*. Sergei Aksakov stayed on to get a degree of sorts, but he seems to have spent most of his time either collecting butterflies or organizing amateur theatricals, stimulated and inspired by a visiting star from Moscow. He was a great one for sudden crazes, which, for a time, would drive everything else out of his head.

Here, then, is the background and most of the subject-matter of Aksakov's composite masterpiece: the story of his memorable grandfather, of a gallery of relations and acquaintances, of his parents' courtship and marriage, followed by memories first of his own infancy, then of his days at school and university. Some thirty years were to pass between his going out into the world and his sitting down to compose this narrative. And in those thirty years there was nothing to suggest the development, the maturing, of a great writer. When the first instalment of *A Family Chronicle* appeared in 1846 in the pages of a Moscow miscellany it was not so much a case of Minerva springing fully armed as of the sloughing of a skin, the emergence of a radiant and perfectly formed imago from the dusty chrysalis. Aksakov was then fifty-six.

What had he been doing with his life? Coming down from Kazan University, he went to St Petersburg and obtained a post as a translator in a government office. This did not last long and for some years he lived on his private income, chiefly in Moscow (very recently recovered from the French occupation), but sometimes in the country. Most of his friends were actors and he himself had aspirations as a dramatist. He did a good deal of translating work—Molière, Boileau—while concocting undistinguished comedies of his own, heavily influenced by French models. At twenty-four he married, but it was not until twelve years later that he decided it was time to find regular employment to supplement his income. He became, of all things, a press-censor under the then Minister of Education, Admiral A. S. Shishkov. Shishkov was one of the most distinguished figures in the land. During the 1812 campaign he had been high among the Tsar's advisers. He also nourished a passion for the Russian language and Russian manners in their antique purity, untainted by foreign importations. He had taken to the young dilettante from Aksakovo, nearly forty years his junior, when they had met long before.

On the face of it, one would have seen Aksakov in his forties as an extremely likeable and intelligent but otherwise unremarkable figure, a minor civil servant with a modest estate to fall back upon, a devoted wife, two clever sons, some very good friends and an amiable but rather hopeless ambition to become a famous writer. It is a common enough ambition, and as a rule it comes harmlessly to nothing. But in Sergei Aksakov there was an unsuspected genius which suddenly, in his fiftieth year, caught fire. In 1840 he began to write seriously; in 1846 came the first published instalment of what was to be his masterpiece. It won instant recognition; and now, while he still worked away at his family chronicle, he brought out two volumes of sketches, one about shooting, the other about fishing (his deepest love); these were widely praised, by Turgenev and Gogol above all— Gogol wrote: 'Your birds and fishes are more real than my men and women.' It was not until 1856 that *A Family Chronicle* at last came out in book form. Aksakov was by now acclaimed as the greatest living Russian writer. He was sixty-five. Turgenev, whose *A Sportsman's Sketches* had appeared in book form four years earlier, was thirty-nine. Tolstoy, who had published *Childhood* in Nekrasov's *The Contemporary (Sovremennik)*, also in 1852, and *Boyhood* in 1854, was twenty-eight.

The accepted story is that Aksakov discovered his genius under the impact of the much younger and extravagantly different Nikolai Gogol. In 1831 Gogol, at twenty-two, had published his first book, a volume of sketches called *Evenings on a Farm near Dikanka*. These sketches were mostly fantasies or legendary tales full of Gogolesque twists and gestures, offering an early preview of the creator of *Dead Souls*. But what caught at Aksakov's imagination was Gogol's simple and matter-of-fact treatment of everyday aspects of rural life—the sort of naturalism implicit in his title: here was the real Russia (in fact Gogol was writing about the Ukrainian countryside of his own youth) speaking in native accents about unconsidered simplicities, almost miraculously free from foreign manners, attitudes, ideas.

The first meeting of the two men was not auspicious: Aksakov did not take to Gogol. But soon he fell under the younger man's spell, making him free of his household, praising his work to the skies, treating him like a prince—an ungrateful prince—until the inevitable disillusionment. But to say that his eyes were suddenly opened by Gogol is to over-simplify. What almost certainly happened was that Gogol acted as a catalyst and at the same time encouraged him to follow his true, his unsuspected bent. The great discovery was the subject-matter, the way to resolve an unconscious conflict between the impulse to imitate Western modes of expression without a true understanding of these modes and the need to find a way of spelling out the peculiarly Russian appreciation of a reality for ever unfolding and unaccented, except by sudden elemental upheavals, like an eternal river.

A Russian Gentleman is a classic example of that essentially Russian *genre*, a factual record faintly disguised as fiction, or a fiction so actual, so apparently inconsequent and uncontrived, that it reads like fact. The first master of this style however, was not Gogol but Pushkin, with his wonderfully matter-of-fact treatment of everyday affairs just as they come, without heroics and with perfect simplicity and transparency of expression. Pushkin died in 1837, misunderstood and unappreciated by Shishkov and his circle, including Aksakov himself: misled by the outward circumstances of the great poet's somewhat rackety life, they saw only the 'cosmopolitan', the Byronic Pushkin. So that Aksakov was in fact carrying on and developing an important part of the Pushkin tradition without being aware of what he was doing, or, indeed, of Pushkin's genius. Gogol, on the other hand, was very much aware. When *The Captain's Daughter*, that marvellous tale of the Pugachev rebellion, appeared in 1836, Gogol wrote as follows:

Compared with *The Captain's Daughter* all our other novels and short stories are like watery gruel. Purity and restraint soar to such heights in it that reality itself seems artificial, a caricature. For the first time we have truly Russian characters: a simple officer commanding a fort, his wife, a sergeant, the fort itself with one solitary cannon, the centurion of the times, the modest grandeur of ordinary men and women. Not only is it reality; it is even better.

Those words—varied only to fit the subject—are perfectly suited to Aksakov's *A Russian Gentleman*. In the later volumes of his family chronicle—*Years of Childhood* and *A Russian Schoolboy*, he applies his artistry and his gift of total recall to a meticulous rendering of his own early years, thus offering the first flowering of that long series of personal memoirs which have become so strong a feature of Russian literature—those of Aksakov, Turgenev, Tolstoy, Korolenko, Gorky, in our own time Paustovsky. In *A Russian Gentleman*, however, Aksakov is moving far outside his own personal experience. He recreates the characters not only of his grandfather (who died when he was five years old), but also of his magnificent great aunt and her wicked husband (whom he did not know even as a child), his grandmother and his father's sisters, to say nothing of his father and his mother themselves at the time of their courtship and in their early married days. All this complicated and emotion-laden family life is recreated with the quiet brilliance of a master novelist and the immediacy of a diarist of genius.

The scene is Catherine's Russia. Grandfather Stepan Mikhailovich rules benevolently but with absolute authority over his own family and all the souls in his employ, for all practical purposes the delegate and viceroy of the great Empress in St. Petersburg, so many days' journey away. In the 1770s he had weathered the storm of the Pugachev rebellion, when the ravaging hordes of Cossacks and rebellious serfs had driven him from his home. But by the time this narrative opens peace has descended on the land and Stepan Mikhailovich has settled down to enjoy in relative tranquillity the last years of a mellowing autocrat, a larger-than-life figure with something of the stature, moral and physical, of an Old Testament patriarch, stern and terrible in his rage, but generous and just at heart.

At first there is only one person he is prepared to respect and treat as an equal, and that is his cousin, the very remarkable Praskovya Ivanovna Kurolesov, who married a fortune-hunting rogue (the perfect model of the most unpleasant kind of Russian landowner), put up with a great deal, but at last broke away with dignity and force, achieving an independence in which she developed unsuspected powers. The interweaving of the story of Stepan Mikhailovich and Praskovya Ivanovna and her appalling husband is quite brilliantly handled to display in intimate detail the good and evil of the serf system. Between the two households we are given as faithful and vivid a picture of rural Russia in the time of Catherine as it is possible to imagine.

And into this complex is injected a new element: the wooing

of Sofya Nikolaevna Zubin by the old man's son, the author's father—the resistance of this strong and spirited character to what seems to her the spinelessness of young Aksakov, whom she nevertheless loves; her introduction to the Aksakovo household and the 'ugly sister' plotting and provocations of her fiancé's family; her winning of the old man's respect and love.

All this occurred before the author was born, so that the entire narrative is based on hearsay—on what his parents, his mother in particular, have told him of their early life—on a childish memory of his grandfather and on his later observation of the characters of his parents, aunts, schoolmasters, servants, peasants, friends. It is a miracle of verisimilitude. It is impossible to tell where hearsay is supplemented by direct observation and where both are quickened by imagination.

The story is told without apparent artifice but in fact, as Gogol said of Pushkin, with a simplicity and restraint which carries it to the highest peak of artistry. It may be read on any number of levels: as an evocation of rural life in eighteenth-century Russia, packed with fascinating characters and twists of fortune; as a detailed historical record, bringing back the forgotten past with the sort of hallucinatory clarity which, for most of us, is captured only in brief and intermittent flashes of scenes remembered against an unfocused background; as a gallery of characters grouped round the portraits of a natural gentleman, virtually illiterate, but possessed of all the dignity of perfect integrity, and a gentlewoman (his cousin) who might have stepped straight out of the Paston Papers; as an argument both for and against the serf system; as a profound psychological study (this most surprising of all in the totally unpretending context of the narrative) of the author's parents, their relations with each other and their families.

Here, I think, is the first example of that truly Russian attitude, neutral and absorbed, towards the infinite complexities of the human character which, through Turgenev, Dostoevsky, Tolstoy and Chekhov in their different ways, was to quicken and enrich the experience of the Western world almost in the moment when the lights went out in Russia.

It may well be that this opening to the soul and to the mind (consider Aksakov's swift and sparing analyses of his parents' differences) will come to be regarded as his supreme contribution. It is an opening sustained and enlarged in the subsequent volumes about his own childhood and youth. Be that as it may, it is for sheer delight in the recreation of old Russia and the *creation* of one of the most memorable larger-than-life characters in all literature that *A Russian Gentleman* will live. In the words of Maurice Baring:

The style flows on like a limpid river; there is nothing superfluous, and not a hesitating touch. It is impossible to put down the narrative after once beginning it, and I have heard of children who read it like a fairy-tale. One has the sensation, when reading it, of being told a story by some enchanting nurse, who, when the usual question, 'Is it true?' is put to her, could truthfully answer, 'Yes, it is true.' The pictures of nature, the portraits of the people, all the good and the bad of the good and bad old times pass before one with epic simplicity and the magic of a fairy-tale. One is spellbound by the charm, the dignity, the good-nature, the gentle, easy accent of the speaker, in whom one feels convinced not only that there was nothing common nor mean, but to whom nothing was common or mean...

'The pictures of nature'... I have left these until last, partly because it is in his treatment of the natural world that Aksakov's genius is most immediately and evidently apparent, partly because it is above all in his exact descriptions of the Russian landscape, the Russian seasons (the torrential coming of spring; the ice-bound winter days; the killing heat of harvest time), the intimate, shimmering, multitudinous life of birds, beasts, butterflies, fish, that I find myself thinking of Aksakov when he is not at hand. And the whole, everything he sees and describes, is true and real down to the last ruffled feather of a bird at odds with the wind, the uneven ring of a horse-shoe that has lost a nail, the creak and rumble of an unsprung waggon. Nothing is abstract. Nothing is generalized.

Russia—Russia—Russia—certainly much of the drive in Aksakov came from the desire to find the essence of Russia and to fix it in words. Certainly the qualities I have tried to indicate, the wonderful acceptance of *what is* (and the honesty to record it for its own sake), we have come to think of as peculiarly Russian. But I wonder. Perhaps the time has come to suggest that Aksakov did much more than give us Russia, and that the qualities we find so finely deployed by him and other great Russian writers are not in fact peculiar to Russia. When all is said, few Russian painters reflect these qualities, while in the painters of the Netherlands, as of Renaissance Florence, we meet them again and again. While the simplicity of Aksakov's prose, the exactitude and sobriety of his observation, the freshness of his vision and the honesty of his purpose are all, surely, to be found in the author of *The Canterbury Tales*.

EDWARD CRANKSHAW

NOTE ON THE TRANSLATOR

JAMES DUFF DUFF was born on 20 November 1860, the son of a retired army officer living in Aberdeenshire. He and his twin brother were among the first boys at Fettes College, Edinburgh. He came as a scholar to Trinity College, Cambridge, in 1878, and was elected a Classical Fellow in 1883. Teaching Latin and Greek at Trinity, and also at Girton, was the main work of his life; and he is best known to classical scholars for what A. E. Housman praised as his 'unpretending school edition' of Juvenal.

He was over forty when he taught himself Russian, in order to read in the original the novels of Tolstoy and especially Turgenev, which he had greatly admired in French translations. He never visited Russia, but had Russian friends, with whom he talked and corresponded in their own language: notably Aleksandra Grigoryevna Pashkova, the wife of a Russian land-owner, whose two sons were Trinity undergraduates.

His admiration for the autobiographical writings of Sergei Aksakov led him to translate them, in three volumes: *Years of Childhood*, *A Russian Gentleman*, and *A Russian Schoolboy*, published by Edward Arnold in 1916 and 1917, and later republished by Oxford University Press in The World's Classics. Paperback editions of *Years of Childhood* and *A Russian Schoolboy* are forthcoming.

The translator died on 25 April 1940.

P. W. DUFF

NOTE ON RUSSIAN NAMES

This list of the principal Russian names in the text indicates the stressed syllable (ë is pronounced *yo* and always stressed).

Afrósinya Andréevna

Aksákov(o)

Aksínya

Aksyútka

Alakáev

Alëna Maxímovna

Alexéi Stepánich (Alësha)

Álkino

Aníchkov

Arína Vasílevna (Arísha)

Astrakhán

Bagróv(o)

Bakhmétev

bátyushka

Baktéev

Bélaya river

Boltunënok

Buguruslán

Bulgákov

Cheprúnov

Chichágov

Churásovo

Dëma river

Efrém Evséich

Erlýkin

Grigóry

Kalpínsky

Kandalíntsev, Véra Ivánovna

Karamzín

Karatáev, Iván

Kazán

Kinél river

kumíss

Kurolésov, Mikháil Maxímovich

Lupenévsky, Flëna

Máina river

mátushka

Mazán

Nasyagái river

Neklyúdov

Nikolái

Níza river

Onúfriev

Orenbúrg

Párashino

Praskóvya Ivánovna (Parásha)

Pugachëv

Rychkóv

Samára

Sergéi Timoféevich

Sergíevsk

Sófya Nikoláevna

Spiridón

Stepán Mikháilovich

Suvórov

Tanaichënok

Tatyána Gorozhána

Timáshev

Timoféi

Tanyúsha

Ufá

Vyátka

Zúbin

CHRONOLOGY OF SERGEI AKSAKOV

1791   20 Sept. Born in Ufa, province of Orenburg.

1799–1807 School and university, Kazan.

1807–11   Employed as translator in government service, St Petersburg.

1811–27   Gentleman of leisure, Moscow and country estate.

1816   Marries: two sons, the future Slavophils Konstantin (b. 1817) and Ivan (b. 1823).

1827   Returns to government service: censorship office.

1831   First meeting with Gogol.

1839   Finally retires from government service.

1840   Begins to write 'A Russian Gentleman', called in Russian *A Family Chronicle*.

1846   Two fragments of 'A Russian Gentleman' appear in *Moskovsky sbornik* (Moscow Miscellany).

1847   *Notes on Angling* published.

1852   *Notes on Shooting in Orenburg Province* published.

1856   'A Russian Gentleman' published in book form, together with 'A Russian Schoolboy', called in Russian *Recollections*.

1858   'Years of Childhood' published, called in Russian *The Childhood Years of the Bagrov Grandson*.

1859   30 Apr. Dies in Moscow.

1890   *Recollections of Gogol* published posthumously.

FRAGMENT I
STEPAN MIKHAILOVITCH BAGROV

1. The Migration

WHEN my grandfather lived in the province of Simbirsk, on the ancestral estate granted to his forefathers by the tsars of Muscovy, he felt cramped and confined. Not that there was really want of room; for he had arable land and pasture, timber, and other necessaries in abundance; but the trouble was that the estate which his great-grandfather had held in absolute possession had ceased to belong to one owner. This happened quite simply: for three successive generations the family consisted of one son and several daughters; and, when some of these daughters were married, their portions took the shape of a certain number of serfs and a certain amount of land. Though their shares were not large, yet, as the land had never been properly surveyed, at this time four intruders asserted their right to share in the management of it. To my grandfather, life under these conditions was intolerable: there was no patience in his passionate temperament; he loved plain dealing and hated complications and wrangles with his kith and kin.

For some time past, he had heard frequent reports about the district of Ufa—how there was land there without limit for the plough and for stock, with an indescribable abundance of game and fish and all the fruits of the earth; and how easy it was to acquire whole tracts of land for a very trifling sum of money. If tales were true, you had only to invite a dozen of the native Bashkir chiefs in certain districts to partake of your hospitality: you provided two or three fat sheep, for them to kill and dress in their own fashion; you produced two or three gallons of whisky, many gallons of strong fermented Bashkir mead and a barrel of home-made country beer—which proves, by the way, that even in old days the Bashkirs were not strict

Mohammedans—and the rest was as simple as A B C. It was said, indeed, that an entertainment of this kind might last a week or even a fortnight: it was impossible for Bashkirs to do business in a hurry, and every day it was necessary to ask the question, 'Well, good friend, is it time now to discuss my business?' The guests had been eating and drinking, without exaggeration, all day and all night; but, if they were not completely satisfied with the entertainment, if they had not had enough of their monotonous singing and playing on the pipe, and their singular dances in which they stood up or crouched down on the same spot of ground, then the greatest of the chiefs, clicking his tongue and wagging his head, would answer with much dignity and without looking his questioner in the face: 'The time has not come; bring us another sheep!' The sheep was forthcoming, as a matter of course, with fresh supplies of beer and spirits; and the tipsy Bashkirs began again to sing and dance, dropping off to sleep wherever they felt inclined. But everything in the world has an end; and a day came at last when the chief would look his host straight in the face and say: 'We are obliged to you, *batyushka*,* ever so much obliged! And now, what is it that you want?' The rest of the transaction followed a regular fashion. The customer began with the shrewdness native to your true Russian: he assured the Bashkir that he did not want anything at all; but, having heard that the Bashkirs were exceedingly kind people, he had come to Ufa on purpose to form a friendship with them, and so on. Then the conversation would somehow come round to the vast extent of the Bashkir territory and the unsatisfactory ways of the present tenants, who might pay their rent for a year or two and then pay no more and yet continue to live on the land, as if they were its rightful owners; it was rash to evict them, and a lawsuit became unavoidable. These remarks, which were true enough to the facts, were followed up by an obliging offer to relieve the kind Bashkirs of some part of the land which was such a burden to them; and in the end whole districts were bought and sold for a mere song. The bargain was clinched by a legal document, but the amount of land was never stated in it, and

* 'Father', a title of respect or affection.

could not be, as it had never been surveyed. As a rule, the boundaries were settled by landmarks of this kind: 'from the mouth of such and such a stream as far as the dead beech-tree on the wolf-track, and from the dead beech-tree in a bee-line to the watershed, and from the watershed to the fox-earths, and from the fox-earths to the hollow tree at Soltamratka,' and so on. So precise and permanent were the boundaries enclosing ten or twenty or thirty thousand desyatinas* of land! And the price of all this might be about one hundred roubles and presents worth another hundred, not including the cost of the entertainments.

Stories of this kind had a great attraction for my grandfather. As a man of strict integrity he disapproved of the deception practised on the simple Bashkirs; but he considered that the harm lay, not in the business itself, but in the method of transacting it, and believed that it was possible to deal fairly and yet to buy a great stretch of land at a low price. In that case he could migrate with his family and transfer half of his serfs to the new estate; and thus he would secure the main object of this design. For the fact was, that for some time past he had been so much worried by unending disputes over the management of the land—disputes between himself and the relations who owned a small part of it—that his desire to leave the place where his ancestors had lived and he himself was born, had become a fixed idea. There was no other means of securing a quiet life; and to him, now that his youth was past, a quiet life seemed more desirable than anything else.

So he scraped together several thousand roubles, and said goodbye to his wife, whom he called Arisha when he was in a good humour and Arina when he was not; he kissed his children and gave them his blessing—his four young daughters and the infant son who was the single scion and sole hope of an ancient and noble family. The daughters he thought of no importance: 'What's the good of *them*? They look out of the house, not in; if their name is Bagrov† today, it may be anything on earth tomorrow; my hopes rest entirely on my boy, Alexei'—such were my grandfather's parting words, when

---

* One desyatina = 2.7 acres.

† Bagrov is a pseudonym for Aksakov.

he started to cross the Volga on his way to the district of Ufa.

But perhaps I had better begin by telling you what sort of a man my grandfather was.

Stepan Mikhailovich Bagrov—this was his name—was under the middle height; but his prominent chest, uncommonly broad shoulders, sinewy arms, and wiry muscular frame, gave proof of his extraordinary strength. When it happened, in the rough-and-tumble amusements of young men, that a number of his brother-officers fastened on him at once, he would hurl them from him, as a sturdy oak hurls off the raindrops, when its branches rock in the breeze after a shower. He had fair hair and regular features; his eyes were large and dark blue, quick to light up with anger but friendly and kind in his hours of composure; his eyebrows were thick and the lines of his mouth pleasant to look at. The general expression of his features was singularly frank and open: no one could help trusting him; his word or his promise was better than any bond, and more sacred than any document guaranteed by Church or State. His natural intelligence was clear and strong. All landowners of that time were ignorant men, and he had received no sort of education; indeed he could hardly read and write his native language. But, while serving in the army, and before he was promoted from the ranks, he had mastered the elementary rules of arithmetic and the use of the reckoning-board—acquirements of which he liked to speak even when he was an old man. It is probable that his period of service was not long; for he was only quartermaster of the regiment when he retired. But in those days even nobles served for long in the ranks or as non-commissioned officers, unless indeed they passed through this stage in their cradles, first enrolled as sergeants in the Guards and then making a sudden appearance as captains in line regiments. Of the career of Stepan Mikhailovich in the army I know little; but I have been told that he was often employed in the capture of the highwaymen who infested the Volga, and always showed good sense in the formation of his plans and reckless courage in their execution; that the outlaws knew him well by sight and feared him like fire. On retiring from the army, he lived for some years on his hereditary estate of Bagrovo* and became very skilful in the management of land. It was not his way to be present from morning to night where his labourers were at work, nor did he stand like a sentry over the grain, when it was coming in and going out; but, when he was on the spot, he looked to some purpose, and, if he noticed anything amiss, especially any attempt to deceive him, he never failed to visit the offender with a summary form of punishment which may rouse the displeasure of my readers. But my grandfather, while acting in accordance with the spirit of his age, reasoned in a fashion of his own. In his view, to punish a peasant by fines or by forced labour on the estate made the man less substantial and therefore less useful to his owner; and to separate him from his family and banish him to a distant estate was even worse, for a man deprived of his family ties was sure to go downhill. But to have recourse to the police was simply out of the question; that would have been considered the depth of disgrace and shame; every voice in the village would have been raised to mourn for the offender as if he were dead, and he would have considered himself as disgraced and ruined beyond redemption. And it must be said for my grandfather, that he was never severe except when his anger was hot; when the fit had passed away, the offence was forgotten. Advantage was often taken of this: sometimes the offender had time to hide and the storm passed by without hurting anyone. Before long, his people became so satisfactory that none of them gave him any cause to lose his temper.

After getting his estate into good order, my grandfather married; his bride was Arina Vasilevna Neklyudov, a young lady of little fortune, but, like himself, of ancient descent. This gives me an opportunity to explain that his pedigree was my grandfather's foible: he was moderately well-to-do, owning only 180 serfs; but his descent, which he traced back, by means of heaven knows what documents, for six hundred years all the way to a Varangian† prince called Shimon, he valued far more

* Bagrovo is a pseudonym for Aksakovo.

† The earliest Russian chronicles report that the Russian empire was founded in the ninth century by certain foreign princes called

than any riches or office in the State. At one time he was much attracted by a rich and beautiful girl, but he would not marry her, merely because her great-grandfather was not a noble.

After this account of Stepan Mikhailovich, let us go back to the course of the narrative.

My grandfather first crossed the Volga by the ferry near Simbirsk, and then struck across the steppe on the farther side, and travelled on till he came to Sergievsk, which stands on a hill at the meeting of two rivers and gives a name to the sulphur springs twelve versts* from the town. The deeper he plunged into the district of Ufa, the more he was impressed by the spaciousness and fertility of that country. The first place where he found trees growing was the district of Buguruslan; and in the town of that name, perched on a high hill above the river, he made a halt, wishing to make inquiries and learn more particulars of the lands that were for sale. Of land belonging to the Bashkirs there was little left in this district: some of the occupiers were tenants of the Crown, whom the Government had settled on lands confiscated for rebellion, though later they granted a general pardon and restored their territory to the Bashkir owners; part of the land had been let to tenants by the Bashkirs themselves; and part had been bought up by migrating landowners. Using Buguruslan as a centre, my grandfather made expeditions to the surrounding districts and spent some time in the beautiful country watered by the Ik and the Dema.†
It is an enchanting region; and even in his old age Stepan Mikhailovich often spoke with enthusiasm of the first impression produced on him by the astonishing richness of that soil. But he did not allow himself to be carried away. Ascertaining on the spot that any purchaser of Bashkir land was quite sure to be involved in endless disputes and lawsuits—for it was impossible for the acquirer to make sure either of his own title or of the number of the former owners—my grandfather, who feared and

Varyagi (Varangians). The nationality of these princes has been a subject of endless controversy, some historians maintaining that they were Norsemen, others denying it.

* A verst is two-thirds of a mile.
† Pronounce Dyaw-ma.

hated like poison the very name of a lawsuit, resolved to buy no land direct from the Bashkirs or without formal legal documents to confirm his ownership. Thus he hoped to exclude the possibility of disputes, and surely he had reason for such a hope; but things turned out very differently, and the last claim was only settled by his youngest grandson when he was forty years old.

My grandfather returned reluctantly from the banks of the Ik and the Dema to Buguruslan, where he bought land from a Russian lady near the river of that name and distant twenty-five versts from the town. The river is rapid and deep and never runs dry. For forty versts, from the town of Buguruslan to the Crown settlement of Fair Bank, the country on both sides of the river was uninhabited, so that there was ample room; and the amenities of the spot were wonderful. The river was so transparent that, if you threw in a copper coin, you could see it resting on the bottom even in pools fifteen feet deep. In some places there was a thick border of trees and bushes—birches, poplars, service-trees, guelder-roses, and bird-cherries, where the hop-bines trailed their green festoons and hung their straw-coloured clusters from tree to tree; in other places, the grass grew tall and strong, with an infinite profusion of flowers, including tall meadowsweet, lords' pride (the scarlet lychnis), kings' curls (the martagon lily), and cat-grass or valerian. The river flows along a valley varying in breadth and bordered on both sides by sloping hills with a steep cliff here and there; the slopes were thickly covered with hardwood trees of all sorts. As you got out of the valley, the level steppe spread out before you, a black virgin soil over two feet in depth. Along the river and in the neighbouring marshes, wild ducks of all kinds, and geese, woodcocks, and snipe made their nests and filled the air with their different notes and calls; while on the table-land above, where the grass grew thick and strong, the music in the air was as rich and quite distinct. Every kind of bird that lives in the steppe bred there in multitudes—bustards, cranes, and hawks; and on the wooded slopes there were quantities of black-game. The river swarmed with every variety of fish that could endure its ice-cold water—pike, perch, chub, dace, and even salmon. Both steppe and forest were filled beyond belief with wild creatures. In a word, the place was, and still is, a paradise for the sportsman.

My grandfather bought about 12,000 acres for 2,500 roubles. That was a large sum in those days, and the price was much higher than was generally paid. When he had assured his title by legal documents, he went back with a light heart to his expectant family in the province of Simbirsk. There he set to work with fierce energy and made all preparations for transferring at once a portion of his serfs to the new estate. It was an anxious and troublesome job, because the distance was considerable—about 400 versts. That same autumn twenty families of serfs started for the district of Buguruslan, taking with them ploughs and harrows with rye for sowing. They chose their ground and set to work on the virgin soil. Two thousand acres were lightly ploughed, then harrowed, and sown with winter rye; two thousand more were ploughed in preparation for the spring sowing; and some cottages were built. When this was done, the men travelled back to spend the winter at home. When winter was over, twenty more labourers again went forth; and, as the spring advanced, they sowed the two thousand acres with spring wheat, erected fences round the cottages and byres, and made stoves for the cottages out of clay. The second party then returned home. These were distinct from the actual settlers, who remained at home, preparing for their move and selling off what they did not need—their houses and kailyards, stock and corn, and all sorts of odds and ends.

The date fixed was the middle of June, that the colonists might reach their destination before St Peter's Day,* when hay-cutting begins. The carts were packed with the women and children and old people, and awnings of bast bent over them to protect them from the sun and rain; the indispensable pots and pans were piled up inside, the cocks and hens perched on the top, and the cows tied on behind; and off they started. The poor settlers shed bitter tears as they parted for ever with their past life, with the church in which they had been christened and married, and with the graves of their fathers and grandfathers. Nobody likes moving, and a Russian peasant least of all; but to

* 29 June.

move in those days to an unknown land inhabited by un-believers, where the churches were so distant that a man might die without confession and infants remain long unchristened, a land of which rumour reported evil as well as good—this seemed a terrible ordeal. When the peasants had gone, my grandfather started after them. He had taken a vow that, when circum-stances allowed, he would build a church dedicated to the Presentation of Our Lady—it was actually built by his son—and he named the new settlement after the festival. But the peasants, whose example was followed by their neighbours, called it New Bagrovo, after their master and in memory of Old Bagrovo, from which they had come; and to this day the formal name is only used in legal documents. No one knows the village, with its fine stone church and high manor-house, by any other name than Bagrovo. With unremitting care and attention my grandfather watched the labour of the people on their own land and on his; the hay was mown, the winter rye and spring corn were cut down and carried, and the right moment was chosen for each operation. The yield of the crops was fabulous. The peasants thought things were not so bad after all. By November, cottages were built for them all, and the beginning of a house for the owner was run up. All this was not done without help from neighbours. In spite of the long distances, they came willingly to lend a hand to the new landowner, who proved to be sensible and friendly; they ate and drank and turned to with a will, and sang as they worked. In that winter my grandfather went to Simbirsk and brought back his wife and children with him.

Next year forty more serfs were transferred and set up in their new abodes; and this proved an easier job. My grandfather's first operation in this year was to build a mill; without it, it had been necessary to drive forty versts to get his corn ground. A spot was chosen where the river was not deep, the bottom sound, and the banks high and solid. Then a dam of earth and brushwood was started from each bank, like a pair of hands ready to clasp; next, the dam was wattled with osiers, to make it more substantial; and all that remained was to stop the swift strong current and force it to fill the basin intended for it. The mill itself, with two pairs of millstones, was built beforehand on the lower bank. All the machinery was ready and even greased. It was the business of the river, when checked in its natural course, to fill the broad dam and pour through wooden pipes down upon the great wheel. When all was ready and four long oaken piles had been firmly driven into the clay bottom of the river, my grandfather invited his neighbours to lend him their assistance for two days; and they came, bringing horses and carts, spades, forks, and axes. On the first day, great piles of brushwood, straw, manure, and fresh-cut sods were heaped up on both banks of the Buguruslan, while the river continued to pour down its waters at its own sweet will. Hardly any one slept that night, and next morning at sunrise about a hundred men set to work to dam the stream; they all looked solemn and serious, as if they had important business before them. They began on both sides at the same moment. With loud cries they hurled with sturdy arms faggots of brushwood into the water; part was carried down by the stream, but part stuck against the piles and sank across the channel. Next came bundles of straw weighted with stones, then soil and manure, then more brushwood, followed by more straw and manure, and, on the top of all, a thick layer of sods. All this accumulation was swallowed up till it rose at last above the surface of the water. At once, a dozen strong and active men sprang on to the barrier and began to tread it and stamp it down. The operation was performed with the utmost speed; and the general excitement was so great and the noise so vociferous, that a passer-by, if he had not known the reason of it, might have been frightened. But there was no one there to be frightened by it: only the uninhabited steppes and dark forests and all the region round re-echoed the shouts of the labourers. The voices of women and children swelled the chorus; for such an important affair aroused interest in every breast, and the noise and excitement were universal. The resistance of the river was not overcome at once. For long it tore away and carried down brushwood and straw, manure and turf; but man at last conquered. The baffled water stopped, as if reflecting; then it turned back, and rose till it poured over its banks and inundated the fields. By evening the mill-pond had taken shape; or one might call it a floating lake, where the banks and all the green grass and bushes had disappeared; only the tops of submerged trees, doomed to die, stuck up here and there. Next day the mill began to work, and goes on working and grinding to this day.

2. The Province of Orenburg

How wonderful in those days was that region, in its wild and virginal richness! It is different now; it is not even what it was when I first knew it, when it was still fresh and blooming and undeflowered by hordes of settlers from every quarter. It is changed; but it is still beautiful and spacious, fertile and infinitely various, the province of Orenburg. The name sounds strange, and the termination 'burg' is inappropriate enough. But when I first knew that earthly paradise, it was still called the 'province of Ufa'.

Thirty years ago, one who was born within it* expressed in verse his fears for the future of the land; and these have been realized in part, and the process still goes on. But still hast thou power to charm, wondrous land! Bright and clear, like great deep cups, are thy lakes—Kandry and Karatabyn. Full of water and full of all manner of fish are thy rivers, whether they race down the valleys and rocky gorges of the Ural Mountains, or steal softly, glittering like a string of jewels, through the prairie-grass of the steppes. Wondrous are these rivers of the steppe, formed by the union of countless little streams flowing from deep water-holes—streams so tiny that you can hardly see the trickle of water in them. And thy rivers that flow swift from fountain-heads and run under the shade of trees and bushes are transparent and cold as ice even in the heat of summer; and all kinds of trout, good to eat and beautiful to see, live there; but they soon die out, when man begins to defile with unclean hands the virgin streams of their clear cool retreats. Fertile is the black soil of thy cornland, and rich thy pastures; and thy fields are covered in spring with the milk-white blossom of the cherry-tree and wild peach, while in summer the fragrant strawberries spread over them like a scarlet cloth, and the small

* Aksakov himself.

cherries that turn purple later when they ripen in autumn. Rich is the harvest that rewards the peasant, however idle and ignorant, when he scratches with his rude ploughshare the surface of thy soil. Fresh and green and mighty stand thy forests of all manner of trees; and buzzing swarms of wild bees fill their self-chosen nests among the leaves with the fragrant honey of the lime blossom. The Ufa marten, with its priceless fur, is still to be found in the wooded head-waters of the great rivers.

The original inhabitants of the land are men of peace, the wandering tribes of Bashkirs. Their herds of horses and cattle and flocks of sheep, though far smaller than they were once, are still numerous. When the fierce storms of winter are over, the Bashkirs crawl forth, thin and wasted like flies in winter. With the first warmth and the first sprouting of the grass they drive out into the open their half-starved herds and flocks, and drag themselves after them, with their wives and children. A few weeks change them beyond recognition, both men and animals. What were mere skeletons have become spirited and tireless horses; and the stallion proudly guards his mares as they graze, and keeps both man and beast at a distance. The meagre cattle have grown fat, and their udders swell with milk. But for cow's milk the Bashkir cares nothing. For the kumiss* is now in season and already fermenting in the bags of horse-hide; and every creature that can drink, from the infant in arms to the tottering old man, swallows the health-giving beverage, a drink for heroes. And the result is marvellous: all the traces of winter and starvation soon disappear, and even the troubles of old age; their faces fill out, and pale sunken cheeks take on the hue of health. But their deserted villages are a sad and even alarming sight. A traveller unfamiliar with the country might well start, appalled by the emptiness and deadness of the place. There stand the deserted huts with their white chimneys, and the empty window-frames look mournfully at him like human faces with no eyes in the sockets. He may hear the bark of a half-starved watch-dog, whom his master visits and feeds at long intervals, or the mewing of a cat that has run wild and finds food for herself; but that is all: not one human being remains.

* Fermented mare's milk.

How varied and picturesque, each in its own way, are the different regions of the land—the forests, the steppes, and, more than all, the hills, where all metals, even gold, are found along the slopes of the Ural ridge! How vast the expanse, from the borders of Vyatka and Perm, where the mercury often freezes in winter, to the little town of Gurev on the edge of Astrakhan, where small grapes ripen in the open air—grapes whose wine the Cossack trades in and drinks himself for coolness in summer and warmth in winter. How noble is the fishing in the Urals, unlike any other both in the fish that are caught and in the manner of catching them! It only needs a faithful and lively description to attract general attention.

But I must ask pardon. I have gone too far in the description of the beautiful country where I was born. Now let us go back and observe the life and unwearied activity of my grandfather.

3. Fresh Scenes

Stepan Mikhailovich had peace at last. Many a time he thanked God from the bottom of his heart, when the move was completed and he found elbow-room on the banks of the Buguruslan. His spirits rose, and even his health was better. No petitions, no complaints, no disputes, no disturbance! No tiresome relations, no divided ownership! No thieves to fell his trees, no trespassers to trample down his corn and meadows! He was undisputed master at last in his own house, and beyond it: he might feed sheep, or mow grass, or cut firewood where he pleased without a word from anyone.

The peasants too soon became accustomed to the new habitation and soon grew to love it. And that was but natural. Old Bagrovo had wood, but little water; meadow-land was so scarce that it was hard for them to find grazing for one horse and one cow apiece; and though the natural soil was good, it had been cropped over and over from time immemorial till its fertility was exhausted. The new site gave them wide and fertile fields and meadows, never touched till now by ploughshare or scythe; it gave them a rapid river with good fresh water, and springs in abundance; it gave them a broad pond with fish in it and the river running through it; and it gave them a mill at their very doors, whereas before they had to travel twenty-five versts to have a load of corn ground, and perhaps to wait after all a couple of days till their turn came.

It surprises you perhaps that I called Old Bagrovo waterless; and you may blame my ancestors for choosing such a spot to settle in. But they were not to blame, and things were different in the old days. Once on a time Old Bagrovo stood on a pretty stream, the Maina, which took its rise from the Mossy Lakes three versts distant; and also along the whole settlement there stretched a lake, not broad but long and clear, and deep in the middle, with a bottom of white sand; and another streamlet, called the White Spring, issued from this lake. So it was in former times, but it is quite another story now. Tradition tells that the Mossy Lakes were once deep round pools surrounded by trees, with ice-cold water and treacherous banks, and no one ventured near them except in winter, because the banks were said to give way under foot and engulf the bold disturber of the water-spirit's solitary reign. But man is the sworn foe of Nature, and she can never withstand his treacherous warfare against her beauty. Ancient tradition, unsupported by modern instances, ceased to be believed. The people steeped their flax on the banks and drove their herds there to water; and the Mossy Lakes were polluted by degrees, and grew shallow at the edges, and even dried up in places where the wood all round was cut. Then a thick scurf formed on the top; moss grew over it, and the vein-like roots of water-plants bound it together, till it was covered with tussocks and bushes and even fir-trees of some size. One of the pools is now entirely covered; of the other are left two deep water-holes, which even now are formidable for a stranger to approach, because the soil, with all its covering of plants and bushes and trees, rises and falls beneath the foot like a wave at sea. Owing to the dwindling of these lakes, the Maina now issues from the ground some distance below the settlement, and its upper waters have dried up. The lake by the village has become a filthy stinking canal; the sandy bottom is covered to a depth of over seven feet by mud and refuse of all kinds from the peasants' houses; of the White Spring not a trace is left, and the memory of it will soon be forgotten.

When my grandfather had settled down at New Bagrovo, he set to work, with all his natural activity and energy, to grow corn and breed stock. The peasants caught the contagion of his enthusiasm and worked so hard and steadily that they were soon as well set up and provided for as if they had been old inhabitants. After a few years, their stackyards took up thrice as much room as the village street; and their drove of stout horses, their herds and flocks and pigs, would have done honour to a large and prosperous settlement.

After the success of Stepan Mikhailovich, migration to Ufa or Orenburg became more fashionable every year. Native tribes came streaming from every quarter—Mordvinians, Chuvashes, Tatars, and Meshchers, and plenty of Russian settlers too—Crown-tenants from different districts, and landowners, large and small. My grandfather began to have neighbours. His brother-in-law, Ivan Neklyudov, bought land within twelve versts of Bagrovo, transferred his serfs there, built a wooden church, named his estate Neklyudovo, and came to live there with his family. This afforded no gratification to my grandfather, who had a strong dislike to all his wife's relations—all 'Neklyudovdom', as he used to call them. Then a landowner called Bakhmetev bought land still closer, about ten versts from Bagrovo, on the upper waters of the Sovrusha, which runs to the south-west like the Buguruslan. On the other side, twelve versts along the river Nasyagai, another settlement was planted, Polibino, which now belongs to the Karamzin family. The Nasyagai is a larger and finer river than the Buguruslan, with more water and more fish in it, and birds still breed there much more freely. On the road to Polibino, and eights versts from Bagrovo, a number of Mordvinians settled in a large village called Noikino, and built a mill on the streamlet of Bokla. Close to the mill, the Bokla runs into the Nasyagai, which rolls its swift strong current straight to the south-west, and is reinforced by the Buguruslan not far from the town of that name. Then the Nasyagai unites with the Great Kinel, and loses thenceforth its sounding and significant* name.

* Nasyagai means 'pursuer'.

The latest arrivals were some Mordvinian colonists, a detachment from the larger settlement at Mordovsky Buguruslan, nine versts from Bagrovo. This smaller settlement, called Kivatsky, was within two versts of my grandfather, down the river; and he made a wry face at first; for it reminded him of old times in Simbirsk. But the result was quite different. They were good-tempered quiet people, who respected my grandfather as much as the official in charge of them.

Before many years had passed, Stepan Mikhailovich had gained the deep respect and love too of the whole district. He was a real benefactor to his neighbours, near or far, old or new, and especially to the latter, owing to their ignorance of the place and lack of supplies, and the various difficulties which always befall settlers. Too often people start off on this difficult job without due preparation, without even providing themselves with bread and corn or the means to buy them. My grandfather's full granaries were always open to such people. 'Take what you want, and pay me back next harvest, if you can; and if you can't—well, never mind!'—with such words as these he used to distribute with a generous hand seed-corn and flour. And more than this: he was so sensible, so considerate towards petitioners, and so inflexibly strict in the keeping of his word, that he soon became quite an oracle in that newly settled corner of the spacious district of Orenburg. Not only did he help his neighbours by his generosity, but he taught them how to behave. To speak the truth was the only key to his favour: a man who had once lied to him and deceived him was ill advised if he came again to Bagrovo: he would be certain to depart with empty hands, and might think himself lucky if he came off with a whole skin. My grandfather settled many family disputes and smothered many lawsuits at their first birth. People travelled from every quarter to seek his advice and hear his decision; and both were punctiliously followed. I have known grandsons and great-grandsons of that generation and heard them speak of Stepan Mikhailovich; and the figure of the strict master but kind benefactor is still unforgotten. I have often heard striking facts told about him by simple people, who shed tears and crossed themselves as they ejaculated a prayer for his soul's rest.

It is not surprising that his peasants loved so excellent a master; but he was loved also by his personal servants who had often to endure the terrible storms of his furious rage. Many of his younger servants spent their last days under my roof; and in their old age they liked to talk of their late master—of his strict discipline and passionate temper, and also of his goodness and justice; and they never spoke of him with dry eyes.

Yet this kind, helpful, and even considerate man was subject at times to fearful explosions of anger which utterly defaced the image of humanity in him and made him capable, for the time, of repulsive and ferocious actions. I once saw him in this state when I was a child—it was many years after the time I am writing about—and the fear that I felt has left a lively impression on my mind to this day. I seem to see him before me now. He was angry with one of his daughters; I believe she had told him a lie and persisted in it. It was impossible to recognize his former self. He was trembling all over and supported on each side by a servant; his face was convulsed, and a fierce fire shot from his eyes which were clouded and darkened with fury. 'Let me get at her!'—he called out in a strangled voice. (So far, my recollection is clear; and the rest I have often heard others tell.) My grandmother tried to throw herself at his feet, to intercede for the culprit; but in an instant her kerchief and cap flew to a distance, and Stepan Mikhailovich was dragging his wife, though she was now old and stout, over the floor by her hair. Meantime, not only the offender, but all her sisters, and even their brother with his young wife and little son,* had fled out of doors and sought concealment in the wood that grew round the house. The rest of them spent the whole night there; but the daughter-in-law, fearing that her child would catch cold, went back and passed the night in a servant's cottage. For a long time my grandfather raged at large through the deserted house. At last, when he was weary of dragging his wife about by the hair, and weary of striking his servants, Mazan and Tanaichenok, he dropped upon his bed utterly exhausted and soon fell into a deep sleep which lasted till the following morning.

* i.e. the author, who in childhood was called Serezha (the familiar form of Sergei).

At dawn Stepan Mikhailovich woke up. His face was bright and clear, and his voice cheerful as he hailed his wife. She hurried in at once from the next room, looking as if nothing had happened the day before. 'I want my tea! Where are the children, and Alexei and his wife? I want to see Serezha'—thus spoke the madman on his waking, and all the family appeared, composed and cheerful, in his presence. But there was one exception. His daughter-in-law was a woman of strong character herself, and no entreaties could induce her to smile so soon upon the wild beast of the day before; and her little son kept constantly saying, 'I won't go to grandfather! I'm frightened!' She really did not feel well and excused herself on that ground; and she kept her child in her room. The family were horrified and expected a renewal of the storm. But the wild beast of yesterday had wakened up as a human being. He talked playfully over his tea and then went himself to visit the invalid. She was really unwell and was lying in bed thin and altered. The old man sat down beside her, kissed her, said kind things to her, and caressed his grandson; then he left the room saying that he would find that day long 'without his dear daughter-in-law'. Half an hour later she entered his room, wearing a pretty dress which he used to say especially became her, and holding her son by the hand. My grandfather welcomed her almost in tears: 'Just see!' he said fondly, 'though she was not well, she got up and dressed, regardless of herself, and came to cheer up an old man.' His wife and daughters bit their lips and looked down; for they all disliked his favourite; but she answered his affectionate greeting with cheerful respect, and looked proudly and triumphantly at her ill-wishers.

But I will say no more of the dark side of my grandfather's character. I would rather dwell on his bright side and describe one of his good days, which I have often and often heard spoken of.

4. My Grandfather on one of his Good Days

It was the end of June, and the weather was very hot. After a stifling night, a fresh breeze set in from the east at dawn, a breeze which always flags when the sun grows hot. Just then my grandfather awoke. It was hot in his bedroom; for the room was not large, and, though the window with its narrow old-fashioned sash was raised as high as it would go, he had curtains of home-made muslin round his bed. This precaution was indispensable: without it, the wicked mosquitoes would have kept him awake and devoured him. Those winged musicians swarmed round the bed, each driving its long proboscis into the fine fabric which protected him, and kept up their monotonous serenade all through the night. It sounds absurd, but I cannot conceal the fact that I like the shrill high note and even the bite of the mosquito; for it reminds me of sleepless nights in high summer on the banks of the Buguruslan, where the bushes grew thick and green and all round the nightingales called; and I remember the beating heart of youth and that vague feeling, half pleasure and half pain, for which I would now give up all that remains of the sinking fire of life.

My grandfather woke up, rubbed the sweat off his high forehead with a hot hand, put his head out between the curtains, and burst out laughing. His two servants, Mazan and Tanaichenok, lay stretched on the floor; their attitudes might have made anyone laugh, and they snored lustily. Confound the rascals! How they snore!' said my grandfather, and smiled again. You could never be sure about Stepan Mikhailovich. It might have been expected that such forcible language would have been followed up by a blow in the ribs from the blackthorn staff which always stood by his bed, or a kick, or even a saluta-tion in the form of a stool. But no: my grandfather had laughed on opening his eyes, and he kept up that mood throughout the day. He rose quickly, crossed himself once or twice, and thrust his bare feet into a pair of faded old leather slippers; then, wearing only his shirt of coarse home-made linen—my grand-mother would not give him any better—he went out upon the stoop to enjoy the freshness and moisture of the morning all around him.

I said just now that Arina Vasilevna would not give her husband finer linen; and the reader will remark with justice that this is inconsistent with the relations between the two. I am sorry, but I cannot help it. It is really true that female persistence triumphed, as it always does, over male violence. My grandmother got more than one beating over the coarse linen, but she continued to supply him with it till at last her husband got used to it. He resorted once to extreme measures: he took an axe and chopped up all his objectionable shirts on the threshold of his room, while my grandmother howled at the sight and implored him to beat *her* rather than spoil his good clothes. But even this device failed: the coarse shirts appeared once more, and the victim submitted. I must apologize for interrupting my narrative, in order to meet an imaginary objection on the part of the reader.

Without troubling anyone, he went himself to the store-room, fetched a woollen mat, and spread it out on the top step of the stoop; then he sat down upon it, meaning to follow his regular custom of watching the sun rise. To see sunrise gives every man a kind of half-conscious pleasure; and my grandfather felt an added satisfaction when he looked down over his courtyard, by this time sufficiently equipped with all the buildings necessary for his farming operations. The court was not, indeed, fenced; and the animals, when turned out of the peasants' yards, used to pay it passing visits, before they were all gathered together and driven to the common pasture. So it was on this morning; and the same thing was repeated every evening. Some pigs, fresh from the mire, rubbed and scratched themselves against the very stoop on which my grandfather was sitting, while they feasted with grunts of satisfaction on shells of crayfish and other refuse from the table, which that unsophisticated household deposited close to the steps. Cows and sheep also looked in, and it was inevitable that these visitors should leave unsightly tokens behind them. But to this my grandfather did not object in the least. On the contrary, he looked with pleasure at the fine beasts, taking them as a certain indication that his peasants were doing well. The loud cracking of the herdsman's long whip soon evicted the trespassers. Now the servants began to stir. The stout groom, Spiridon—known even in advanced old age as 'little Spirka'—led out, one after another, three colts, two bays and one brown. He tied them to a post, rubbed them down, and exercised them at the end of a long halter, while my grandfather admired their paces and also admired in fancy the stock he hoped to raise from them—a dream which he realized with entire success. Then the old housekeeper came forth from the cellar in which she slept, and went down to the river to wash herself. First she sighed and groaned, according to her invariable custom; then she turned towards the sunrise and said a prayer, before she set to work at washing and scrubbing plates and dishes. Swallows and martins twittered cheerfully as they cut circles in the air, quails called loudly in the fields, the song of the larks rained down from the sky, the hoarse note of the sitting landrails came from the bushes, and the bleat of the snipe from the neighbouring marsh, the mocking-birds imitated the nightingales with all their might; and forth from behind the hill issued the bright sun! Blue smoke rose in columns from the peasants' houses and then swayed in the breeze like the fluttering flags of a line of ships; and soon the labourers were plodding towards the fields.

My grandfather began to feel a desire for cold water to wash in and then for his tea. He roused his two servants from their ungainly attitudes; and they jumped up in a great fright at first, but were soon reassured by his good-humoured voice: 'Mazan, my washing things! Tanaichenok, wake Aksyutka and your mistress, and then tea!' There was no need to repeat these orders: clumsy Mazan was already flying at top speed to the spring for water, carrying a glittering copper basin, while handy Tanaichenok woke up Aksyutka, a young but ugly maid; and she, while she put straight the kerchief on her head, called her mistress, Arina Vasilevna, now grown old and stout. In a few minutes all the household were on their legs, and all knew by this time that the old master had got out of bed on the right side! A quarter of an hour later, a table was standing by the stoop—the white tablecloth was home-made and adorned with a pattern—a samovar in the shape of a large copper teapot, was hissing on the table, and Aksyutka was busy about the tea. Meanwhile Arina Vasilevna was greeting her husband. On some mornings it was the etiquette to sigh and look sorrowful; but today she asked after his health in a loud cheerful voice: How had he slept? What dreams had he had? Stepan Mikhailovich greeted his wife affectionately and called her

'Arisha'; he never kissed her hand, but sometimes gave her his to kiss as a sign of favour. Arina Vasilevna, in her pleasure, looked quite young and pretty; one forgot her stout awkward figure. She brought a stool at once and sat down on the stoop beside my grandfather, which she never ventured to do unless he was in a very good humour. 'Come, Arisha, let us have a cup of tea together before it gets hot,' said Stepan Mikhailovich; 'it was a stifling night, but I slept so sound that I have forgotten all my dreams. How did you sleep?' This question was a signal mark of favour, and my grandmother replied at once that, when Stepan Mikhailovich had a good night, she of course had one too, but that Tanyusha* was restless all night. Tanyusha was the youngest daughter and, as often happens, her father's favourite. He was vexed to hear this account of her, and ordered that she was not to be called but to sleep on till she woke. She had been called at the same time as her sisters Alexandra and Elizabeth, and was dressed already; but no one ventured to mention this fact. She made haste to undress, got into bed, and had the shutters drawn. She could not get to sleep, but she lay in the dark for two hours; and her father was pleased that Tanyusha had had her sleep out. The only son,† who was now nine, was never wakened early. But the two elder daughters appeared immediately; and Stepan Mikhailovich gave them his hand to kiss and called them by their pet names, Lexanya and Lizanka. They were both clever girls, and Alexandra had also inherited her father's active mind and violent temper but none of his good qualities. My grandmother, a very simple woman, was entirely under the thumb of her daughters; and whenever she ventured to play tricks upon Stepan Mikhailovich, it was because they had put her up to it; but she was so clumsy that she seldom succeeded, and her husband knew very well who was at the bottom of it. He knew also that his daughters were prepared to deceive him whenever they got the chance—though, for the sake of a quiet life, he let them suppose that he was

* A diminutive form of Tatyana.

† The author's father, called throughout Alexei; his real name was Timofei (Timothy). So his mother, whose name was Marya (Mary) is called Sofya (Sophia).

blind to their goings on. But this only lasted while he was in a good temper: as soon as he got angry, he stated his view of their conduct in the most unsparing and uncomplimentary terms, and sometimes even chastised them. But, like true daughters of Eve, they were not discouraged. When the fit of anger passed and the cloud lifted from their father's brow, they started again upon their underhand schemes, and pretty often they were successful in carrying them out.

When he had drunk his tea and talked about things in general with his womenfolk, my grandfather got ready to drive out. Some time before, he had said to Mazan, 'My horse!'—and an old brown gelding was already standing by the steps, harnessed to a long car, a very comfortable conveyance, with an outer framework of netting and a plank, covered with felt, to sit on. Spiridon, the driver, wore a simple livery: he had bare feet and nothing on but his shirt, with a red woollen belt, from which hung a key and a copper comb. On a similar occasion on the previous day, he had worn no hat; but this had been disapproved of, and he now wore some head-gear which he had woven out of broad strips of bast. My grandfather made merry over this 'sun-bonnet'. Then he put on his own cap and long coat of unbleached home-made cloth, placed his heavy cloak beneath him in case of rain, and took his seat on the car. Spiridon also folded his coat and sat upon it; it was made of unbleached cloth but dyed bright red with madder. Madder grew freely in the fields round Bagrovo, and was so much used that the servants about the house were called by the neighbours 'redbreasts'; I have heard the nickname myself fifteen years after my grandfather's death.

In the fields, Stepan Mikhailovich found everything to his mind. He examined the rye-crop; it was now past flowering and stood up like a wall, as high as a man; a light breeze was blowing, and bluish-purple waves went over it, now lighter and now darker in the sunlight; and the sight gladdened his heart. He visited the young oats and millet and all the spring-sown crops, and then went to the fallow, where he ordered his car to be driven backwards and forwards over the field. This was his regular way of testing the goodness of the work: any spot of ground that had not been properly ploughed and harrowed gave the light car a jolt, and, when my grandfather was not in a good humour, he stuck a twig or a stick in the ground at the place, sent for the bailiff if he was not present, and settled accounts with him on the spot. But today all went well: his wheels may have encountered such obstacles, but he took no notice of them. His next point was the hayfields, where he admired the tall thick steppe-grass which was to fall beneath the scythe before many days were past. He paid a visit to the peasants' fields also, to see for himself who had a good crop and who had not; and he drove over their fallow to test it. He noticed everything and forgot nothing. Passing over an untilled strip, he saw some wild strawberries nearly ripe; he stopped and, with Mazan's help, picked a large handful of splendid big berries, which he took home as a present for his 'Arisha'. In spite of the great heat he was out till nearly noon.

As soon as my grandfather's car was seen descending the hill, dinner was set on the table, and all the family stood on the steps to receive him. 'Well, Arisha,' he called out cheerfully, 'what splendid crops God is giving us this year! Great is His goodness! And here are some strawberries for you; they are nearly ripe; the pickers must go out tomorrow.' This attention was almost too much for my grandmother. As he spoke, he walked into the house, and the smell of the hot cabbage soup came to meet him from the parlour. 'Ah! I see dinner's ready; good!' said Stepan Mikhailovich more cheerfully than before, and walked straight into the parlour and sat down at table, without visiting his own room. I should mention that my grandfather had a rule: at whatever hour, early or late, he returned from the fields, dinner must be on the table, and heaven help the women, if they did not notice his coming and failed to serve the meal in time! There were occasions when such neglect gave rise to sad consequences; but on this happy day, everything went without a hitch. Behind my grandfather's chair stood a stout lad, holding a birch bough with the leaves on to drive away the flies. The hottest weather will not make a true Russian refuse cabbage soup, and my grandfather supped his with a wooden spoon, because silver would have burnt his lips. Soup was followed by a fish salad, made of kippered sturgeon as yellow as wax, and shelled crayfish. All the courses were of this light kind, and were washed down with kvass* and home-made beer; the drinks were iced and so was the salad. There were days when dinner was eaten in terrible stillness and silent dread of an explosion; but this was a cheerful meal, with much loud talking and laughing. Every boy and girl about the place had heard that the master was in a cheerful temper, and they all crowded into the parlour in hopes of a 'piece'. He gave them all something good to eat; for there was five times as much food on the table as the family could eat.

Immediately after dinner he went to lie down. All flies were expelled from the bed-curtains, and the curtains drawn round him with the ends tucked under the mattress; and soon his mighty snoring proclaimed that the master was asleep. All the rest went to their rooms to lie down. Mazan and Tanaichenok, when they had had their dinner and swallowed their share of the remnants from the dining-room table, also lay down in the passage, close to the door of my grandfather's bedroom. Though they had slept before dinner, they went to sleep again at once; but they were soon wakened by the heat and the burning rays of the sun coming through the windows. They felt a strong desire to cool their parched throats with some of their master's iced beer; and the bold scamps managed to get it in the following way. My grandfather's dressing-gown and nightcap were lying on a chair near the half-open door of his room. Tanaichenok put them on and sat down on the stoop, while Mazan went off to the cellar with a jug and wakened the old housekeeper, who like every soul in the house was fast asleep. He said his master was awake and wanted an iced tankard at once. She was surprised at his waking so soon, but Mazan then pointed to the figure in the dressing-gown and nightcap sitting on the stoop. The beer was drawn at once and ice added; and Mazan went quickly back with his prize. The cronies shared the jug between them and then replaced the garments. An hour later their master awoke in excellent humour, and his first words were, 'Iced beer!' This frightened the rascals; and when

* A drink made of malt and rye.

Tanaichenok hurried off to the cellar, the housekeeper guessed at once where the previous jug had gone. She produced the liquor, but followed the messenger back herself, and found the real master sitting on the stoop and wearing the dressing-gown. The truth came out at once; and Mazan and Tanaichenok shaking with fear fell at their master's feet. And what do you think my grandfather did? He burst out laughing, sent for his wife and daughters, and told them the story with loud bursts of laughter. The culprits breathed again, and one of them even ventured to grin. But Stepan Mikhailovich noticed this and very nearly grew angry: he frowned, but the composing effect of his good day was so strong that his face cleared up, and he said with a significant look, 'Well, I forgive you this once, but if it happens again . . .'—there was no need to end the sentence.

It is certainly strange that the servants of a man so passionate and so violent in his moments of passion should dare to be so impudent. But I have often noticed in the course of my life that the strictest masters have the most venturesome and reckless servants. My grandfather had other experiences of a similar kind. This same servant, Mazan, was sweeping out his master's room one day and preparing to make the bed, when he was suddenly tempted by the soft down of the bedding and pillows. He thought he would like a little taste of luxury; so down he lay on his master's bed and fell asleep. My grandfather himself came upon him sound asleep, and only laughed! He did, indeed, give the man one good rap with his staff; but that was nothing —he only did it in order to see how frightened Mazan would be. Worse tricks than these were played upon Stepan Mikhailovich in his time. During his absence from home, his cousin and ward, Praskovya Ivanovna Bagrov, was given in marriage to a dangerous and disreputable man whom he detested; the girl, who was only fourteen and a great heiress, was an inmate of Bagrovo and very dear to its owner. It is true that the plot was executed by the girl's relations on her mother's side; but Arina Vasilevna gave her consent, and her daughters were actively engaged in it. But I shall return to my narrative for the present and leave this incident to be told later.

He woke up at five in the afternoon and drank his iced beer.

Soon afterwards he wanted his tea, in spite of the sultry heat of the day; for he believed that a very hot drink makes hot weather more bearable. But first he went down to bathe in the cool waters of the river, which flowed under the windows of the house. When he came back, the whole family were waiting for him at the tea-table—the same table set in the shade, with the same hissing teapot and the same Aksyutka. When he had drunk his fill of his favourite sudorific beverage, with cream so thick that the curd on it was yellow, my grandfather proposed that the whole party should make an expedition to the mill. The plan was received with joy; and Alexandra and Tatyana, who were fond of angling, took fishing-rods with them. Two cars were brought round in a minute. Stepan Mikhailovich and his wife took their seats on one, and placed between them their one boy, the precious scion of their ancient and noble line; while the other carried the three daughters, with a boy to dig for worms on the mill-dam and bait their hooks for the young ladies. When they reached the mill, a seat was brought out for Arina Vasilevna, and she sat down in the shade of the building, not far from the mill-race where her daughters were fishing. Meanwhile Elizabeth, the eldest, partly to please her father and partly from her own interest in such matters, went with Stepan Mikhailovich to inspect the mill and the pounding-machine. The little boy either watched his sisters fishing—he was not allowed to fish himself in deep places—or played beside his mother, who never took her eyes off him, in her fear that the child would somehow tumble in.

Both sets of millstones were at work, one making wheat-flour for the master's table, and the other grinding rye for a neighbour; and there was millet under the pounding-machine. My grandfather was well acquainted with all farming operations: he understood a mill thoroughly and explained all the details to his attentive and intelligent companion. He saw in a moment any defect in the machinery or mistake in the position of the stones. One of them he ordered to be lowered half a notch, and the rye-meal came out finer, to the great satisfaction of its owner. At the other stone, his ear detected at once that one of the cogs on the small wheel was getting worn. He stopped the current, and Boltunenok,* the miller, jumped down beside the wheel. He looked at it and felt it and then said, 'You are quite right, *batyushka* Stepan Mikhailovich! One of the cogs is a little worn.' 'A little you call it!'—said my grandfather, not at all vexed: 'but for my coming, the wheel would have snapped this very night!' 'I am sorry I did not notice it, Stepan Mikhailovich.' 'Well, never mind! Bring a new wheel, and take the worn cog off the other; and mind the new cog is neither thicker nor thinner than the rest; the whole secret lies in that.' The new wheel, fitted and tested beforehand, was fixed at once and greased with tar; and the current was turned on by degrees, also by my grandfather's instructions; at once the stone began to hum and grind smoothly and evenly, with no stumbling or knocking. The visitors went next to the pounding-machine, where my grandfather took a handful of millet from the mortar. He blew the chaff away and said to the man who had brought the grain to the mill, a Mordvinian and an old acquaintance: 'Have a care, friend Vaska! If you look, every grain is pounded already, and if you go on, you will have less of it.' Vaska tried it himself and saw that my grandfather was right. He said, 'Thank you,' ducked his head by way of bowing, and ran off to stop the current. Their last visit was to the poultry-yard, where a large number of ducks and geese, hens and turkeys, were looked after by an old woman and her little granddaughter. Everything here was in excellent order. As a sign of special favour, my grandfather gave both of them his hand to kiss, and ordered that the hen-wife should get an extra allowance of twenty pounds of wheat-flour every month to make pies with. Stepan Mikhailovich rejoined his wife in good spirits. Everything had gone right: his daughter had shown intelligence, the mill was working well, and the hen-wife, Tatyana Gorozhana,† was attending to her duties.

The heat had long been abating; coolness came from the water and from the approach of evening; a long cloud of dust drifted along the road and came nearer the village with the bleating of

* A nickname: 'Little Chatterer', a dimunitive of *boltun*.

† She had got this nickname ('the townswoman') because she had spent part of her youth in some town (*author's note*).

sheep and lowing of cattle; the sun was losing light and sinking behind the steep hill. Stepan Mikhailovich stood on the mill-dam and surveyed the wide mirror of the pond as it lay motionless in the frame of its sloping banks. A fish jumped from time to time; but my grandfather was no fisherman. 'Time to go home, Arisha,' he said at last: 'I expect the bailiff is waiting for me.' Seeing his good humour, his daughters asked leave to fish on: they said the fish would take better at sunset, and they would walk home in half an hour. Leave was given, and the old couple started for home on one of the cars, while Elizabeth took her little brother in the other. As Stepan Mikhailovich had expected, the bailiff was awaiting for him by the stoop, and some peasants and their wives were there with him; they had got a hint from the bailiff, who knew already that his master was in the right mood, and now seized the opportunity to state some exceptional needs or prefer some exceptional requests. Not one of them was disappointed. To one my grandfather gave corn, and forgave an old debt which the man could have paid; another was allowed to marry his son before the winter* and to a girl of their own choosing; he gave leave to a soldier's wife, who was to be turned out of the village for misconduct, to go on living with her father; and so on. Nor was that all: strong home-made spirits were offered to each of them, in a silver cup which held more than an ordinary dram. Then my grandfather gave his orders to the bailiff, shortly and clearly, and went off to his supper which had been standing ready some time. The evening meal did not differ much from the midday dinner; but the cooler air probably gave a keener edge to appetite. It was a custom with Stepan Mikhailovich to send his family off to bed and sit up for half an hour or so on the stoop, with nothing on but his shirt, for the sake of coolness. This day he stayed there longer than usual, laughing and jesting with Mazan and Tanaichenok; he made them wrestle and fight with their fists, and urged them on till they began to hit out in earnest and even clutched each other by the hair. He had laughed his fill; and now a word of command, and the tone it was spoken in, brought them to their senses and parted them.

* After harvest was the normal time for peasants' marriages.

All the landscape lay before him, still and wonderful, enfolded by the summer night. The glow of sunset had not yet disappeared, and would go on till it gave place to the glow of dawn. Hour by hour, the depths of the vault of heaven grew darker; hour by hour, the stars flashed brighter, and the cries of the night birds grew louder, as if they were becoming more familiar with man; the clack of the mill sounded nearer in the misty damp of the night air. My grandfather rose from his stoop, and crossed himself once or twice, looking at the starry sky. Then, though the heat in his bedroom was stifling, he lay down on the hot feather-bed and ordered his curtains to be drawn round him.

FRAGMENT II

MIKHAIL MAXIMOVICH KUROLESOV

I PROMISED to give a separate account of Mikhail Maximovich Kurolesov and his marriage with my grandfather's cousin, Praskovya Ivanovna Bagrov. This story begins about 1760, earlier than the time described in the First Fragment of this history, and ends much later. I shall now fulfil my promise.

Stepan Mikhailovich was the only son of Mikhail Bagrov; Mikhail had a brother Peter, whose only daughter was Praskovya Ivanovna. As she was his only cousin and the sole female representative of the Bagrov family in that generation, my grandfather was much attached to her. While still in the cradle she lost her mother, and her father died when she was ten. Her mother, one of the Bakteev family, was very rich and left to her daughter 900 serfs, a quantity of money, and still more in silver and valuables, and her father's death added 300 serfs to her property. Praskovya Ivanovna was therefore a rich orphan, and would bring a great fortune to her future husband. After her father's death she lived at first with her grandmother, Mme Bakteev; then she paid a long visit to Bagrovo; and finally Stepan Mikhailovich took her to his house as a permanent inmate. He was quite as fond of his orphan cousin as of his daughters and was very affectionate to her in his own way. But she was too young, too babyish, one might say, to appreciate her cousin's love and tenderness, which never took the form of spoiling, while, under her grandmother's roof, where she had spent some time, she had grown accustomed to indulgence. So it is not surprising that she grew tired of Bagrovo and wished to go back to old Mme Bakteev. Praskovya Ivanovna, though she was not beautiful, had regular features and fine intelligent grey eyes; her dark eyebrows, long and rather thick, were a sign of her masculine strength of character; she was tall and well-made, and looked eighteen when she was only fourteen. But, in spite of her physical maturity, her mind and feelings were still those of a mere child: always lively and merry, she capered and frisked, gambolled and sang, from morning till night. She had a remarkable voice and was passionately fond of joining with the maids in their singing or dancing or swinging; or, when nothing of that kind was to be had, she played with her dolls all day, invariably accompanying her occupation with popular songs of all sorts, of which she knew even then an immense number.

A year before Praskovya Ivanovna went to live at Bagrovo, Mikhail Kurolesov, an officer in the army, came on leave to the province of Simbirsk. He belonged to a noble family in the district, and was then twenty-eight years old. He was a fine-looking fellow, and many people called him handsome; but some said that, in spite of his regular features, there was something unpleasing about him; and I remember to have heard as a child debates on this point between my grandmother and her daughters. Entering the army at fifteen, he had served in a regiment of high reputation in those days and had risen to the rank of major. He did not often come home on leave, and he had little reason to come, because the serfs—about 150 in all—who formed his property, owned little land and were scattered about. As a matter of course, he had received no proper education, but he had a ready tongue and wrote in an easy correct style. Many of his letters have passed through my hands; and they prove clearly that he was a man of sense and tact and also firm of purpose and businesslike. I don't know his exact relationship to our immortal Suvorov;* but I found in the correspondence some letters from the great captain, which always begin thus—

'Dear Sir and cousin, Mikhail Maximovich,' and end—

'With all proper respect for you and my worthy cousin, Praskovya Ivanovna,

'I have the honour to be,' &c.

Kurolesov was little known in the province of Simbirsk.

* A. V. Suvorov (1720–1800), most famous of all Russian soldiers.

But 'rumour runs all over the earth', and perhaps the young officer on leave permitted himself some 'distractions', as they are called; or perhaps the soldier servant whom he brought with him, in spite of his master's severity, let something leak out at odd times. Whatever the reason, an opinion gradually took shape about him, which may be summed up in the following statements—'Toe the line, when you parade before the Major' —'Mind your Ps and Qs, when talking to Kurolesov'—'When one of his men is caught out, he shows no mercy, though he may try to shield him'—'When he says a thing, he means it'— 'He's the very devil when his temper's up.' People called him 'a dark horse' and 'a rum customer'; but everyone admitted his ability as a man of business. There were also rumours, probably proceeding from the same sources, that the Major had certain weaknesses, which, however, he gratified with due regard to time and place. But these feelings were excused by the charitable proverbs—'A young man must sow his wild oats', and 'It's no crime in a man to drink', and 'The man who drinks and keeps his head/Scores two points, it must be said.' So Kurolesov had not a positively bad reputation; on the contrary many people thought highly of him. Insinuating and courteous in his address, and respectful to all persons of rank and position, he was a welcome guest in every home. As he was a near neighbour of the Bakteev family, and indeed a distant connexion, he soon managed to make his way into their good graces; they took a great liking to him and sounded his praises everywhere. At first he had no special object, but was merely following his invariable rule—to make himself agreeable to persons of rank and wealth; but later, when he met in their house Praskovya Ivanovna, lively, laughing, and rich, and looking quite old enough to be married, he formed a plan of marrying her himself and getting her wealth into his hands. With this definite object in view, he redoubled his attentions to her grandmother and aunt, till the two ladies quite lost their heads about him; at the same time he paid court so cleverly to the girl herself, that she soon had a liking for him, as she naturally would for a man who agreed to everything she said, gave her everything she asked, and spoiled her in every possible way. Next he showed his hand to her relations: he professed that he had fallen in love with the orphan girl, and they believed that he was suffering all a passionate lover's pangs, mad with longing, and haunted by his darling's image day and night. They approved of his plan and took the poor victim of love under their protection. The favour and connivance of her relations made it easy for him to proceed along his path: he did everything he could to entertain and amuse the child—taking her out for drives behind his spirited horses, pushing her in the swing and sitting beside her in it himself, singing with her the popular songs which he sang very well, giving her many trifling presents, and ordering amusing toys for her from Moscow.

Kurolesov knew, however, that the consent of her cousin and guardian was a necessary preliminary to complete success, and therefore tried to get into the good graces of Stepan Mikhailovich. Under various pretexts and provided with introductory letters from Praskovya Ivanovna's relations, he paid a visit at Bagrovo; but the visit proved a failure. At first sight this may seem strange; for some of the young officer's qualities were likely to appeal to Stepan Mikhailovich. But my grandfather, as well as his quick eye and sound sense, had that instinct, peculiar to men who are perfectly honest and straightforward themselves, which is instantly conscious of the hidden guile and crooked ways even of a complete stranger—the instinct which detects evil under a plausible exterior and surmises its future development. Kurolesov's respectful manner and polite speeches did not take him in for a moment: he guessed at once that there was some knavery underneath. There were other objections. My grandfather's own life was very strict, and the reports of the Major's peccadilloes which had casually come to his ear, though many people treated them lightly enough, filled his honest breast with disgust; and, though he was himself capable of furious anger, he hated deliberate unkindness and cold cruelty. For all these reasons his reception of his guest was cool and dry, though Kurolesov talked in a sensible practical way on all subjects and especially the management of land. Praskovya Ivanovna had now come to live with my grandfather; and when the Major began, on the strength of their old acquaintance, to pay her compliments which she accepted with pleasure, his host's head bent a little to one side, his eyebrows met, and he shot a look at his guest which was hardly hospitable. Arina Vasilevna, on the contrary, and her daughters had been charmed straight off by the young man's seductions and were quite inclined to say kind things to him; but the storm-signals on the face of Stepan Mikhailovich quenched their ardour and made them all hold their tongues. The guest tried to restore the harmony of the party and to resume their agreeable conversation. But it was no use: he received short answers from them all, and his host was not even quite polite. Though it was getting late and an invitation to stay the night would have been the natural thing, there was nothing for it but to take his leave. 'The man is a knave and rotten all through,' said Stepan Mikhailovich to his family; 'but perhaps he won't come here again.' No voice was raised to contradict him; but, behind his back, the women went on for a long time praising the dashing young officer; and one who liked to listen to his merits and to tell of them herself, was the orphan girl with the large fortune.

With the taste of this rebuff in his mouth, Kurolesov went back and told Mme Bakteev of his failure. The people there knew my grandfather well, and at once abandoned all hope that he would give his consent. Long consideration brought no solution of the difficulty. The bold Major suggested that her grandmother should invite the girl on a visit, and that the marriage should take place without the consent of Stepan Mikhailovich; but both Mme Bakteev and her daughter, Mme Kurmyshev, were convinced that Stepan Mikhailovich would not let his cousin go alone, or, if he did, would be slow about it, and the Major's leave was nearly at an end. Then he proposed a desperate scheme—to induce Praskovya Ivanovna to elope with him, and to get married in the nearest church; but her relations would not hear of such a scandalous expedient, and Kurolesov went back to his regiment. The ways of Providence are past finding out, and we cannot judge why it came about that this nefarious scheme was crowned with success. Six months later, Mme Bakteev heard one day that Stepan Mikhailovich was called away to some distance by very important business and would not return for some time. His destination and errand I do not know; but it was some distant place, Astrakhan or Moscow, and the business was certainly legal, because he took with him his man of business. A letter was sent at once to Stepan Mikhailovich, begging that the child, during the absence of her cousin and guardian, might stay with her grandmother. A curt answer was received—that Parasha* was very well where she was, and if they wished to see her they were welcome to visit Bagrovo and stay as long as they liked. Stepan Mikhailovich sent this plain answer, and gave the strictest injunctions to his always submissive wife, that she was to watch Parasha as the apple of her eye and never let her go out of the house alone; and then he started on his journey.

Mme Bakteev was constantly sending letters and messages to Praskovya Ivanovna and my grandfather's womenfolk; and she sent news of his departure at once to Kurolesov, adding that the absence would be a long one, and asking whether the Major could not come on leave, to take a personal share in the promotion of their scheme. She herself and her daughter went at once to Bagrovo. She had always been on friendly terms with Arina Vasilevna, and now, on discovering that she also liked Kurolesov, revealed the fact that the young officer was passionately in love with Parasha; she launched out into praise of the suitor, and said, 'There is nothing I wish so much as to see the poor little orphan comfortably settled in my lifetime; I am sure she will be happy. I feel that I have not long to live, and therefore I should like to hurry on the business.' Arina Vasilevna, on her side, entirely approved of the plan but expressed doubts whether Stepan Mikhailovich would consent: 'Heaven knows why,' she said, 'but he took a strong dislike to that delightful Kurolesov.' Arina Vasilevna's elder daughters were summoned to a council presided over by Mme Bakteev and her daughter, a strong partisan of the Major's; and it was settled that the grandmother, as the girl's nearest relation, should manage the affair, without involving Arina Vasilevna and her daughters; it was to appear that they knew nothing

* A familiar form of Praskovya, which itself represents the Greek name Paraskeva.

about it and took no hand in it. I have said already that Arina Vasilevna was a kind-hearted and very simple woman; her daughters sympathized entirely with Mme Bakteev, and it is not surprising that she was persuaded by them to promote a scheme which was sure to provoke the furious rage of Stepan Mikhailovich.

Meantime the innocent victim laughed and sang, with no suspicion that her fate was being decided. They often spoke of Kurolesov in her presence, praised him to the skies, and assured her that he loved her more than his own life, was constantly studying how to please her, and would certainly bring her a number of presents from Moscow on his next visit. All this she heard with pleasure, and often said that she loved Kurolesov better than anyone in the world. While Mme Bakteev was at Bagrovo, she had a letter forwarded to her, in which Kurolesov assured her that he would come, as soon as he could get leave. Arina Vasilevna promised to say nothing when writing to her husband, and also to send Parasha to her grandmother's house, in spite of her husband's strict orders to the contrary, on the pretext that her nearest relative was dangerously ill. When the two ladies left Bagrovo and went home, Praskovya Ivanovna cried and asked to go with them; the Major was expected soon, and that was an additional attraction; but permission was refused, out of respect, it was said, to her guardian's strict orders. Kurolesov had some difficulty in getting leave, and it was two months before he arrived. Immediately afterwards a special messenger was dispatched to Bagrovo with a letter from Mme Kurmyshev to Arina Vasilevna; the lady wrote that her mother was desperately ill and wished to see her granddaughter and give her her blessing; she therefore asked that Parasha might be sent, with an escort. She also wrote that Stepan Mikhailovich would certainly have sent the child to see the last of her grandmother, and could not possibly resent this infraction of his commands. The letter was clearly intended to be shown by Arina Vasilevna, in order to protect herself from her husband's displeasure. True to her promise and reassured by this letter, Arina Vasilevna made her preparations at once and took Parasha herself to the place where the grandmother was supposed to be dying; she stayed there a week and returned home charmed by the politeness of Kurolesov and also by some presents which he had brought from Moscow for her, and for her daughters as well. Praskovya Ivanovna was very happy: her grandmother took a sudden turn for the better; that fairy godmother, the Major, had brought her a number of presents and toys from Moscow and stayed in the house continually. He flattered her in every possible way, and soon took her fancy so completely, that, when her grandmother told her he wished to marry her, she was charmed. She ran up and down through the house like a perfect child, telling everyone she met that she was going to marry the Major and would have capital fun—driving all day with him behind his fine trotters, swinging on a swing of immense height, singing, or playing with dolls, not little dolls, but big ones that were able to walk and bow. You can judge by this, how far the poor little bride realized her position. Fearing that reports might reach Stepan Mikhailovich, the plotters went to work quickly: they invited the neighbours to a formal betrothal, at which the pair exchanged rings and kisses, sat side by side at table, and had their healths drunk. At first, the bride got tired of the ceremony where she had to sit still so long and listen to so many congratulations; but when she was allowed to have her new doll from Moscow beside her, she quite cheered up, introducing the doll to everyone as her daughter, and making it curtsey when she did, in acknowledgement of their kind wishes. A week later, the marriage took place with all due formality; the bride's age was given as seventeen instead of fifteen, but no one would have guessed the truth, to look at her.

Though Arina Vasilevna and her daughters knew what the end must be, yet the news of the marriage, which came sooner than they expected, filled them with horror. The scales fell from their eyes, and they now realized what they had been about, and that neither the grandmother's sham illness nor her letter would serve to cover them from the just wrath of Stepan Mikhailovich. Before she heard of the marriage, Arina Vasilevna had written to her husband that she had taken the child to her grandmother: 'It was quite necessary', she wrote, 'because the old lady was in a dying state. I stayed there a whole week, and mercifully the invalid took a good turn; but they insisted on keeping Parasha till her grandmother got well. I was helpless: I could not take her by force, so I agreed against my will and hurried back to our own children, who were quite alone at Bagrovo. And now I am afraid that you will be angry.' In answering, he said she had done a foolish thing and told her to go back and fetch Parasha home at all costs. Arina Vasilevna sighed and shed tears over this letter, and was puzzled how to act. The young couple soon came to pay her a visit. Parasha seemed perfectly happy and cheerful, though some of her childish gaiety had gone. Her husband seemed happy too, and at the same time so composed and sensible that his clever arguments had power to lull Arina Vasilevna's fears to rest. He proved to her convincingly that her husband's wrath must all fall upon the grandmother: 'And she,' said he, 'owing to that dangerous illness—though now, thank God! she is better—had a perfect right not to wait for the consent of Stepan Mikhailovich; she knew that he would be slow in giving it, though of course he must have given it in time. It was impossible for her to delay, owing to her critical condition, and it would have been hard for her to die without seeing her orphan granddaughter settled in life; her place could not be filled even by a brother, far less by a mere cousin.' Many soothing assurances of this kind were forthcoming, backed by some very handsome presents which were received by the Bagrovo ladies with great satisfaction and some sinking of heart. Other presents were left, to be given to Stepan Mikhailovich. Kurolesov advised Arina Vasilevna not to write to her husband till he answered the letter of intimation from the young couple; and he assured her that he and his wife would write this at once. He did not really dream of writing: his sole object was to delay the explosion and get time to take root in his new position. Immediately after his marriage, he applied for leave to retire from the army, and got it very soon. He then began by paying a round of visits with his bride to all the relations and friends on both sides. At Simbirsk he began by calling on the Governor and neglected no one of any importance who could be useful to him. All were enthusiastic in praise of the handsome young couple, and they were so popular everywhere that the marriage was soon sanctioned by public opinion. Thus several months passed away.

Stepan Mikhailovich had had no news from home for a long time, and his lawsuit dragged on interminably. He was suddenly seized by a longing to see his family again, and returned one fine day to Bagrovo. Arina Vasilevna trembled all over when she heard the awful words, 'The master has come!' Hearing that all were alive and well, he entered his house in high spirits, kissed his Arisha and daughters and son, and then asked in an easy tone, 'But where on earth is Parasha?' Encouraged by her husband's kind manner, Arina Vasilevna answered: 'I don't know for certain where she is; perhaps with her grandmother. Of course you heard long ago, *batyushka*, that she was married.' I shall not describe my grandfather's amazement and fury; but his fury became twice as hot, when he heard the name of the bridegroom. He was proceeding to settle accounts with his wife on the spot, when she and all her daughters fell at his feet and showed him Mme Bakteev's letter; thus she had time to convince him that she knew nothing about it and had been deceived herself. The fury of Stepan Mikhailovich was now diverted to Mme Bakteev; he ordered fresh horses to be ready, rested two hours, and then galloped straight off to her house. The battle royal that took place between the two may be imagined. The old lady stood the first torrent of unmeasured abuse without flinching; then she drew herself up, grew hot in her turn, and delivered her own attack upon my grandfather. 'How dare you make this furious assault on me,' she asked, 'as if I was your bond-slave? Do you forget that my birth is quite as good as yours, and that my late husband held a much higher rank than you? I am a nearer relation to Parasha, I am her own grandmother, and her guardian as much as you are. I arranged for her settlement without waiting for your consent, because I was dangerously ill and did not wish to leave her dependent upon you. I knew your infernal temper; under your roof, the child would have had a taste of the stick some day. Kurolesov is an excellent match for her, and Parasha fell in love with him of herself. Everybody likes him and praises him. I know he did not take your fancy; but just ask your own family, and you will soon find out that they can't say enough in his praise!'

'You lie, you old swindler!' roared my grandfather; 'you deceived my wife by pretending that you were dying! Kurolesov has bewitched you and your daughter by the power of the devil, and you have sold your granddaughter into his hands!'

This was too much for Mme Bakteev, and she let out in her rage that Arina Vasilevna and her daughters were in league with her and had themselves accepted presents at different times from Kurolesov. This disclosure turned the whole force of my grandfather's rage back upon his own family. He threatened that he would dissolve the marriage on the ground that Parasha was not of age, and then started home. On the way he turned aside to visit the priest who had performed the ceremony, and called him to account. But the priest met his attack very coolly, and showed him without hesitation the certificate of affinity, the signatures of the grandmother, the bride, and the witnesses, and also the baptismal certificate which alleged that Praskovya Ivanovna was seventeen. This was a fresh blow to my grandfather, for it deprived him of all hope of breaking the hateful marriage; and it increased enormously his anger against his wife and daughters. I shall not dwell upon his behaviour when he got home: it would be too painful and repulsive. Thirty years later, my aunts could never speak of that day without trembling. I shall only say, that the culprits made a full confession, that he sent back all the presents, including those intended for himself, to Mme Bakteev, to be forwarded to the proper quarter, that the elder daughters long kept to their beds, and that my grandmother lost all her hair and went about for a whole year with her head bandaged. He sent a message to the Kurolesovs forbidding them to dare to appear before him, and ordered that their names should never be mentioned in his house.

Time rolled on, healing wounds whether of mind or body, and calming passions. Within a year Arina Vasilevna's head was healed, and the anger in the heart of Stepan Mikhailovich had cooled. At first he refused either to see or hear of the Kurolesovs, and would not even write to Praskovya Ivanovna; but when a year had passed and he heard from all quarters good accounts of her way of life, and was told that she had suddenly become sensible beyond her years, his heart softened and he became anxious to see the cousin whom he loved. He reasoned that she, as a perfect child, was less to blame than any of the rest, and gave her leave to come, without her husband, to Bagrovo; and, as a matter of course, she came at once. The reports were true: one year of marriage had wrought such a change in Praskovya Ivanovna, that Stepan Mikhailovich could hardly believe it. It was puzzling also, that she now showed towards her cousin a kind of love and gratitude which she had never felt in her girlhood, and was still less likely, one would think, to feel after her marriage. In his eyes, which filled with tears when they met, did she read how much love was concealed under that harsh exterior and that arbitrary violence? Had she any dark foreboding of the future, or did she dimly realize that here was her one support and stay? Or did she feel unconsciously, that the rough cousin who had opposed her happiness and still disliked her husband, loved her better than all the women who had indulged her by falling in with all her childish wishes? I cannot answer these questions; but all were struck by the change. In her careless childhood she had been indifferent to her cousin, thinking little of his rights and her duties; and now she had every reason to resent his treatment of her grandmother; yet she felt to him now as a devoted daughter feels to a tender father when both have long known and loved one another. Whatever the cause of it, this sudden feeling ended only with her life.

But what was the remarkable change that had come over so young a woman as Praskovya Ivanovna, after one year of married life? The foolish child had turned into a sensible but cheerful woman. She frankly confessed that they had all behaved badly to Stepan Mikhailovich. For herself only she pleaded youth and ignorance, and for her grandmother, her husband, and the rest, their blind devotion to her. She did not ask him to pardon the chief criminal at once; but she hoped that in time, when he saw her happiness and the unwearied care with which her husband managed her property and looked after her estates, her cousin would forgive the culprit and admit him at Bagrovo.

My grandfather, though he made no answer at the time, was completely conquered by this appeal. He did not keep his 'clever cousin'—as he now began to call her—long at his house; he said that her place was now elsewhere, and soon sent her back to her husband. At parting, he said: 'If you are as well satisfied with your husband a year hence, and if he behaves as well to you as he does now, I shall be reconciled to him.' A year later, as he knew that Kurolesov was behaving well and paying the utmost attention to the management of his wife's property, and found his cousin, when he saw her, looking healthy and happy and cheerful, Stepan Mikhailovich told her to bring her husband with her to Bagrovo. He received Kurolesov cordially, frankly confessed his former doubts, and ended by promising to treat him as a kinsman and friend, on condition of continued good conduct. The guest behaved very cleverly: he was less furtive and less insinuating than he used to be, but just as respectful, attentive, and tactful. His bearing was clearly more confident and self-assured; he was giving the closest attention to agricultural problems, on which he asked advice from my grandfather —advice which he took in very quickly and followed with remarkable skill. He was connected in some distant way with Stepan Mikhailovich, and addressed him as 'uncle' and treated the rest of the family as relations. Even before the scene of reconciliation or forgiveness, he had rendered a service of some kind to Stepan Mikhailovich; my grandfather was aware of this and thanked him for it now; he even gave him a similar commission to execute. In fact, the visit passed off very well. But, though all the circumstances seemed to speak in favour of Kurolesov, my grandfather still said: 'The lad is all right: he is clever and sensible; but somehow I don't take to him.'

It was in the course of the next year that Stepan Mikhailovich made his move to the district of Ufa. For three years after his marriage, Kurolesov behaved with discretion and moderation, or at least concealed his conduct with such care that nothing got round. Besides, he was constantly moving about and spent little time at home. There was only one report, which spread everywhere with exaggeration—that the young landowner was a very strict master. During the next two years he did wonders in the way of improving his wife's property, and established his character for unceasing activity, bold enterprise, and steadfast perseverance in the execution of his schemes. The property had been mismanaged previously: the land had been injured by neglect, and the peasants brought in very little income, not because there was no market for their grain, but because they were spoilt and lazy, and had too little land; and another difficulty was that some of them belonged to three different owners—Mme Bakteev and her daughter as well as Praskovya Ivanovna. Kurolesov began by transferring some of the peasants to new ground, while he sold the old land at a good profit. He bought about 20,000 acres of steppe in the province of Simbirsk (now Samara) and the district of Stavropolsk—excellent arable land, level and easy to plough, with over three feet of black soil. The land lay on the river Berlya, which had some coppices on its banks near the source; and there was also 'Bear Hollow', which was left untouched for some time and is now the only forest on the property. He settled 350 serfs here. This estate turned out highly profitable, because it was only a hundred versts from Samara and about fifty from a number of ports on the Volga. It is well known that the value of an estate in our country depends entirely upon the market for grain.

Next, Kurolesov went off to the district of Ufa and bought from the Bashkirs 60,000 acres. The soil, though good, was not as productive as that in Simbirsk, but there was a considerable quantity of wood, not only firewood, but timber for building. He planted two colonies there, one of 450 serfs and the other of 50; and he called the larger 'Parashino' and the smaller 'Ivanovka'. As the Simbirsk estate was called 'Kurolesovo', each of the properties bore one of the names of his wife. Such a romantic fancy has always seemed to me curious, considering the sort of man that Kurolesov turned out to be; but some will maintain that these inconsistencies are common enough. He also made a seat for himself and his wife in the village of Churasovo, fifty versts from Simbirsk; this was a separate property of 350 serfs which his wife had inherited from her mother. He built there a splendid mansion, according to the ideas of those days, with all the usual appurtenances; it was finely decorated and furnished, and painted with frescoes inside and out; the chandeliers and bronzes, the silver plate and china, were a wonder to behold. The house was situated on the slope of a hill, from which more than twenty excellent springs came bubbling out. The house and the hill stood in the centre of an orchard, very large and productive, stocked with apple-trees and cherry-trees of every possible sort. The internal arrangements—the service and cooking, the horses and carriages—were luxurious and substantial. There was a constant succession of visitors at Churasovo, either country neighbours, of whom there were a good many, or people from Simbirsk; they ate and drank, took walks and played cards, sang and talked, and were generally noisy and merry. Kurolesov dressed his wife up like a doll, anticipated all her wishes, and entertained her from morning till night, that is, when he happened to be at home. In short, after a few years, he had attained such a position all round, that good people admired him and bad people envied him. Nor did he forget the claims of religion: in place of an old tumbledown wooden erection, he built a new church of stone and equipped it splendidly; he even formed an excellent choir out of the household servants. Praskovya Ivanovna was quite contented and happy. She gave birth to a daughter in the fourth year of her marriage, and to a son a year later, but she soon lost them, the girl in infancy, and the boy when he was three. She had become so attached to the boy that this loss cost her dear. For a whole year her eyes were never dry, her excellent constitution was seriously affected, and she had no more children. Meanwhile her husband's reputation and influence grew by leaps and bounds. It is true that his behaviour to the small landowners was arbitrary and harsh; yet they, if they did not like him, were exceedingly afraid of him; and people of importance thought it only to his credit, that he made his inferiors know their proper place. His absence from home became more frequent and longer, from year to year, especially after the sad year in which Praskovya Ivanovna lost her son and would not be comforted. It is probable that he grew weary of tears and sighs and solitude; for she refused to have any visitors for a whole year.

But indeed the most cheerful and noisy society at Churasovo was no attraction to Kurolesov.

Little by little, certain rumours began to spread abroad and gain strength. According to these reports, the Major was not merely strict, as was said before, but cruel; in the privacy of his estates at Ufa he gave himself up to drink and debauchery; he had gathered round him a band with whom he drank and committed excesses of every kind; and, worse still, several victims had already been killed by him in the fury of his drunken violence. The police and magistrates of the district, it was said, were all his creatures: he had bribed some with money and others with drink and terrorized them all. The small land-owners and inferior officials went in terror of their lives: if any dared to act or speak against him, they were seized in broad daylight and imprisoned in cellars or corn kilns, where they were fed on bread and water and suffered the pangs of cold and hunger; and some were unmercifully flogged with an instrument called a 'cat'. Kurolesov had a special fancy for this imple-ment, which was merely a leather whip with seven tails and knots at the end of each tail. Some specimens were kept long after Kurolesov's death in a store-room at Parashino, for show, not for use; and I saw them there myself; they were burnt by my father when he inherited the property. These reports were only too well founded: the reality far surpassed the timid whisper of rumour. Kurolesov's thirst for blood, inflamed to madness by strong drink, grew unchecked to its full proportions, till it presented one of those horrible spectacles at which humanity shudders and turns sick. The instinct of the tiger is terrible indeed, when combined with the reasoning power of a man.

At last the rumours were changed into certain knowledge; and of all the people with whom Praskovya Ivanovna lived—relations, neighbours, and servants,—everyone knew the real truth about Kurolesov. When he returned to Churasovo from the scene of his exploits, he always showed the same respect to rank, the same friendly attention to his equals, the same anxiety to please his wife. She had now got over her loss and had recovered health and spirits; the house was as full of visitors as it used to be, and something was always going on. At Churasovo, Kurolesov never struck any of the servants, leaving the bailiff and the butler in sole possession of this amusement; but they all knew about him and trembled at a mere look. Even relations and intimate friends showed some discomfort and embarrassment in his company. But Praskovya Ivanovna noticed nothing, or, if she did, ascribed it to a quite different cause—the involuntary respect which everyone felt for her husband's remarkable success as a landowner, his splendid establishment, and his general intelligence and firmness of purpose. Sensible people who loved Praskovya Ivanovna, when they saw her perfectly composed and happy, were glad of her ignorance and hoped it might last as long as possible. There were, no doubt, some women among her dependants and humble neighbours whose tongues itched uncommonly, and who felt a strong desire to pay the Major out for his contemptuous treatment of them, by disclosing the truth; but, apart from the fear they could not help feeling, which would probably not have deterred them, there was another obstacle which prevented the fulfilment of their kind intentions. It was simply impossible to bring any tales against her husband to Praskovya Ivanovna. She was clever, keen-sighted, and determined; and, as soon as she detected any hidden innuendo to the detriment of Kurolesov, she knitted her dark eyebrows and said in her downright way that any offence of the kind would be punished by perpetual exclusion from her house. As the natural result of such a significant warning, nobody ventured to interfere in what was not their business. There were two servants in the house, a favourite attendant of her late father's and her own old nurse, whom she specially favoured, though they were not admitted to such close intimacy as old servants often were in those days; but they too were powerless. To them it was a matter of life and death that their mistress should know the real truth about her husband; for they had near relations who were personal attendants of Kurolesov's and were suffering beyond endurance from their master's cruelty. At last they determined to tell the whole story to their mistress. They chose a time when she was alone, and went together to her room; but the old nurse had hardly mentioned Kurolesov's name, when Praskovya Ivanovna flew into a violent passion. She told the woman that if she ever again ventured to open her mouth against her master, she would banish her from her presence for ever and send her to live at Parashino. Thus all possible channels were blocked, and all mouths were stopped, that might have informed against the criminal. Praskovya Ivanovna loved her husband and trusted him absolutely. She knew that people like to meddle with what does not concern them, and like to trouble the water, that they may catch fish; and she had made up her mind at once and laid down an absolute rule, to listen to no tales against her husband. It is an excellent rule, and indispensable for the preservation of domestic peace. But there is no rule that does not admit of exceptions; and perhaps, in the present case, the resolute temper and strong will of the wife, added to the fact that all the wealth belonged to her, might have checked the husband at the outset of his career. As a sensible man, he would not have cared to deprive himself of all the advantages of a luxurious life; he would not have gone to such extremes or given such free play to his monstrous passions. It is more likely that, like many other men, he would have taken his pleasures in moderation and with precaution.

Thus several years went by, during which Kurolesov gave himself up without restraint to his evil tendencies. His degeneration was rapid, and at last he began to commit incredible crimes, and always with impunity. I shall not describe in detail the kind of life he led on his estates, especially at Parashino, and also in the villages of the district; the story would be too repulsive. I shall say no more than is necessary to convey a true conception of this formidable man. During the early years when his whole attention was given to organizing his wife's estates, he deserved to be called the most far-seeing, practical, and watchful of agents. To all the infinitely various and troublesome business, involved in removing peasants and settling them down in distant holdings, he gave his personal and unremitting attention. He kept constantly in view one object only, the well-being of his dependants. He could spend money where it was needed; he saw that it came to hand at the right time and in the right quantity; he anticipated all the wants and requirements of the settlers. He accompanied them himself for a great part of their journey, and met them himself at the end of it, where they found everything prepared for their reception. It is true that he was too severe and even cruel in the punishment of culprits; but he was just, and could keep his eyes shut at times. From time to time he allowed himself a little relaxation, when he disappeared for a day or two to amuse himself; but he could throw off the effects of his debauchery like water off a duck's back, and come to work again with fresh vigour.

So long as he had the burden of his work upon his shoulders, it took up all his powers of mind and kept him from the fatal passion for drink, which robbed him of his senses and removed the curb from his monstrous inhuman passions. Work was his salvation; but when he had got both the new estates, Kurolesov and Parashino, into order, and built manor-houses at both, with a second smaller house at Parashino, then came the season of little work and much leisure. Drunkenness, with its usual consequences, and violence, gained complete mastery over him, and developed by degrees into an insatiable thirst for human blood and human suffering. Encouraged by the passive fear of all around him, he soon ceased to set any limit to his arbitrary violence. He chose from among his dependants a score of ruffians, fit instruments for his purposes, and formed them into a band of robbers. They saw that their master bore a charmed life, and believed in his power; drunken and debauched themselves, they carried out all his insane orders willingly and boldly. If any man offended Kurolesov by the slightest independence in word or action—if, for example, he failed to turn up when invited to one of their drunken revels—the gang set off at once at a sign from their master, seized the culprit either secretly or openly wherever they found him, and brought him back to Parashino, where he was treated with insult and chained up in a cellar underground or flogged by their master's orders. Kurolesov was a man of taste: he liked good horses, and he liked good pictures—he thought them good at least—to adorn his walls. If anything of the kind took his fancy in a neighbour's house or in any house where he happened to be, he at once proposed an exchange; in case of a refusal, he would sometimes, if he was in a good humour, offer money; but if this also was refused, he gave warning that he would take it and give nothing for it. And he did actually turn up with his gang a short time after, pack up whatever he wanted, and carry it off. Complaints were made, and the preliminary steps for an inquiry were taken. But Kurolesov saw this must be stopped at once. He sent a message to the district magistrate, that he would flay with the 'cat' any officer of the law who dared to present himself; and he remained master of the situation. Meantime the man who had dared to complain was seized and beaten, on his own estate and in his own house, with his wife and children kneeling round and imploring mercy. It was Kurolesov's custom to make it up with his victims after a time: sometimes he offered them pecuniary compensation, but more often he restored peace by terrorizing them; in any case, the stolen goods remained his lawful property. During his carouses he liked to boast that he had taken 'that pretty thing in the gilt frame' from so-and-so, and that inlaid writing-table from someone else; and often these very people were sitting at the table, pretending to be deaf or plucking up heart to laugh at their own losses. There were even worse acts of violence, but these also went scot-free.

Kurolesov had a very powerful constitution: though he drank a great deal, it never disabled him but only put him on the move and roused a horrible activity in his clouded brain and inflamed body. One of his favourite amusements was to harness teams of spirited horses to a miscellaneous assortment of carriages, to pack the carriages with his ragtag and bobtail of men and women, and then scour over the fields and through the villages at full gallop, with the jingling of bells and the singing and shouting of his drunken rabble. He took a stock of liquor with him on these occasions and made everyone he met, without regard to calling or sex or age, drink till they were intoxicated; and anyone who dared to refuse was first flogged, and then tied to a tree or a post, though it might be raining or freezing at the time. Of more revolting acts of violence I say nothing. One day he was driving in this state of mind through a village, and, as he passed a threshing-floor, noticed a woman of remarkable beauty. 'Stop!' he called out. 'Petrushka, what do you think of that woman?' 'She's uncommonly pretty,' said Petrushka. 'Would you like to marry her?' 'How can I marry another man's wife?' asked Petrushka with a grin on his face. 'I'll show you how! Seize her, my lads, and put her in the carriage beside me!' They did so; the woman was taken straight to the parish church, and there, though she protested that she had a husband living and two children, was married to Petrushka; and no complaints were made either in Kurolesov's lifetime or in that of his widow. When the estate came into my father's hands, he restored this woman with her husband and children to her former owner; her first husband had long been dead. My father also distributed various articles of property to their former owners when they asked for them; but many of the things had got worn out by tossing about in lumber-rooms. It is hard to believe that such things could happen in Russia, even eighty years ago; but the truth of the narrative it is impossible to dispute.

This life of drunken and criminal violence, horrible and disgusting enough in itself, led on to worse, till the man's natural cruelty became a ferocious thirst for blood. To inflict torture became with him a necessity as well as a pleasure. On the days when he could not gratify this passion, he was depressed and listless, uneasy and even ill; and this was why his visits to Churasovo grew steadily rarer and his stay there shorter. But, on his return to the solitude of Parashino, he made haste to reward himself for his abstinence. He had only to watch the labourers at their work, to secure a sufficient number of victims; no excuses were accepted, and it is always possible to find trifling cases of neglect on the land if you are determined to hunt for them. Yet it was the personal servants and people about the house who suffered most from his ferocity. He seldom flogged a peasant, unless the man had committed a serious offence or was personally known to him; but his bailiffs and clerks suffered as much at his hands as the household servants. He spared no one: everyone of his favourites had, some time or other, been flogged within an inch of his life, and some of them many times. It is remarkable that, when Kurolesov got violently angry, which seldom happened, he did not use violence; but, when he had got hold of a man and intended to torture him for his own amusement, he would say in a quiet and even affectionate tone: 'Well, my good friend Grigory Kuzmich,'—Grishka* being his usual name—'it can't be helped; come, and I will settle accounts with you.' Thus he would speak to his head-groom, who for some unknown reason was put to the torture more often than others. 'Scratch him up a bit with the cat,' said the master with a smile, and then the torture went on for hours, while the master drank tea with brandy in it, smoked his pipe, and from time to time passed jests on his victim till unconsciousness supervened. Trustworthy witnesses have assured me that only one expedient proved successful in saving life after such an ordeal: the lacerated body of the victim was wrapped up in sheepskins taken warm from the animals' backs as soon as they were slaughtered. Kurolesov would carefully examine his victim; then, if content, he would say, 'Well, that's enough; take him away'—and then he became cheerful, jocular, and amiable for the whole day and sometimes for several days. In order to complete the portrait of this monster, I shall quote his own words which he repeated more than once among his boon companions: 'Don't talk to me of the knout or the stick! They kill a man before you mean it. The "cat" is the thing for me: it gives pain without taking life!' I have told here only a tithe of what I know, but perhaps I have said enough. It is remarkable, as an instance of the inexplicable inconsistencies of corrupt human nature, that Kurolesov, at a time when he had reached the extreme limit of debauchery and cruelty, was zealously engaged in building a stone church at Parashino. At the time I am about to describe, the outside of the church was finished, and workmen had been hired for the internal decoration: carpenters, carvers, gilders, and ikon-painters had been at work for some months and were occupying all the smaller manor-house of Parashino.

Praskovya Ivanovna had now been married fourteen years. She noticed something strange about her husband, whom for two years she had only seen at long intervals for a few days at a

* A familiar form of Grigory (Gregory).

time, but she did not even suspect anything like the truth. She went on with her easy cheerful way of life: in summer she gave great attention to her orchard and the water-springs which she left in their natural state and liked to clean out with her own hands; at other seasons she spent her time with her visitors and became a great lover of cards. Suddenly she received, by post or special messenger, a letter from an old lady for whom she had great respect, a distant relation of her husband's. This letter gave a full description of Kurolesov's life, and ended by saying, that it would be sinful not to open the eyes of the mistress of a thousand serfs, when they were suffering such monstrous cruelty and she could protect them by cancelling the legal authority she had given her husband to manage her estates. 'Their blood cries to heaven,' she wrote, 'and at this moment a servant known to you, Ivan Onufriev, is dying in consequence of cruel maltreatment. You have nothing to fear yourself from Kurolesov: he will not venture to show his face at Churasovo, and your good neighbours and the Governor himself will protect you.'

This letter fell like a thunderbolt on Praskovya Ivanovna. I have heard her say myself that she was quite stunned for some minutes; but she was supported by her firm faith in God and the uncommon strength of her will, and soon determined on a step from which most brave men would have shrunk. She ordered horses to be harnessed, saying that she was going to Simbirsk, and then, with one maid and a man and the coachman, drove straight to Parashino. It was a long journey of 400 versts, and she had plenty of leisure to think over what she was doing. She used to say herself that she had formed no plan of action whatever; she merely wished to see with her own eyes and find out for certain what her husband was doing and how he lived. She did not entirely trust the letter from his kinswoman, who lived at a distance and might have been deceived by false reports; and she did not choose to question her old nurse at Churasovo. The thought of danger never entered her head: her husband had always been so gentle and respectful with her, that it seemed to her quite natural and quite possible to induce him to return in her carriage to Churasovo. She timed herself to arrive at Parashino in the evening, left her carriage outside the village, and walked unrecognized—few of the people there knew her—accompanied by her maid and man, to the court of the mansion-house. She passed through the back entrance, made her way to a wing from which loud sounds of singing and laughter were issuing, and opened the door with a steady hand.

Fortune, as if on purpose, had brought together everything that could reveal at one flash the kind of life her husband was leading. More intoxicated than usual, he was carousing with his boon companions. Dressed in a shirt of red silk, he had a glass of punch in one hand and with his other arm held a beautiful girl on his knee,* while a tipsy herd of servants, retainers, and country women danced and sang before him. Praskovya Ivanovna nearly fainted at the sight. She understood all now. Unnoticed, because the room was crowded with people, she shut the door and left the house. On the steps she came face to face with one of Kurolesov's servants, not a young man, and, fortunately, sober. He recognized his mistress and was just calling out, '*Matushka*† Praskovya Ivanovna, is it you?'—when she put her hand over his mouth and led him to the centre of the courtyard. She said in an ominous voice, 'Is this the way you go on behind my back? The days of your feasting and dancing are done.' The man fell at her feet weeping and said: '*Matushka*, do you suppose that *we* find pleasure in his goings-on, that *we* are responsible? God himself has brought you here.' She told him to be silent and take her to see Ivan Onufriev; she had heard that he was still living. She found him dying, lying in a cow-byre in the backyard. He was too weak to tell her anything; but his brother, Alexei, a mere lad, who had been flogged only the day before, crawled somehow from his pallet, fell on his knees, and told her what had befallen his brother and himself and others as well. Praskovya Ivanovna's heart swelled with pity and horror. She felt that she also was to blame, and she formed a firm resolve to put an end to the crimes and atrocities of

* The sentence 'and with...his knee' was censored in the edition Duff used, but appears in later editions.

† i.e. Mother, a term of affection and respect.

Kurolesov. She thought there would be no difficulty, She gave strict orders that her presence should be kept secret. Then, as she heard that the smaller house, which had been built some years before, but from some caprice of her husband's, never furnished, contained one habitable room unoccupied by the workmen, she went off, intending to pass the remainder of the night there and to speak next morning to her husband when he was sober. But the secret of her arrival was not strictly kept. The report reached the ear of one of the most desperate of Kurolesov's gang, and he, moved by devotion or by fear, whispered it to his master. Kurolesov was dumbfounded by the news; it sobered him in a moment; he felt uneasy and scented danger ahead. His wife's firm and masculine temper had found few opportunities to display itself hitherto, but he guessed that it was there. Dismissing his band of revellers, he had two or three buckets of cold water poured over his head; and then, braced up and invigorated by this expedient, he changed into ordinary clothing and went to see if his wife was asleep. He had had time to reflect and fix on a line of action. He guessed the truth, that Praskovya Ivanovna had received from some quarter information as to his way of life, but that she was incredulous and had come to Parashino to ascertain the truth herself. He knew that her eye had rested for a moment on his revels, but he did not know that she had seen Onufriev and that Alexei had told her the whole story. He intended to play the repentant sinner, to excuse himself as best he could for his riotous debauch, to pour oil on the troubled waters by his delicate attentions, and to take his wife away as soon as possible from Parashino.

It was morning by now, and the sun had actually risen. Kurolesov stole on tiptoe to the room occupied by Praskovya Ivanovna and softly opened the door. A bed had been made for her on the top of a chest, but the sheets were still smooth and no one had lain down on them. He looked all round the room and saw Praskovya Ivanovna. She was kneeling in prayer; there was no ikon in the room, and her eyes, full of tears, were fixed upon the cross on the church, which was just opposite the window and glittered in the rays of the rising sun. He remained standing a few moments, and then said in a playful voice: 'You have prayed long enough, my dear! I am delighted to see you. What made you think of coming?' Praskovya Ivanovna rose from her knees with no sign of confusion; she refused her husband's embrace; then, concealing the flame of her just anger under a cold determined manner, she told him that she knew all and had seen Ivan Onufriev. She expressed in plain terms her aversion to the monster whom she could no longer regard as her husband, and she passed sentence upon him: he was to return the document which gave him authority over her estates. to leave Parashino at once, never to appear before her again, and never to set foot on any of her lands; if he refused, she would petition the Governor of the province, and reveal all his crimes; and his fate would be Siberia and penal servitude. Kurolesov was taken by surprise; he foamed at the mouth with rage and anger. 'So that is the way you talk to me, my beauty! Then I shall change my tune too!' roared the infuriated ruffian. 'You shall not leave Parashino till you sign a document transferring all your estates to me; if you refuse, I shall shut you up in a cellar and starve you to death.' Then he caught up a stick from a corner of the room, felled his wife to the floor with his first blows, and went on beating her till she lost her senses. Next he ordered some of his trusted servants to carry their mistress to a stone cellar, which he locked with a huge padlock and put the key in his pocket. He was a formidable figure when he appeared before the assembled household; he had summoned them all, in order to discover the culprit who had led his mistress to the cow-byre; but the man had already sought safety in flight, accompanied by the coachman and manservant who had come from Churasovo. The fugitives were pursued at once. Kurolesov did no injury to the maid, who had refused to desert her mistress: he gave her directions for exhorting the prisoner to submission, and then locked her up with his own hands in the same cellar. What did Kurolesov do next? He began to drink and riot more furiously than before. But alas! in vain did he swallow brandy like water, in vain did his revel rout dance and sing before him—he had turned gloomy and sullen. Yet this did not prevent him from working indefatigably for the attain-

ment of his purpose. He procured from the local town a legal
document by which Praskovya Ivanovna professed to sell
Parashino and Kurolesovo to one of his disreputable friends—
Churasovo he was kind enough to leave to her—and twice a day
he went down to the cellar and pressed his wife to sign the
paper; he begged pardon for his violence in the heat of the
moment, promised that if she consented she should never see
him again, and took an oath that he would restore all her
property to her by his will. But Praskovya Ivanovna, though
bruised and half-starved and suffering from fever, refused even
to listen to any compromise whatever. So things went on for
five days, and God only knows how it would all have ended.

All this time my grandfather Stepan Mikhailovich was living
and prospering on his estate of New Bagrovo, which was 120
versts distant from Parashino. As I have mentioned already, he
had frankly made it up with Kurolesov and was satisfied with
him in general, though he felt no fancy for him. Kurolesov, on
his side, showed great deference to Stepan Mikhailovich and all
his family, and was ready to perform any services for them.
When he had planted his colony at Parashino and was engaged
in organizing it, he came every year to Bagrovo and made
himself very agreeable. He appealed to Stepan Mikhailovich,
as a man of practical experience in colonizing, for his advice;
he received it gratefully, wrote it all down word for word, and
really followed it. He even invited Stepan Mikhailovich twice to
Parashino, to judge of his pupil's proficiency; and each time
my grandfather approved entirely of what he saw; and on his last
visit, when he had inspected the arable land and all the farming
arrangements, he said to Kurolesov, 'You are young, friend,
but you've got on fast; I can teach you nothing.' And, as a
matter of fact, everything at Parashino was in excellent order.
Of course, the host received the old man as if he had been his
own father, with all possible deference and attention. As years
went on, ugly rumours about Kurolesov found their way to
Bagrovo. As my grandfather disliked gossip, nothing was said
to him at first; but the rumours grew steadily. The womenfolk
at Bagrovo knew of them; and Arina Vasilevna ventured at last
to tell her husband that Kurolesov was leading a terribly wicked

life. He would not believe it. He said: 'Once you believe what people say, you will soon accuse your neighbour of robbing a church! I know what the Bakteev servants were like—thieves and shirkers, to a man! And my cousin's serfs too got spoilt, with no master to look after them. It's not surprising if they're terrified of honest work and decent order. Friend Mikhail may have gone to work too fast: what of that? they'll learn to bear it. As to his drinking—if he takes a glass after his work, a man's none the worse for that, provided he doesn't neglect his business. There *are* beastly things a man shouldn't do; but there, I fancy, they're lying. You women are too fond of listening to gossip.' For a long time after this, Stepan Mikhailovich heard nothing more of the rumours. At last, some Bagroff serfs, who had been transferred from the province of Simbirsk to Parashino together with the serfs of the Bakteev family, came to visit their relations at New Bagrovo and told terrible stories of their master. Arina Vasilevna again appealed to her husband, and begged that he would himself question one of these men who was now at Bagrovo; he was an old man with an established character for speaking the truth; and Stepan Mikhailovich had known him all his life. My grandfather consented. He sent for the man and questioned him, and heard a story which made his hair stand on end. He could not think what to do, or how to mend matters. Praskovya Ivanovna's occasional letters showed that she was quite happy and undisturbed; and he concluded that she knew nothing of her husband's conduct. In the old days he had warned her himself never to listen to tales against her husband; and he felt sure that she was following his advice only too well. He reflected that, if she learnt the truth, it was doubtful if she could do anything; she would distress herself terribly, all to no purpose. It was therefore desirable that her eyes should never be opened. He could not now interfere; and he thought interference useless in the case of such a man. 'I hope he will break his neck or be tried for a murder; he deserves it. No hand but God's can mend a man like that. He is not so hard upon his peasants and labourers, and the house-servants are a pack of scoundrels; let them suffer for their sins! I have no mind to soil my fingers with this dirty business.' Thus Stepan

Mikhailovich reasoned in his own way. He broke off all relations with Kurolesov, however, and ceased to answer his letters. This hint was understood, and the correspondence came to an end. But to Praskovya Ivanovna, Stepan Mikhailovich began to write oftener and more intimately than before.

So matters remained till the morning when the three fugitives from Parashino made their appearance before my grandfather as he sat on his stoop. They had spent the first day concealed in an inaccessible swamp which joined on to the stackyards of Parashino; in the evening they learnt from someone in the village exactly what had happened, and made their way straight to Bagrovo, considering Stepan Mikhailovich as the only possible protector and champion of Praskovya Ivanovna. His feelings may be imagined when he heard what had happened at Parashino. He loved his one cousin not less, perhaps more, than his own daughters. The image of Parasha half-killed by her ruffian of a husband, of Parasha confined in a cellar for three days and perhaps dead already, presented itself so vividly to his lively imagination that he sprang up like one demented, and rushed down the courtyard and through the village, summoning his retainers and labourers in accents of frenzy. Those who were not in the cottages came running from the fields. When all were assembled, they were full of sympathy for their master's passionate despair and cried with one voice that they would go on foot, if need be, to the rescue of Praskovya Ivanova. In a short time three cars, drawn by teams of spirited horses from the stables of Bagrovo, and carrying a dozen men chosen for strength and courage, were galloping along the road to Parashino. The party included the fugitives from Parashino, and they were armed with guns and swords, pikes and pitchforks. Later in the day two more cars followed to reinforce Stepan Mikhailovich; the men were armed in the same way; the horses were the best the peasants could produce. By the evening of the second day, the vanguard was within seven versts of Parashino. They fed the jaded horses, and in the first light of the summer dawn dashed into the wide courtyard and drove straight up to the cellar. It was close to the rooms occupied by Kurolesov. Stepan Mikhailovich jumped out and began to beat his fist

against the wooden door of the cellar. A voice faintly asked,
'Who is there?' My grandfather recognized his cousin's voice;
dropping a tear of joy that he had found her alive, and crossing
himself, he called out in a loud voice, 'Thank God! It is your
cousin, Stepan Mikhailovich; you are safe now! He sent off the
servants from Churasovo to get ready Praskovya Ivanovna's
carriage, and posted six armed men to defend the gate, while he
himself and the rest of his men applied axes and crowbars to the
cellar door. It gave way in a moment; and Stepan Mikhailovich
himself carried out Praskovya Ivanovna, placed her on a car
between himself and her faithful maid, and drove unmolested
out of the courtyard with all his retainers. The sun was rising as
they drove past the church, and its first beams lit up the cross
on the roof. It was just six days since Praskovya Ivanovna had
prayed with her eyes fixed on that cross; and now she prayed
again and thanked God for her deliverance. The carriage caught
them up when they were five versts from Parashino; and Stepan
Mikhailovich moved his cousin into the carriage and drove with
her back to Bagrovo.

But I shall be asked, 'How did all this happen? did no one
see it? what had become of Kurolesov and his trusty retainers?
is it possible that he was unaware of it or absent at the time?'
No: the liberation of Praskovya Ivanovna took place before
many witnesses; and Kurolesov was at home and knew what
was going on, but did not venture to show his face.

The explanation is quite simple. His men had spent the
whole evening carousing with their master, and some of them
were so drunk that they could not be roused. There was one
sober man, a complete abstainer and a favourite. He wakened
his master with some difficulty, and, trembling with fear, told
him of the raid of Stepan Mikhailovich and the guns pointing
straight at the windows. 'But where are all our fellows?' asked
Kurolesov. 'Some are asleep, and others are hiding,' said the
man; but this was not true; for the drunken rabble was muster-
ing near the outside steps. Kurolesov thought a moment; then
with a gesture of despair he said, 'Let her go, and the devil go
with her! Lock the door, go to the window, and watch what
happens.' In a few minutes, the man cried out. 'They are carry-

ing away the mistress!—They're off!'—'Go to your bed,' said his master; then he rolled himself up in his blankets and either fell asleep or made a pretence of it.

Yes, right has a moral strength before which wrong must bend, for all its boldness. Kurolesov knew the stout heart and fearless courage of Stepan Mikhailovich, and he knew that he himself was in the wrong; and therefore, in spite of his furious temper and unscrupulous impudence, he let his victim go without a struggle.

Tenderly and carefully Stepan Mikhailovich conveyed the sufferer, whom he had always loved and who now roused in him deep sympathy and a still greater affection. No question passed his lips on the journey; and, when he brought her in safety to Bagrovo, he forbade his womenfolk to trouble her with inquiries. But in a fortnight Praskovya Ivanovna was herself again, thanks to her strong constitution and high spirits; and then Stepan Mikhailovich determined to cross-examine her. In order to act, he must know the real truth, and he never trusted second-hand information. She told him the whole truth with perfect frankness, but begged that he would keep it from his family and that she should be asked no questions by anyone else. She put herself altogether in his hands; but she feared his hot temper and implored him not to take vengeance on Kurolesov. She said positively that, on reflection, she had decided not to bring shame on her husband, or to stain the name which she must continue to bear throughout her life. She added that she now repented of the words which had burst from her lips at her first interview with Kurolesov at Parashino, and that nothing would induce her to make a complaint to the Governor against him. Yet she considered it her duty to rescue her serfs from his cruelty, and therefore intended to cancel the document which gave him authority over her estates. She asked Stepan Mikhailovich to take over the management himself, and also to write to Kurolesov demanding the document and stating that, if he refused to give it up, she would take legal steps to cancel it. She asked Stepan Mikhailovich to express this in plain terms but without any abusive epithets: and she offered to sign the letter herself to make it more convincing. I should mention that she could hardly read and write her native language. Stepan Mikhailovich loved his cousin so well that he bridled his rage and assented to her wishes. But he would not hear of taking over the management. 'No, my dear,' he said; 'I don't want to meddle in other people's affairs, and I don't want your relations to be saying that I feather my own nest while looking after your multitude of serfs. The land will be badly managed in your hands, I don't doubt; but you are rich and will have enough. I don't mind saying in the letter that I am to take over the management; that will give your sweet pet a turn! All the rest you ask shall be done.'

Strict orders were accordingly issued to the womenfolk to ask no questions of the lady. My grandfather wrote the letter to Kurolesov with his own hand, Praskovya Ivanovna added her signature, and a special messenger was dispatched with it to Parashino. But, while they were considering and wondering and writing at Bagrovo, all was already over at Parashino. The messenger returned on the fourth day and reported that, by God's will, Kurolesov had died suddenly and was already buried.

Stepan Mikhailovich heard the news first. Involuntarily he crossed himself and said, 'Thank God!' And so said all his family: in spite of their former weakness for Kurolesov, they had long looked on him with horror as a criminal and a ruffian. With Praskovya Ivanovna it was different. Judging by their own feelings, they all supposed she would welcome the news, and told her at once. But to the surprise of everyone she was utterly prostrated by it, and became ill again; and when her strength got the better of the illness, her depression and wretchedness were extreme: for some weeks she wept from morning till night, and she grew so thin that Stepan Mikhailovich was alarmed. No one could understand the cause of such intense sorrow for a husband whom she could not love and who had treated her so brutally—'a disgrace to human nature', as they called him. But there was an explanation, and this is it.

Many years later, my mother, who was a great favourite with Praskovya Ivanovna, was talking with her of past days—a thing which Praskovya Ivanova generally avoided—and in the open-hearted frankness of their conversation she asked: 'Please tell me, aunt, why you took on so after your husband's death. In your place, I should have said a prayer for his soul, and felt quite cheerful.' 'You are a little fool, my dear,' answered Praskovya Ivanovna: 'I had loved him for fourteen years and could not unlearn my feeling in one month though I had found out what he was; and, above all, I grieved for his soul: he had no time to repent before he died.'

After six weeks, Praskovya Ivanovna's good sense mastered her grief to some extent; and she consented, or, I should rather say, did not refuse, to travel with all the Bagrov family to Parashino, in order to attend a memorial service at Kurolesov's grave. To the general surprise, she dropped no tear at Parashino or during the sad ceremony; but one may imagine how much this effort cost her, in her condition of sorrow and bodily weakness. By her wish, only a few hours were spent at Parashino, and she did not enter that part of the house where her husband had lived and died.

It is not difficult to guess the cause of Kurolesov's sudden death. When Stepan Mikhailovich had rescued his cousin from the cellar, the people at Parashino all plucked up heart, believing that the end of Kurolesov's rule had come. They all supposed that the owner of Bagrovo, who was in the position of a father to their mistress, would turn her husband neck and crop out of a place that did not belong to him. No one dreamed that their young mistress, insulted and beaten and half-starved in an underground cellar in her own house, would fail to appeal to the law for redress. Every day they expected an irruption from Stepan Mikhailovich with the sheriff at his back; but week followed week, and no one came. Kurolesov was as drunken and violent as ever: everyone of his retainers he flogged till they were half-dead, for having betrayed him, not sparing even the sober man who had awakened him on the night of the rescue; and he boasted that Praskovya Ivanovna had given up to him the title-deeds of her estates. It was past the power of human endurance; and the future seemed hopeless.* Two of the

* From here to the end of the paragraph was removed by the censor from the early editions of the work.

scoundrels, who had been favourites, and, strangely enough, two who had suffered less than the rest from his cruelty, ventured upon a horrible crime. They poisoned him with arsenic, putting it into a decanter of kvass, which Kurolesov generally emptied during the night; and they put in so much that he was dead in two hours. As they had taken no one into their confidence, the catastrophe startled and terrified the whole household. The servants suspected one another, but the real criminals remained unknown for some time. Six months later one of them became desperately ill and confessed his crime before he died; and his accomplice, though the dying man had not betrayed him, made off and was never seen again.

The sudden death of Kurolesov would certainly have been followed by an inquest but for the presence at Parashino of a young clerk called Mikhail Maximich, who had only lately come to the place. By cleverness and good management, he contrived to get the affair hushed up. He became later Praskovya Ivanovna's man of business and the chief agent on all her estates, and enjoyed her full confidence. Under the name of 'Mikhail-ushka' he was known to all and sundry in the provinces of Simbirsk and Orenburg. He was a man of remarkable ability; though he made a large fortune, he lived discreetly and modestly for many years; but when he received his freedom on the death of his mistress, and lost his wife to whom he was much attached, he took to drinking and died in poverty. One of his sons, if I remember rightly, entered the official class and was eventually ennobled.

I should not conceal the fact that forty years later, when I became the owner of Parashino, I found the recollection of Kurolesov's management still fresh among the peasants, and they spoke of him with gratitude, because they felt every day the advantage of many of his arrangements. His cruelty they had forgotten, and they had felt it less than his personal attendants; but they remembered his power of distinguishing guilt and innocence, the honest workman and the shirker; they remembered his perfect knowledge of their needs and his constant readiness to give them help. The old men smiled as they told me that Kurolesov used often to say: 'Steal and rob as you please, if you keep it dark; but if I catch you, then look out.'

When she went back to Bagrovo, Praskovya Ivanovna, soothed by the sincere and tender love of her cousin and by the assiduous attentions of his womenfolk (whom she did not much like but who expected great favours and benefits from her), gradually got over the terrible blow she had suffered. Her good health came back, and her peace of mind; and at the end of a year she resolved to go back to Churasovo. It was painful to Stepan Mikhailovich to part with his favourite: her whole nature appealed to him, and he had become thoroughly accustomed to her society. Not once in his whole life was he in a rage with Praskovya Ivanovna. But he did not try to keep her: on the contrary, he pressed her to go as soon as possible. 'It's no sort of life for you here, my dear,' he used to say; 'it's a dull place, though we have got accustomed to it. You are young still'—she was thirty—'and rich and used to something different. You should go back to Churasovo, and enjoy your fine house and splendid garden and the springs. You have plenty of kind neighbours there, rich people who live a gay life. It is possible that God will send you better fortune in a second venture; you won't want for offers.' Praskovya Ivanovna put off her departure from day to day—so hard did she find it to part from the cousin who had saved her life and been her benefactor from her childhood. At last the day was fixed. Early on the previous morning, she came out to join Stepan Mikhailovich, who was sitting on his stoop and thinking sad thoughts. She kissed and embraced him; the tears came to her eyes as she said: 'I feel all your love for me, and I love and respect you like a daughter. God sees my gratitude; but I want men to see it too. Will you let me bequeath to your family all my mother's property? What I have from my father will come to your son in any case. My relations on my mother's side are rich, and you know that they have given me no reason to reward them with my wealth. I shall never marry. I wish the Bagrov family to be rich. Say yes, my dear cousin, and you will comfort me and set my mind at rest.' She threw herself at his feet and covered with kisses the hands with which he was trying to raise her up.

'Listen, my dear,' said Stepan Mikhailovich in a rather stern voice: 'You don't know me aright. That I should cover what does not belong to me, and cut out the rightful heirs to your estates—no! that shall never be, and never shall anyone be able to say that of Stepan Bagrov! Mind you don't ever mention it again. If you do, we shall quarrel; and it will be the first time in our lives.'

Next day Praskovya Ivanovna left Bagrovo and began her own independent life at Churasovo.

FRAGMENT III

THE MARRIAGE OF THE YOUNG BAGROV

MANY years passed by and much happened during that time —famine and plague, and the rebellion of Pugachev.* The landowners of the Orenburg district scattered before the bands of the usurper, and Stepan Mikhailovich also made off with his family, first to Samara, and then down the Volga to Saratov and as far off as Astrakhan. But by degrees all disturbances passed over and calmed down and were forgotten. Children became boys, boys became men, and men came to grey hairs; and among these last was Stepan Mikhailovich. He saw this himself, but he hardly believed it. He would sometimes allude to the ravages of time, but he did so without uneasiness, as if there were no personal reference to himself. Yet my grandfather had ceased to be his old self: his herculean strength and tireless activity had gone for ever. This sometimes surprised him; but he went on living precisely in the old way—eating and drinking to his heart's content, and dressing with no regard to the weather, though he sometimes suffered for this neglect. Little by little, his keen clear eye became clouded and his great voice lost its power; his fits of anger were rarer, but so were his bright and happy moods. His elder daughters had all married, and the eldest had been dead some time, leaving a daughter of three years old. Aksinya,† the second, had lost one husband and married again; Elizabeth, a clever but arrogant woman, had somehow married a General Erlykin, who was old and poor and given to drinking; and Alexandra had found herself a husband in Ivan Karataev, well-born, young, rich, but a passion-

* Pugachev was a Cossack who raised a formidable rebellion in East Russia; taken prisoner by Suvorov, he was executed at Moscow in 1775.

† The popular form of Xenia; the diminutive is Aksyutka.

ate lover of the Bashkirs and their wandering life—a true Bashkir himself in mind and body. The youngest daughter, Tanyusha, had not married. The only son* was now twenty-six, a handsome youth with a complexion of lilies and roses: his own father used to say of him, 'Put a petticoat on him, and he'd be a prettier girl than any of his sisters!' Though his wife, Arina Vasilevna, shed bitter tears and would not be comforted, Stepan Mikhailovich sent his son into the army as soon as he was sixteen. He served for three years, and, owing to the influence of Mikhail Kurolesov, acted as aide-de-camp for part of the time to Suvorov. But Suvorov left the district of Orenburg and was succeeded by a German general (I think his name was Treubluth); and he sentenced the young man to a severe flogging, from which his entire innocence, if not his noble birth, should have protected him. His mother nearly died of grief, when she heard it; and even my grandfather thought this was going too far. He withdrew his son from the army and got him a place in the law court at Ufa, where he earned promotion by long and zealous service.

I cannot pass over in silence a strange fact that I have noticed: most of the Germans and foreigners in general who held posts in the Russian service in those days were notorious for their cruelty and love of inflicting corporal punishment. The German who punished young Bagrov so cruelly was a Lutheran himself, but at the same time a great stickler for all the rites and ceremonies of the Russian Church. This historic incident in the annals of the Bagrov family happened in the following way. The general ordered a service to be performed in the regimental chapel on the eve of some unimportant saint's day; he was always present himself on these occasions, and all officers were expected to attend. It was summer, and the chapel windows were open. Suddenly, a voice in the street outside struck up a popular song. The general rushed to the window: three subalterns were walking along the street, and one of them was singing. He ordered them under arrest and sentenced each of them to 300 lashes. My unfortunate father, who was not singing but merely walking with his friends, pleaded his noble birth;

* The author's father.

but the general said with a sneer, 'A noble is bound to show special respect to divine service'; and then the brute himself looked on till the last stripe was inflicted on the innocent youth. This took place in a room next the chapel, where the solemn singing of the choir could be distinctly heard; and the tyrant forbade his victim to cry out, 'for fear of disturbing divine worship'. After his punishment, he was carried off unconscious to hospital, where it was found necessary to cut off his uniform, owing to the swelling of his tender young body. It was two months before his back and shoulders healed up. What it must have cost his mother to hear such news of her only son whom she simply worshipped! My grandfather lodged a complaint in some quarter; and his son, who had sent in his papers at once, got his discharge from the army before he left the hospital, and entered the Civil Service as an official of the fourteenth or lowest class. Eight years had now gone by, and the incident was by this time forgotten.

Alexei Stepanich was now living peacefully at Ufa and performing his duties there. Twice a year he paid a visit to his parents at Bagrovo, 240 versts away. His life was quite uneventful. Quiet, bashful, and unassuming, this young heir to a landed estate lived on good terms with all the world, till suddenly the modest course of his existence became disturbed.

There was a permanent military administration in the town of Ufa, and next in authority to the Lieutenant-Governor was Nikolai Zubin, who resided regularly in the town. M. Zubin was an honest and able man, but his character was weak. His wife had died, leaving three children—Sonechka,*a girl of twelve, and two younger boys. He was devoted to his daughter; and it was no wonder he should love a child so beautiful and so clever, who, in spite of her tender years, soon became her father's companion and assisted him in the management of the household. Eighteen months after the death of his first wife, whom he had loved and sincerely mourned, M. Zubin found consolation by falling in love with the daughter of M. Rychkov, a landowner in Orenburg, well-known for his descriptions of

* A pet name for Sofya (Sophia). This is the author's mother, whose real name was Marya.

that country. The marriage soon took place; and the young wife, Alexandra, by her intelligence and beauty, soon gained entire control over her submissive husband. But she was hard and unfeeling, and conceived a hatred for her stepdaughter, her father's darling, who bade fair to grow up into a beautiful woman. The thing is common enough. The name of stepmother has long been proverbial for cruelty, and it fitted Mme Zubin precisely. But it was by no means easy to tear Sonechka from her place in her father's heart: she was not a girl who could be put down easily, and the contest which followed inflamed the stepmother's anger to an extraordinary pitch. She swore that this hussy of thirteen, who was the idol of her father and all the town, should some day live in the maid's room, wear the coarsest clothes, and carry the slops out of the children's nursery. She kept her oath to the letter: after two or three years, Sonechka was living with the servants and clothed like a scullion, and she scrubbed and cleaned the nursery which was now inhabited by two half-sisters. But what was the father doing? He had once loved her dearly; but now for whole months he never saw her; and when he did meet her going about in rags, he turned away with a sigh, wiped away a furtive tear, and made off as soon as possible. It is the way of many elderly men who have married again and are dominated by young wives. As I do not know exactly the ways and methods by which Mme Zubin attained her object, I shall not speak of them; nor shall I dwell upon the cruelties and sufferings inflicted upon the bereaved girl, with her sensitive temper and strong will; nothing was spared her, not even the most humiliating punishments and beatings for imaginary offences. I shall merely say, that the stepdaughter was not far from suicide, and was only saved from it by a miracle. It happened thus. When she had decided to put an end to an intolerable existence, the poor child wished to say her last prayer before a picture of Our Lady of Smolensk, the picture with which her mother on her deathbed had blessed her. She fell on her knees in her garret before the ikon, and, with floods of bitter tears, pressed her face on the dirt-stained floor. Suffering deprived her of consciousness for some minutes; when she recovered and got up, she saw the candle, which she had put out the night before, still burning before the ikon. At first she cried out with surprise and involuntary fear; but soon she recognized that she had seen a miracle wrought by divine power. She took courage; she was conscious of a strength and composure she had never felt before; and she firmly resolved to suffer and endure and live. From that day the helpless child wore armour proof against the increasing exasperation of her stepmother: whatever she was told to do, she did; whatever was inflicted upon her, she bore. Degrading punishment no longer forced the tears from her eyes, no longer made her turn sick and faint, as it used to do. 'Mean slut' had long been her title, and 'desperate wretch' was now added to it. But the measure of God's patience now brimmed over, and his thunder pealed: Mme Zubin, in the prime of life and in the pride of her health and beauty, died ten days after giving birth to a son. Twenty-four hours before the end, knowing that she must die, she was eager to take the load off her conscience. Sonechka was suddenly wakened in the night and summoned to her stepmother's bedside. The dying woman confessed in the presence of witnesses her guilty conduct towards her stepdaughter, begged her forgiveness, and conjured her in the name of God to be good to the children. The girl forgave her and promised to care for the orphans; and she kept that promise. Mme Zubin confessed also to her husband that the accusations which had been brought against his daughter were all calumnies and falsehoods.

Her death caused a complete reversal of affairs. M. Zubin also had a paralytic stroke, and, though he survived for some years, never left his bed again. The oppressed and ragged Cinderella, whom the servants—and especially those belonging to Mme Zubin—had been mean enough to humiliate and insult to their heart's content, suddenly became the absolute mistress of the household, her sick father having put everything under her control. The reconciliation between the guilty father and the injured daughter was touching and even distressing to the daughter and all who saw it. For long, M. Zubin was wrung by remorse: his tears flowed day and night, and he repeated the same words over and over, 'No, Sonechka, it is impossible you should forgive me!' To each one of his acquaintance in the town he formally confessed his misconduct towards his daughter; and 'Sofya Nikolaevna', as she was now called, became the object of general respect and admiration. Made wise by years of suffering, this girl of seventeen developed into a grown woman, a mother to the children, and the manager of the household. She even discharged public duties; for, owing to her father's illness, she received all heads of departments, officials, and private citizens; she discussed matters with them, wrote letters and official documents, and at last became the real manager of the business in her father's office. Sofya Nikolaevna nursed her father with anxious care and tenderness; she looked after her three brothers and two sisters, and even took trouble about the education of the elder children. Her own brothers, Sergei and Alexander, were now boys of twelve and ten; and she contrived to find teachers for them—a kind old Frenchman called Villemer, whom fortune had somehow stranded at Ufa, and a half-educated Little Russian who had been exiled to the town for an attempted fraud. She availed herself of the opportunity to study with her brothers, and worked so hard that she could soon understand a French book or conversation and even talk French a little herself. Eighteen months later she sent her brothers to Moscow for their education. Through a certain M. Anichkov who lived at Ufa, she had become acquainted with his cousin who lived at Moscow, and they often corresponded. The well-known writer, Novikov, shared a house at Moscow with this M. Anichkov; and both friends were so struck by the letters from this young lady on the banks of the river Belaya, that they sent her regularly all new and important books in the way of Russian literature; and this did much for her mental development. This M. Anichkov had a special respect for her, and considered it an honour to carry out her request. He undertook to receive both her brothers and place them at a boarding-school connected with Moscow University, and performed his undertaking punctiliously. The boys got on well at school, but their studies were broken off when the summons came for them to enter the Guards, in which they had been enrolled while still in the cradle.

All clever and educated people who came to Ufa hastened to make the acquaintance of Sofya Nikolaevna, were attracted by her, and never forgot her. Many of these acquaintances became in course of time the intimate friends of her children, and the relation was severed only by death. I shall name only those of them whom I knew myself—V. Romanovsky, A. Avenarius, Peter Chichagov, Dmitry Mertvavo, and V. Ichansky. Scholars also, and travellers attracted by the novelty and beauty of the district, invariably made the young lady's acquaintance and left written testimony of their admiration for her beauty and wit. It is true that her position in society and her home helped her, and served, one might say, as a pedestal for the statue; but the statue itself was a noble figure. I remember especially the verses of Count Manteuffel, a traveller; he sent them to Sofya Nikolaevna with a most respectful letter in French; and he also sent a copy of an immense work in five quarto volumes, by a Dr Buchan,* which had just been translated from English into Russian and made a great sensation in the medical world of that day. Buchan's *Domestic Medicine* was a real treasure to Sofya Nikolaevna: she was able to make use of its directions to make up medicines for her father's benefit. In his verses Count Manteuffel compared the fair lady of Ufa to both Venus and Minerva.

In spite of his enfeebled state, M. Zubin did not resign his office for several years. Twice a year he gave a ball; he did not appear himself in order to welcome the ladies, but the men went to see him where he lay in his study; and the young hostess had to receive the whole town. Several times a year her father insisted on her going out to balls in the houses of the leading people, and she yielded to his earnest entreaties and put in a short appearance at the ball. She wore fine dresses and was an excellent dancer in the fashion of the time. When she had gone through a Polish minuet and a single country-dance or schottische, she went away at once, after flashing through the room like a meteor. All who had the right to be so, were in love with Sofya Nikolaevna, but they sighed at a respectful distance;

* Buchan's *Domestic Medicine* was published in 1769; the author died in 1805.

for this young lady gave none of them any encouragement whatever.

And with this peerless creature the son of Stepan Mikhailovich fell in love! He could not understand and appreciate her fully, but her appearance alone and her lively cheerful temper were enough to bewitch a man; and bewitched he accordingly was. He saw her first in church, and the first sight was enough for his susceptible heart. Alexei Stepanich—henceforth we shall give him both his names—soon discovered that the fair lady received all officials who visited at her father's house; and, being himself an official in the law-court, he began to appear regularly in her drawing-room, to pay his respects on high days and holidays. He saw her every time, and his passion grew steadily. His calls were so regular and so prolonged—though he hardly opened his mouth—that they soon attracted general notice; and it is probable that the first person to notice them was the young hostess herself. Rapturous looks, flaming cheeks, helpless confusion—these are the symbols by which love has always spoken. A frank passion has been an object of ridicule from time immemorial, and all Ufa laughed at Alexei Stepanich. He was humble and shy and as bashful as a country girl; and his only reply to all jests and allusions to the subject was to blush the colour of a peony. But Sofya Nikolaevna, so cold and even snubbing in her manner to her fashionable admirers, was surprisingly indulgent to this speechless worshipper. Perhaps she was sorry for this young man who had no armour against all the ridicule he suffered on her behalf; perhaps she understood that his was no idle or passing fancy and that his whole life was at stake; anyhow, the severe young beauty not only bowed graciously and looked kindly at him, but tried also to start conversation; and his timid incoherent replies and agitated voice did not seem to her ridiculous or repulsive. I should say, however, that Sofya Nikolaevna, though she stood on her dignity with self-assertive people, was always kind and condescending to humility and modesty.

Things went on thus for some time. Suddenly, a bold thought flashed on the brain of Alexei Stepanich—the thought of getting Sofya Nikolaevna for his wife. At first he was frightened by his own ambition, so bold and so unlikely to be realized. How could he raise his eyes to Sofya Nikolaevna, the chief personage in Ufa, and in his opinion the cleverest and most beautiful woman in the world? He abandoned his intention entirely for a time. But by degrees the lady's constant goodwill and attention, her friendly glances which seemed to him to hold out some encouragement, and, above all, the passion which mastered his whole being, recalled the abandoned ideal; and it soon grew familiar and became part of his life. There was an old lady called Mme Alakaev, then living at Ufa to look after a lawsuit, who used to visit at the Zubins' house; she was distantly related to Alexei Stepanich and had always taken a great interest in him. He now began to visit her oftener, and did his best to please her; and at last he confessed his love for a certain person, and his intention to seek her hand. His love was the talk of the town and therefore no news to Mme Alakaev; but his intention of marrying her was a surprise. 'She won't have you,' said the old lady, shaking her head; 'she's too clever, too proud, too highly educated. Plenty of people have been in love with her, but not one has ever dared ask the question. You're a handsome lad, certainly, well-born and fairly well off, and you will be rich in course of time—everybody knows that; but then you're a plain country fellow, no scholar or man of the world, and you're terribly bashful in society.' Alexei Stepanich was aware of all this himself; but love had entirely confused his brain, and a voice whispered in his ear day and night that Sofya Nikolaevna would accept him. Though the young man's hopes seemed to her unfounded, Mme Alakaev consented to go to Sofya Nikolaevna's house, where, without making any allusion to his wishes, she would turn the conversation on to him and take note of all that was said. She started at once, and Alexei Stepanich remained in the house till she should come back. She was absent for some time, and the lover became so distressed and despondent that he began to cry, and then fell asleep, tired out, with his head leaning against the window. When the old lady came back, she wakened him and said with a cheerful air: 'Well, Alexei Stepanich, there is really something in it! When I began to speak about you, and was rather hard upon you, Sofya Nikolaevna took up the cudgels in earnest on your behalf, and ended by saying that she was sure you were very kind and modest and gentle, and respectful to your parents; and she said that God sent his blessing on such people, and they were much better than your pert and forward talkers.' Alexei Stepanich was so enraptured by this report that he hardly knew where he was. Mme Alakaev gave him time to recover, and then said with decision: 'If your mind is quite made up about this, I will tell you what you had better do. Go home at once, tell the whole story to your parents, and ask for their consent and blessing, before kind people put their oar in. If they give you one and the other, I don't refuse to work in your cause. Only don't be in a hurry: begin by getting on the soft side of your sisters; your mother won't go against your wishes. Of course, your father's consent matters most of all. I know him: he is masterful to a degree, but he has good sense; have a talk to him when he is in a good humour.' Alexei Stepanich did not see the need of all this caution and manœuvring: he said that his parents would be delighted, and asked what possible flaw could be found in Sofya Nikolaevna. 'Two terrible flaws,' said the shrewd old lady: 'she has only twopence to her fortune, and her grandfather was a simple sergeant in a Cossack regiment.' The significance of her words was entirely lost upon Alexei Stepanich, but the old lady was not wrong in her presentiment, and her warning came too late.

Within a week Alexei Stepanich got leave of absence. He called on Sofya Nikolaevna to say goodbye, and she treated him kindly, wishing him a pleasant journey, and hoping he might find his parents in good health and happy to see him. Her kind words encouraged him to hope, and off he went home. The old people were glad to see him, but they were puzzled by the time of his visit and looked at him inquiringly. His sisters—who lived near Bagrovo and came there in hot haste on a summons from their mother—kissed their brother and made much of him, but kept on smiling for some reason. The youngest sister, Tatyana, was his favourite, and he revealed his passion to her ears first. Being a rather romantic girl and fonder of her brother than the elder sisters were, she listened to him with sympathy, and at last went so far as to confide in him a great secret: the family knew already of his love affair and were opposed to it. It had happened in this way.

Two months before, Ivan Karataev had travelled to Ufa on business and brought back this piece of news to his wife. Alexandra Karataev—I have spoken already of her character— boiled over with rage and indignation. She took the lead in the family, and could twist them all, except, of course, her father, round her little finger. She set one of her brother's servants to spy on his master, and made him report to her every detail concerning his love affair and his life at Ufa; and she found a female friend in the town, who first rummaged and ferreted about, and then, with the help of a discarded attorney's clerk, sent her a long letter composed of town talk and servants' gossip. As her chief authorities were the servants of the late Mme Zubin, it is easy to guess the kind of portrait which these enemies drew of Sofya Nikolaevna.

It is a well-known fact that in the good old days of the Empress Catherine—perhaps it is the case still—there was little love lost between a man's wife and his sisters; and the case was worse when the sisters had only one brother, because his wife must become the sole and undisputed mistress of the household. A great deal of selfishness underlies human nature; it often works without our knowledge, and no one is exempt from it; honourable and kind people, not recognizing selfish motives in themselves, quite honestly attribute their actions to other and more presentable causes; but they deceive themselves and others unintentionally. Where there is no kindness of heart or refinement of manners, selfishness shows itself without any concealment or apology; and so it was with the womenfolk of Stepan Mikhailovich. It was inevitable that they should all resent their brother's marriage, irrespective of his choice. 'Alesha will change towards us and love us less than before; his bride will be a cuckoo in the nest and push out the birds born there'—such would certainly have been the language of the sisters, even if Alexei Stepanich had chosen a bird of his own feather; but Sofya Nikolaevna was worse than anything they could imagine. Alexandra summoned her sister Elizabeth and hurried to

Bagrovo to communicate to her mother and sisters—of course, with suitable embellishments—all the information she had received of her brother's goings on. They believed every word she said, and their opinion of Sofya Nikolaevna was to the following effect. In the first place, the Zubin girl—this was her regular name in the secret meetings of the family council—was of mean birth: her grandfather had been a Ural Cossack, and her mother, Vera Ivanovna Kandalintsev, had belonged to the merchant class; the alliance was therefore a degradation to an ancient and noble family. In the second place, the Zubin girl was a mere pauper: if her father died or was dismissed from his post, she would depend on charity for her bread, and all her brothers and sisters would be a stone round her husband's neck. Thirdly, the Zubin girl was proud and fashionable, a crafty adventuress who was accustomed to lord it over the town of Ufa; and she would turn up her nose with no ceremony at plain people living in the country, however long their pedigree. Fourthly and lastly, the Zubin girl was a witch who used magic herbs to keep all the men running after her with their tongues hanging out; and their poor brother was one of her victims; she had scented out his future wealth and his easy temper, and had determined to marry into a noble family by hook or by crook. Alexandra managed the whole affair; her glib and wicked tongue frightened them all and soon proved to them, beyond all possibility of doubt, that such a marriage was a terrible misfortune for them. 'Likely enough, she will get round Stepan Mikhailovich himself, and then we're all done for: we must leave no stone unturned to prevent the marriage.' It was clearly of the first importance to impress upon Stepan Mikhailovich the worst possible opinion of Sofya Nikolaevna; but who was to bell the cat? Their conscience was not clear, and they dared not go to work openly. If their father suspected that they had any concealed purpose, he would not believe even the truth in that case; once before, when there had been some talk of choosing a daughter-in-law, he had seen through their repugnance to the scheme and had told them so plainly.

They had recourse therefore to the following stratagem. Arina

Vasilevna had a married niece living near; her name was Flena Lupenevsky; she was short and stout, a notorious fool and gossip, and not averse to strong liquors. She was instructed to come to Bagrovo as if on an ordinary visit, and to bring in, among other topics, the love affairs of Alexei Stepanich: she was, of course, to represent Sofya Nikolaevna in the most unfavourable light. Alexandra spent a long time coaching this lady in what she was to say and how she was to say it. When she had learnt it as well as she could, Mme Lupenevsky turned up at Bagrovo and had dinner there; after dinner, hosts and guests slept for three hours and then assembled for tea. The master of the house was in good humour and himself gave his guest an opening to begin the performance. 'Come now, Flena,' he said, 'tell us the news you got from the travellers to Ufa'—her sister, Mme Kalpinsky, had just been there with her husband—'I warrant they brought home a good budget, and you will add as much more out of your own head.'

'You will always have your joke, dear uncle,' said the lady; 'but they brought plenty of news, and I have no need to invent.' Then off she started on a string of silly gossip, true and untrue, which I shall spare my readers. My grandfather pretended to disbelieve her throughout, even when she was telling the truth; he made fun of her stories, threw her out on purpose, and teased her till all the hearers laughed heartily. The stupid woman, who had taken a stiff glass on waking to give her courage, got vexed at last and said with some heat: 'Uncle, why do you keep on laughing and believe nothing I say? Wait a moment; I have kept one special bit of news for the end, and that won't make you laugh, though you can't help believing it.' The family exchanged glances, and my grandfather laughed. 'Come out with it!' he said coolly; 'I shan't believe it; and, if I don't laugh at it, it's because I'm bored by your stories.' 'O uncle, uncle,' she began, 'you're quite in the dark about my dear cousin, Alexei Stepanich. He's a perfect wreck: the witch of Ufa, the daughter of a great man there, Governor or Commander-in-Chief, I don't know which, has used devilish arts to fascinate him. She's a perfect beauty, they say, and has captivated all the men, young and old; she has bewitched them with magic herbs, and they all run after her. And my poor cousin, Alexei Stepanich, is so bad that he can neither eat nor drink nor sleep. He's constantly sitting beside her, he can't take his eyes off her, he just looks and sighs; and at night he's always walking past her house, carrying a gun and a sword and keeping guard over her. They say that the Zubin girl is very sweet upon him; of course he's handsome and well-born; she knows what she's about and means to marry him. It's natural enough: she has no money, and her father is a Cossack's son who rose from the ranks; though he has worked his way up and held great posts, he has put nothing by; he has spent every penny on dinners and fine parties and dresses for his daughter. The old man is at death's door, and there is a swarm of children—half a dozen of them by his two wives. They will all settle on your shoulders, uncle, if my cousin marries her; she has no portion but the clothes she wears; they have silk to their backs, but nothing to put in their bellies. And Alexei Stepanich, they say, is changed out of all knowledge: he looks terrible; the very servants weep to see him and dare not inform you. Believe me, uncle, every single word is gospel truth. Question his servants, and they won't deny it.'

At this, Arina Vasilevna began to cry and her daughters to rub their eyes. My grandfather was rather taken aback, but soon recovered himself. Then he smiled and said coolly: 'Plenty of lies there, and perhaps a grain of truth. I have heard myself that the young lady is pretty and clever; and that's all the magic there is about it.* It's little wonder if Alexei's eyes were dazzled. All the rest is rubbish. Mlle Zubin has no idea of marrying Alexei; he is no match for her; she will find a better man and a more pushing man to marry her. And now, that's enough: not a word more on the subject! Let us go and drink tea out of doors.' As a matter of course, neither Mme Lupenevsky nor anyone else dared to refer again to the news from Ufa. The

---

* In general, my grandfather had little belief in witchcraft. A wizard once told him that a gun was charmed and would not go off. He took out the shot secretly and fired at the wizard, who got a great fright. But he recovered and said that my grandfather himself was 'a man of power'; and this was generally believed, except by Stepan Mikhailovich (*author's note*).

visitor departed in the evening. After supper, when Arina Vasilevna and her daughters were about to take a silent farewell of Stepan Mikhailovich, he stopped them and said: 'Well, Arisha, what do you think about it? Though that stupid Flena added plenty of lies, yet it seems to me there is truth in the story too. The boy's letters have been quite different of late. The thing needs some looking into. The best plan would be to summon Alesha here; we shall learn all the truth from him.' At this point Alexandra offered to send a special messenger to Ufa to find out the truth through a relation of her husband's: 'She is a very honest woman,' she said, 'and nothing would make her tell a lie.' Her father agreed not to send for his son till the fresh report arrived. Alexandra started at once for her own house, which was not more than thirty versts from Bagrovo, and returned in a week, bringing with her the letter I have mentioned already, which she had received long before from her gossiping female friend at Ufa. This letter was shown and read aloud to Stepan Mikhailovich; and though he put little faith in the women as detectives and informers, some statements in the letter seemed to him probable, and he was displeased. He said positively, that if Mlle Zubin did wish to marry Alesha, he would forbid it, on the ground of her birth. 'Write by the next post to Alesha,' he said, 'and tell him to come home.' A few days passed, and were used by the women to prejudice Stepan Mikhailovich as strongly as possible against the marriage; and then, as we know already, the young man turned up at Bagrovo without having received the letter.

Alexei Stepanich heard the whole of this story from Tatyana, and it made him very serious and uneasy. He was not by nature strong-willed, and had been brought up in blind obedience to his family and his father. In his alarm, he did not know what to do. At last he decided to speak to his mother. Arina Vasilevna was devoted to her only son; but as she was accustomed to look on him as still a child and convinced that this child had taken a fancy to a dangerous toy, she met his avowal of strong feeling with the words one would use to a child who begged to hold the hot poker; and when this treatment brought the tears to his eyes, she tried to comfort him in the way that a child is comforted for the loss of a favourite toy. He might say what he chose, he might try as he pleased to refute the slander brought against Sofya Nikolaevna—his mother either did not listen at all or listened without attending. Two more days passed by; the young man's heart was breaking; though his love and longing for Sofya Nikolaevna increased every hour, it is probable that he would not easily have plucked up courage to broach the subject to his father; but Stepan Mikhailovich took the first step. Early one fine morning, he was sitting as usual on his stoop, when Alexei Stepanich, looking rather pale and worn after an almost sleepless night, came out to join his father. The old man was in a cheerful mood; he greeted his son affectionately, and then, looking attentively at his face, he read what was going on within. He gave him his hand to kiss, and then said, not in anger but with energy: 'Listen to me, Alexei! I know the burden on your mind, and I see that this fancy has taken a strong hold of you. Just tell me the story now, the whole truth and nothing but the truth.' Alexei Stepanich felt more fear than love for his father, and was not in the way of speaking to him frankly; but his love for Sofya Nikolaevna lent him courage. He threw himself at his father's feet and repeated the whole story, omitting no details and keeping nothing back. Stepan Mikhailovich listened with patience and attention. When any of the family appeared in the distance and evidently meant to come and say 'good morning', he waved his blackthorn staff with a significant gesture, and then nobody, not even Aksyutka with the tea, dared approach before he summoned them. Though his son's story was ill-arranged, confused, long, and unconvincing, yet Stepan Mikhailovich with his clear head made out the gist of the matter. But unfortunately he did not and could not approve of it. Of the romantic side of love he had small appreciation, and his masculine pride was offended by his son's susceptibility, which seemed to him degrading weakness in a man, and a sign of worthlessness; and yet at the same time he saw that Sofya Nikolaevna was not in the least to blame, and that all the evil he had heard about her was merely malicious falsehood, due to the ill-will of his own womenfolk. After a little reflection, he said, with no sign of anger, even affectionately, but firmly: 'Listen to me, Alexei! You are just at the time of life when a pretty girl may easily take a man's fancy. In that there is no harm whatever; but I see that you have gone too far, and that does not do. I don't blame Sofya Nikolaevna in the least; she seems to me a very worthy girl; but she's not a good match for you, and she won't suit us. In the first place, her nobility dates from yesterday, while you are the descendant of an ancient and noble line. Then she is accustomed to town life, highly educated, and independent; since her stepmother died she has ruled a household; and, though poor herself, she is used to luxury; but we are plain country people, and you know yourself how we live. And you ought to know your own character; you're too compliant. But her cleverness is the chief objection to her; to marry a wife cleverer than one's self is a mistake; she is sure to rule her husband; and you are so much in love that you are certain to spoil her at first. Well, as your father, I now bid you clear your head of this notion. I confess I don't believe myself that Sofya Nikolaevna would accept you. Choose your shoe of the right size, and it won't pinch your foot. We will find out a wife for you here—some gentle quiet girl, well-born and with some money. Then you can give up your office and live here in comfort. You know, my boy, we're not rolling in wealth. We get enough to eat, but very little money comes in. As to the Kurolesov legacy, about which people made such a noise, I never give it a thought; we can't count on it: Praskovya Ivanovna is young enough to marry and have children of her own. Now, mind what I say, Alesha: throw all this off like water off a duck's back, and don't let me hear again of Sofya Nikolaevna.' Then Stepan Mikhailovich gave his hand graciously to his son, who kissed it as respectfully as usual. The old man ordered tea to be served and the family to be summoned; he was more than usually cheerful and friendly to them all, but Alexei Stepanich was terribly depressed. No anger on his father's part would have produced such an effect; that was soon over and was always followed by indulgence and kindness, but the old man's quiet determination deprived him of all hope. There was a change in his expression, so sudden and complete, that his mother was frightened to see it and plied him

with questions—'Was he unwell? What had happened to him?'
His sisters noticed the change also, but they were more cunning
and held their tongues. None of this was lost on Stepan
Mikhailovich. He looked askance at Arina Vasilevna and muttered through his teeth, 'Don't worry the boy!' So they took no
more notice of him but left him in peace, and the day went on
with its usual routine.

The conversation with his father made a deep impression on
Alexei Stepanich; one may say that it crushed him. His appetite
and sleep failed, he lost interest in everything, even his bodily
strength was affected. His mother shed tears, and even his sisters
were uneasy. Next day his mother found it difficult to get from
him any account of the interview with his father. To all inquiries
he returned the same answer: 'My father won't hear of it; I am
a lost man, and life will soon be over for me.' And within a
week he did really take to his bed; he was very weak and often
half-conscious; and though his skin was not hot, he was constantly delirious. No one could understand what was the matter
with him; but it was simply a nervous fever. The family were
terribly alarmed. As there were no doctors in the neighbourhood, they treated him with domestic remedies; but he grew
steadily worse till he was so weak that his death was expected
hourly. His mother and sisters screamed and tore their hair.
Stepan Mikhailovich, though he shed no tears and was not
always sitting by the bedside, probably suffered more than
anyone: he understood perfectly what had caused this illness.
But youth at last asserted itself, and the turn came after exactly
six weeks. Alexei Stepanich woke up to life an absolute child,
and life was slow in resuming its normal course with him; his
convalescence lasted two months, and all the past seemed to
have been blotted out from his memory. Everything that he saw,
both indoors and out, pleased him as much as if it were new and
strange. At last he got perfectly well; his face filled out and got
back the healthy colour which it had lost for more than a year;
he went out fishing and shooting quails, ate and drank heartily,
and was in good spirits. His parents felt more joy than they
could express, and were convinced that the illness had expelled
all former thoughts and feelings from his head and heart.

And perhaps this would really have been the case, if they had taken him away from Ufa, kept him a whole year at home, and found a pretty girl for him to marry. But their fears were lulled to rest by his present condition, and they sent him back to the same place and the same duties after six months. This settled his fate once and for all. The old passion revived and blazed up with far greater power. I do not know whether love came back to his heart all at once or by degrees; I only know that he went seldom at first to the Zubins' house, and then oftener, and at last as often as he could. I know also that his old friend, Mme Alakaev, continued her visits to Sofya Nikolaevna, sounding her cautiously as to her sentiments and bringing back favourable reports, which confirmed her own hope that the proud beauty was not indifferent to her humble worshipper. A few months after Alexei Stepanich had returned to Ufa, a letter from him suddenly arrived at Bagrovo, in which he declared to his parents, with his usual affection and respect, but also with a firmness not characteristic of him, that he loved Sofya Nikolaevna more than his own life and could not live without her; he had hopes of her accepting him, and asked his parents to give him their blessing and their consent to the match. This letter was a great surprise and shock to the old people. Stepan Mikhailovich knitted his brows but did not express his feelings by a single word. The family all sat round in perfect silence till he dismissed them by a gesture. When he was alone, my grandfather sat there a long time, tracing patterns on the floor of his room with his blackthorn staff. He soon realized that it was a bad business, that they had been mistaken, and that no fever would cure the lad of his passion. His impulsive and kindly nature shook his resolve and made him inclined to give his consent, as may be inferred from what he said to his wife. When they were alone together next morning, he said: 'Well, Arisha, what do you think of it? If we refuse, we shall see no more of Alesha than of our own ears. He will die of grief, or go off to the wars, or become a monk—and that's the end of the Bagrov family!' But Arina Vasilevna had been primed already by her daughters, and she answered, as if her son ran no risk: 'As you please, Stepan Mikhailovich; your will is mine too. But how can you hope they will respect you in future, if they resist your positive commands now?' This mean and cunning trick was successful: the old man's pride was touched, and he resolved to stand firm. He dictated a letter, in which he expressed surprise that his son should begin the old business over again, and repeated what he had already said by word of mouth. In short, the letter contained a positive refusal.

Two or three weeks passed, and brought no reply from Alexei Stepanich. Then there came one stormy autumn morning, when my grandfather was sitting across his bed in his own room; he was wearing his favourite dressing-gown of fine camel's hair over a shirt buttoning up at the side, and had slippers on his bare feet. Arina Vasilevna was sitting near him with her spinning-wheel, spinning goat's down and carefully drawing out the fine long threads with which she intended to make cloth —cloth to provide her son with light, warm, comfortable garments. Tanyusha was sitting by the window, reading a book. Elizabeth, who was on a visit to Bagrovo, was sitting on the bed near her father, telling him of her troubles—her husband's poor prospects, and the shifts they had to practise at home to make ends meet. The old man listened sadly, with his hands on his knees, and his head, now turning white, bent down over his breast. Suddenly the door opened; and Ivan, a tall handsome lad, wearing a travelling jacket, entered the room with a quick step and delivered a letter which he had brought from the post-town twenty-five versts away. The stir among the party showed that the letter was eagerly expected. 'From Alesha?' asked the old man quickly and uneasily. 'From my brother,' answered Tanyusha, who had gone to meet Ivan, taken the letter quickly from him, and looked at the address. 'You have lost no time, and I thank you. A dram for Ivan! Then go and have your dinner and rest.' The spirit-case was opened at once; Tanyusha took out a long cut-glass decanter, filled a silver cup with brandy, and handed it to Ivan. Ivan crossed himself and drank it, then coughed, bowed, and left the room. 'Read it aloud, Tanyusha,' said her father; she did his reading and writing for him. She placed herself by the window; her father left his bed and her mother her spinning-wheel, and all crowded round the reader, who had unsealed the letter by this time but dared not take a preliminary peep. After a moment's silence, the letter was read slowly and audibly. It began with the form of address usual in those days: 'Dear and honoured Father, and dear and honoured Mother,' and then went on in this fashion:

In answer to my last letter, I had the misfortune to receive a refusal of my request, my dearest parents. I cannot go against your will; I submit to it, but I cannot long drag the burden of my life without my adored Sofya Nikolaevna; and therefore a fatal bullet shall ere long pierce the head of your unhappy son.*

The letter produced a powerful effect. My aunts began to whimper; my grandmother, who was taken utterly by surprise, turned pale, threw out her hands, and flopped down on the ground like a corn-sheaf. Even in those days fainting-fits were not unknown. Stepan Mikhailovich never stirred; but his head bent a little to one side, as it used to do when a fit of anger was coming on, and began to tremble slightly; and the same tremulous motion went on from that hour till his death. The daughters rushed to their mother's aid and soon brought her back to her senses. At once, Arina Vasilevna threw herself at her husband's feet, raising the cry of mourning for the dead; and her daughters followed her example. Taking no notice of the storm-signals on his brow, and quite forgetting that she herself had egged him on to disappoint his son, she cried at the top of her voice: '*Batyushka* Stepan Mikhailovich! have pity and do not be the death of your own child, our only son! Give Alesha leave to marry! If anything happens to him, I will not live one hour longer!' The old man never stirred. At last he said in an unsteady voice: 'Enough of that howling! Alesha deserves a good whipping. But we'll leave it till tomorrow; morning brings good counsel. Now go and order dinner to be served.' Dinner my grandfather regarded as a sedative at every domestic crisis. Arina Vasilevna tried to begin again—'Mercy! Mercy!'—but

---

* I know the letter nearly by heart. It probably still exists among the old papers of one of my brothers. Some expressions in it are clearly borrowed from the novels which Alexei Stepanich was fond of reading (*author's note*).

Stepan Mikhailovich called out loudly, 'Leave the room, all of you!'—and in his voice was audible the roar that goes before a storm. The room was cleared instantly, and no one ventured near him before the dinner-hour.

It is hard to imagine the thoughts that passed through his mind in the interval, the struggle that took place in that iron heart between love and prudence, and the final defeat of the stubborn spirit; but when Mazan's voice was heard outside the door, announcing dinner, my grandfather came out of his room quite composed. His face was rather pale, but his wife and daughters, who were standing, each by her own chair, till he appeared, could not see the faintest sign of anger; on the contrary, he was quieter and more cheerful than he had been in the morning, and made a hearty meal. Arina Vasilevna had to harden her heart and suit her conversation to his mood; she dared not even sigh, far less ask questions; in vain she tried to guess what was passing through her husband's mind; the little chestnut-brown eyes in her fat face might ask what questions they pleased, but the dark-blue eyes of Stepan Mikhailovich, for all their frank good-humoured expression, gave no answer. After dinner he lay down as usual, and woke in a still more cheerful mood, but not a syllable did he utter about his son or the letter. Yet it was clear that no wrath was brooding in the old man's heart. When he said goodnight to his wife after supper, she ventured to say, 'Please say something about Alesha.' He smiled and answered: 'Did I not say that morning thoughts are best? Go to sleep, and God bless you!'

Morning did indeed bring good counsel and kindly action. My grandfather got up at four o'clock when Mazan was kindling his fire, and his first words were: 'Tanaichenok, you are to take a letter at once to Ufa for Alexei Stepanich. Get ready immediately, and no one is to know your errand or where you are going. Put the young brown horse in the shafts, and the roarer abreast of him. Take six bushels of oats with you and a loaf of bread. Ask the housekeeper for two roubles in copper for your expenses. See that all is ready when my letter is written, and don't lose a moment!' When my grandfather demanded haste, he always got it. Then he opened the oak desk which served him as a writing-table, got writing materials, and with some effort—for ten years past he had written nothing but his signature—he wrote as follows in a stiff old-fashioned hand:

Dear Son Alexei,

Your mother, Arina Vasilevna, and I, give you our permission to marry Sofya Nikolaevna Zubin, if that be God's will, and we send you our blessing.

Your father,

STEPAN BAGROV

Half an hour later, long before it was light, Tanaichenok had reached the top of the long hill and passed the stackyard, and was trotting briskly along the road to Ufa. At six o'clock Stepan Mikhailovich ordered Aksyutka to bring the samovar but to wake no one in the house. In spite of this, the mistress was called, and told in confidence that Tanaichenok had started very early with a pair of horses from the stable; he was carrying a letter from the master, but his destination was unknown. She did not venture to join her husband at once: she waited an hour or so, and appeared when he had finished his tea and was chatting with Aksyutka, the maid, who had been plain as a child and was now still plainer in middle life. 'Well, what did they wake you for?' said Stepan Mikhailovich, holding out his hand to his wife. 'I dare say you had a bad night.' Arina Vasilevna kissed his hand respectfully: 'No,' she said, 'no one called me, I woke of myself; and I had a good night, for I hoped you would be kind to our poor boy.' He looked attentively at her; but her face was accustomed to wear a mask, and he could not read her thoughts. 'In that case', he said, 'I have good news for you. I have sent a special messenger to Ufa and written to Alexei that he has permission from us both to marry Sofya Nikolaevna.'

Arina Vasilevna had been horrified by her son's tragic intentions, and had sincerely begged and prayed her stern husband to consent to the marriage. Yet, when she heard how Stepan Mikhailovich had decided, she felt more fear than joy; or rather, she did not dare to feel joy, because she feared her daughters. She knew already what Elizabeth thought of the letter, and guessed what Alexandra would say. For these reasons she received the decision, which her husband hoped would delight her, rather coldly and strangely; and this did not escape him. Elizabeth expressed no satisfaction whatever, but merely respectful submission to her father's will; but Tanyusha, who took her brother's letter quite seriously, rejoiced with all her heart. Elizabeth was not alarmed even at first by her brother's threat; she shed tears and interceded for him, merely because it would not look well to act differently from her mother and youngest sister. She wrote at once to Alexandra, who was furious when she heard of the decision and came with all speed to Bagrovo. She too treated her brother's letter as an empty threat, a trick suggested by Sofya Nikolaevna; and the two together soon converted their mother and even Tanyusha to this belief. But the matter was settled, and open rebellion was now out of the question. Stepan Mikhailovich had thought that Sofya Nikolaevna would refuse his son; but no one else at Bagrovo believed this. But it is time now to leave Bagrovo and see what was going on at Ufa.

I shall not take upon myself to decide positively whether Alexei Stepanich really intended to shoot himself, if his parents were obdurate, or took a hint from some incident in a novel and tried to excite their fears by suggesting the awful result of their refusal. Judging by the later development of his character —and I knew it well—I cannot think him capable of either course of action. Therefore, as I suppose, the young man was not playing a trick in order to frighten his parents; on the contrary, he sincerely intended to blow out his brains, if he was forbidden to marry Sofya Nikolaevna. But at the same time I do not think he could ever have brought himself to carry out his fatal purpose, although your mild quiet people, who are often called faint-hearted, are sometimes more capable of desperate actions than men of bold and energetic temperament. The idea of suicide was certainly borrowed from some novel; it was quite out of keeping with the character of Alexei Stepanich, his view of life, and the circle of ideas in which he had been born and brought up. However that may be, when he had launched the fatal letter, he became greatly agitated and was soon laid up with fever. His friend and confidante, Mme Alakaev, knew

nothing of the letter; she came to see him daily and soon per-
ceived that his illness and his love affair were not enough to
account for his excessive agitation. She was sitting beside him
one day, knitting a stocking and talking about trifles, in order to
amuse the invalid and distract his mind from his hopeless
passion; he was lying on the sofa, with his hands behind his
head, looking out of the window. Suddenly he turned as white
as a sheet. A cart with a pair of horses had turned off the
street into the courtyard, and he recognized the horses and
Tanaichenok. He sprang to his feet, cried out, 'A message from
my father, from Bagrovo!' and made for the door. Mme Alakaev
seized his arm, and, with the help of a servant, prevented him
from hurrying to the steps; it was wet and cold autumn weather.
Meanwhile Tanaichenok came quickly into the room and
delivered the letter. Alexei Stepanich broke the seal with trembling fingers, read the few lines, burst into tears, and fell on his
knees before the ikon. Mme Alakaev was puzzled until he
handed her the letter; but when she had read it, she too shed
tears of joy. The young man was beside himself with happiness.
He now confessed the nature of the letter he had written to his
parents, and she shook her head when she heard it. Tanaichenok
was called in and closely questioned; when he told how he had
been sent off, they saw that Stepan Mikhailovich had settled the
matter by himself, without the knowledge of his womenfolk
and probably against their wishes.

Mme Alakaev was entirely taken by surprise: even when she
had read the letter over again she could not believe her own
eyes, because she knew Stepan Mikhailovich of old and quite
realized the opposition of the family. But when the first excitement of surprise and joy was over, the two began to discuss how
they should set to work. So long as opposition from their own
side made the marriage seem remote and impossible, they had
been sanguine as to the feelings of the lady; but now a doubt
seized on Mme Alakaev. When she recalled and examined all
the favourable signs, she felt that perhaps she had attached more
importance to them than they deserved; and like a sensible
woman, she made haste to moderate the young man's confident
hopes, prudently calculating that if he were seduced by them,

he would find it harder to bear the sudden collapse of those radiant dreams. A refusal now seemed to her quite possible, and her fears had effect upon her companion. Still, she did not back out of her promise to help him: on the contrary, she went next day and laid his proposal before Sofya Nikolaevna.

Simply, clearly, and with no exaggeration, she described the constant and ardent attachment of Alexei Stepanich—all the town had long known it, and certainly Sofya Nikolaevna did; she spoke warmly of the fine character of her young relative, his kind heart, his rare modesty; she gave true and exact details of his financial position and prospects; she told the facts about his family, not forgetting to state that he had received by letter yesterday his parents' blessing and their full consent to seek the hand of a lady so worthy and highly respected as Sofya Nikolaevna; she added, that the young man had caught a fever in the excitement of waiting for his parents' reply, but found it impossible to postpone the decision of his fate, and therefore had asked her, as his kinswoman and a friend of Sofya Nikolaevna's, to find out whether a formal proposal for her hand, laid before her father, would be distasteful to her or not.

Sofya Nikolaevna had long been accustomed to act for herself: without confusion and without any of the affectation and prudery expected of women in those days, she replied as follows:

'I thank Alexei Stepanich for the honour he has done me, and you, dear lady, for your interest in the matter. I say frankly that I noticed long ago his partiality for me and have long expected that he would make me a proposal; but I have never decided whether I would accept or reject it. His last visit to his parents, the suddenness—you told me this yourself—of his long and dangerous illness at home, and the change in him when he came back to Ufa—these were signs that his parents disapproved of me as a daughter-in-law. This, I confess, I did not expect; it seemed more natural to fear opposition on the part of my father. Later I saw that Alexei Stepanich had revived his former feeling for me; and now I suppose that he has been able to induce his father and mother to consent. But you must admit yourself, my dear lady, that the matter now assumes quite a new aspect.

To enter a family where one is not welcome is too great a risk. Certainly, my father would not oppose my choice; but can I venture to conceal the truth from him? If he were to learn that an obscure country squire thought twice before admitting me to the honour of alliance with his family, he would consider it a degradation, and nothing would induce him to consent. I am not in love with Alexei Stepanich: I only respect his good qualities and his constant affection, and I believe he might make the woman he loved happy. Allow me, therefore, to think it over; and also, before I speak of this to my father and trouble him in his feeble state with such news, I wish to speak myself to Alexei Stepanich. Let him come and see us, when he is well enough.'

Mme Alakaev reported this answer exactly to the young man. He did not think it promising, but she disagreed with him and tried to soothe his anxiety.

After parting on very friendly terms with her visitor, Sofya Nikolaevna sat for a long time alone in her drawing-room, and thought hard. Her bright lively eyes were clouded; sombre thoughts raced through her brain and were reflected on the mirror of her beautiful face. All that she had said to Mme Alakaev was perfectly true: the question, whether she should marry Alexei Stepanich or not, was really not settled. But the proposal had now been made, and it was necessary to make the great decision, so critical in every woman's life. Sofya Nikolaevna had an unusually clear head; in later years, the trials of life and her own passionate temperament may have warped her judgement, but she was able then to see everything exactly in its true light. Her prospects were not bright. Her father was a hopeless invalid, and Zanden, their best doctor, declared he could not live more than a year. His property consisted of two villages near Ufa, Zubkova and Kasimovka—forty serfs in all and a small amount of land; he had also scraped together a sum of 10,000 roubles which he intended as a portion for his daughter. To see her married was his constant and eager desire; but strange things do happen, and Sofya Nikolaevna had never before received a formal offer. He would leave behind him six orphans, the children of his two marriages, and separate

guardians would have to be appointed. The three youngest
would go to their grandmother, Mme Rychkov; their mother's
fortune consisted of a small estate of fifty serfs. Sofya
Nikolaevna's own brothers were at a boarding-school in
Moscow; she would be left absolutely alone without even distant
relations to take her under their roof. In short, she had nowhere
to lay her head. To face poverty and want, to live on the charity
of strangers and in complete dependence upon strangers—such
a fate might distress anyone; but to a girl who had lived in
comfort and held a high position in society, a girl proud by
nature and flattered by general attention and popularity, a girl
who had experienced all the burden of dependence and then all
the charm of authority—such a change might well seem
intolerable. And here was a young man, good-looking, honest,
modest, the heir of an ancient line and an only son, whose
father possessed 180 serfs and who was himself to inherit wealth
from an aunt; and this young man worshipped her and offered
her his hand and heart. At first sight, hesitation seemed out of
the question. But, on the other hand, they were ill-matched in
mind and temperament. No one in the town could believe that
Sofya Nikolaevna would accept Alexei Stepanich, and she
realized the justice of public opinion and could not but attach
importance to it. She was considered a marvel of beauty and
intelligence: her suitor was certainly pretty in a boyish way—
which was no recommendation to Sofya Nikolaevna—but rather
simple and stupid, and passed with everyone for a plain country
lad. She was quick and enterprising: he was timid and slow.
She was educated and might almost be called learned, had read
much, and had a wide range of intellectual interests: he was
quite ignorant, had read nothing but a few silly novels and a
song-book, and cared for little beyond snaring quails and flying
his hawks. She was witty and tactful and shone in society: he
could not string three words together; clumsy, shy, abject, and
ridiculous, he could only blush and bow and squeeze into a
corner or against a door, to escape from the talkative and
sociable young men whom he positively feared, though he was
in truth far cleverer than many of them. She had a firm,
positive, unbending temper: he was humble and wanting in

energy, easily silenced and easily discomfited. Was he the man to support and defend his wife in society and in domestic life?

Such were the contradictory thoughts and ideas and fancies which swarmed in the young girl's mind, mingling and jostling one another. Long after darkness had come down, she was still sitting there alone. At last a feeling of extreme misery, a terrible certainty that her reason was utterly baffled and growing less and less able to solve her problem, turned her thoughts to prayer. She hurried to her room to beg for the light of reason from on high, and fell on her knees before the ikon of Our Lady of Smolensk, who had once before by a miracle lightened her darkness and pointed out to her the path of life. For a long time she prayed, and her hot tears fell. But by degrees she felt a kind of relief, a measure of strength, a power of resolve, though she did not know yet what her resolve would be; and even this feeling helped her. She went downstairs to look at her father in his sleep; then she came back to her own room, lay down, and went peacefully to sleep. When she woke next morning, she was perfectly composed; she reflected for a few minutes, gave a thought to her hesitation and perplexity of the night before, and then kept quietly to her purpose, which was, first to have a conversation with her suitor, and then to settle the matter definitely, in accordance with the impression left on her mind by their interview.

Alexei Stepanich, wishing to know his fate as soon as possible, sent for the doctor and begged to be put on his legs without delay. The doctor promised to let him out soon and kept his promise for once. Within a week Alexei Stepanich, though still pale, thin, and feeble, was sitting in Sofya Nikolaevna's drawing-room. Touched by the loss of colour and change in his young face, she was not quite as outspoken and rigorous as she meant to be. In substance she repeated to him what she had said to Mme Alakaev, but she added two points—that she would not part from her father while he lived, and that she would not live in the country. She wished to live in a town, in Ufa for choice, where she was acquainted with many worthy and cultivated people, and hoped to enjoy their society after her marriage.

She ended by saying that she would like to see her husband in the public service and holding a position in the town, which, if not brilliant, should at least secure deference and respect. To all these conditions and anticipations of a wife's rights, Alexei Stepanich replied, with abject humility, that her will was law to him, and that his happiness would consist in the fulfilment of all her wishes. Such an answer no man should have given: it proved that his love was not to be depended on, and that he could not assure a woman's happiness; yet it pleased Sofya Nikolaevna, clever as she was. Reluctantly I must confess that love of power was one of her ruling passions; and the germs of this passion, now that she had been released from the cruel oppression of her stepmother, were sprouting actively at this time. Love of power did really, though she herself did not know it, help her to her decision.

She expressed a wish to see the letter of consent which he had received from his parents; and he produced it from his pocket. She read it and was convinced that she was right in guessing that his wishes had at first been opposed. The young man was incapable of dissimulation, and also so much in love that he could not resist a kind look or word from his idol. So, when Sofya Nikolaevna demanded perfect frankness, he made a clean breast of everything; and I believe that this frankness finally settled the question in his favour. Sofya Nikolaevna was clever, but still she was a woman; and she was filled with the idea of reshaping and remoulding in her own way this good-tempered young man, so modest and sincere and uncorrupted by society. How delightful to think of the gradual awakening and enlightenment of this savage! He had no lack of sense; and feeling, though wrapt in unbroken slumber, was there too. He would love her still better, if that were possible, in gratitude for his transformation. This vision took hold of her eager imagination; and she parted very graciously from her adorer, promising to talk the matter over wtih her father and communicate the result through Mme Alakaev. Alexei Stepanich was 'swimming in bliss' —to use an expression of that day. That evening Sofya Nikolaevna again had recourse to prayer, and prayed for a long time with great mental strain and fervour. She was exhausted when she went to sleep; and she had a dream which she interpreted, as people often do, as a confirmation of her purpose. Men are clever enough to interpret anything according to their desires. This dream I forget; but I remember that it was capable, with much more probability and much less forcing, of the opposite interpretation. Next morning Sofya Nikolaevna lost no time in telling her father, who was now in a very feeble state, of the proposal she had received. M. Zubin did not know Alexei Stepanich, but had somehow come to think of him as a person of no importance; and he was not pleased, in spite of his eager desire to see his daughter settled before he died. But she proved to him, with her usual eagerness and convincing eloquence, that it was unwise to show the door to such a suitor. She urged all the advantages of the match which we know already, and above all, that, far from parting with him, she would continue to live in the same house. She painted her helpless condition when it should please God to remove her father, till the sick man shed a tear and said: 'Do as you please, my dear clever child. I consent to everything. Bring your future husband to see me soon: I wish to become better acquainted with him. And I insist on receiving a proposal in writing from his parents.'

Sofya Nikolaevna then sent a note to Mme Alakaev, asking Alexei Stepanich to call on her father at a fixed hour. He was still 'swimming in bliss', which he shared only with his old friend and supporter; but he was much disconcerted by this invitation which he had never expected from such a confirmed invalid. M. Zubin, in the absence of the Lieutenant-Governor the most important and powerful personage in the whole district of Ufa! M. Zubin, whom he had always approached with reverence and awe! His name seemed now more formidable than ever. What if he frowned on this proposal for his daughter's hand from one of the humblest of his subordinates? Might he not treat it as insolence, and thunder out: 'How dared you think of my daughter? Are you a fit match for her? Off with him to prison and to judgement!' However wild these notions may appear, they did really pass through the young man's head; and he often told the story afterwards himself. Plucking up his spirits and encouraged by Mme Alakaev, he put on his uniform, which hung loosely on his limbs from loss of flesh, and set off to wait on the great man. With his three-cornered hat under his arm, and clutching his troublesome sword in a trembling hand, he entered M. Zubin's study, so nervous that he could hardly breathe. M. Zubin who had once been clever, lively, and energetic, now lay on his couch hardly able to move and shrunk to a mere skeleton. The visitor bowed low and remained standing by the door. This in itself was enough to annoy the invalid. 'Step this way, M. Bagrov, and take a chair near my bed; I am too weak to talk loud.' Alexei Stepanich, with a profusion of bows, sat down on the edge of a chair close to the bed.'I understand that you seek my daughter's hand,' the old man went on. The suitor jumped up, bowed, and said that he did in fact venture to seek this happiness.

I could report the whole of this interview in detail, as I have often heard it fully described by Alexei Stepanich himself; but part of it would be a repetition of what we know already, and I am afraid of wearying my readers. The important points are these. M. Zubin questioned the young man about his family, his means, and his intentions with regard to his profession and place of residence; he said that Sofya Nikolaevna would have nothing but her portion of 10,000 roubles, two families of serfs as servants, and 3,000 roubles in cash for initial expenses; and he added: 'Though I am quite sure that you, as a dutiful son, would not have made such a proposal without the consent of your parents, yet they may change their minds; and social usage requires that they should write to me personally on the subject; and I cannot give you a positive answer till I receive a letter to that effect.' Alexei Stepanich got up repeatedly, bowed, and sat down again. He agreed to everything and promised to write that very day to his parents. In half an hour the invalid said that he was tired—which was perfectly true—and dismissed the young man rather dryly. The moment he left, Sofya Nikolaevna entered her father's study; he was lying with closed eyes, and his face expressed weariness and also anxiety. Hearing his daughter's approach, he threw an imploring glance at her, pressed his hands to his breast, and ejaculated: 'Is it possible, Sonechka, that you intend to marry him!' But Sofya Nikolaevna had anticipated the result of the interview and was prepared for an even worse impression. 'I warned you, father,' she said in a gentle but firm voice, 'that Alexei Stepanich, owing to utter ignorance of society, awkwardness, and timidity, was bound to appear to you at first somewhat of a simpleton; but I, who have seen him often and had long conversations with him, will vouch for it that he is no fool and has more sense than most people. I beg you to have two more interviews with him; and I am sure you will agree with me.' M. Zubin looked long at his daughter with a keen and penetrating gaze, as if he wished to read some secret hidden in her heart; then he sighed heavily and consented to do what she asked.

By the next post Alexei Stepanich sent a very affectionate and respected letter to his parents. He thanked them for having given him life a second time, and humbly begged them to write at once to M. Zubin and request the hand of his daughter for their son; he added that this was the regular custom, and without such a letter the father would not give a positive answer. The fulfilment of this simple request gave some trouble to the old people at Bagrovo. They were no hands at composition, and for want of previous experience had no idea how to set about it, while they were exceedingly loath to commit themselves before the Governor's Deputy and their future relation, who was sure to be a skilful man of business and a practised writer. It took them a whole week to compose their letter; at last it got written somehow and was dispatched to Alexei Stepanich. It was not a skilful production, having none of those polite phrases and professions of affection which are indispensable in such cases.

While waiting for the answer from home, Alexei Stepanich received two more invitations from M. Zubin. The second visit did not remove the unfavourable impression produced by the first. On the next occasion, however, Sofya Nikolaevna was present. Returning from a call earlier than usual, she walked into her father's room, as if she did not know that her suitor was sitting there. Her presence made all the difference. She could make him talk and knew what he could talk about, so as to display to advantage his natural good sense, high principle, and goodness of heart. M. Zubin was obviously pleased: he spoke kindly to the young man and invited him to come to the house as often as he could. When they were alone, the old man embraced his daughter with tears, called her by many fond names, and said she was a witch whose spells could draw out a man's good qualities, even when they were so deeply hidden that no one suspected their existence. She too was much pleased; for she had not dared to hope that Alexei Stepanich would do so much to support her favourable opinion and justify the character she had given him.

The letter containing the formal proposal arrived at last, and Alexei Stepanich delivered it in person to M. Zubin. Alas! without the magic presence and aid of Sofya Nikolaevna the suitor failed again to please his future father-in-law, who was also far from satisfied with the letter. Next day he had a long conversation with his daughter, in which he set before her all the disadvantages of marrying a man inferior to herself in intelligence, education, and force of character; he said that the Bagrov family would not take her to their hearts—they would be much more likely to hate her, because coarse and cruel ignorance always hates refinement; he warned her not to rely on the promises of a lover; for these as a rule are not kept after marriage, and Alexei Stepanich, even if he wished, would not have the power to keep them. To all this sage advice, drawn directly from the experience of life, she had an answer of surprising adroitness; and at the same time she depicted in such lively colours the advantages of marrying a man who, if he lacked energy and refinement, was at least kind-hearted, honourable, loving, and no fool, that her father was carried away by her confidence and gave his full consent. She clasped her father in her arms and kissed his wasted hands; then she gave him the ikon and received his blessing, kneeling by his bed and weeping. 'Father,' she cried in her excitement, 'with God's help, I hope that in a year's time Alexei Stepanich will be a different creature: the reading of good books, the society of clever people, and constant conversation with his wife—these will make up for defects of education; his bashfulness will pass away, and the power to take a place in society will come of itself.' 'May it be so!' he answered. 'Now send for the priest. I wish that we should pray together for your happiness.'

That same evening Alexei Stepanich was invited to the house, with Mme Alakaev and some old friends of the Zubins—M. Anichkov and the Misailovs; and the favourable answer was given. The young man's bliss no words can describe: Sofya Nikolaevna, even in extreme old age, used to speak of his joy at that moment. He threw himself at M. Zubin's feet and kissed his hands, cried and sobbed like a child, and nearly fainted from the effect of this immense good fortune which down to the last moment had seemed beyond his reach. She too was deeply moved by such a frank expression of ardent and entire devotion.

The official betrothal came two days later, and all the town was invited to the ceremony. There was general surprise, because many had disbelieved the reports of the engagement. But all sceptics were convinced at last, and came to express their congratulations and good wishes. Alexei Stepanich was radiant with happiness; he was quite unaware of any hidden meaning in congratulations, of any mockery in looks and smiles. But Sofya Nikolaevna let nothing pass unnoticed: she saw everything and heard everything, though in speaking to her, everyone was cautious and polite. Though she knew beforehand the view society would take of her action, she could not help being vexed by this expression of their opinion. But no one detected her vexation; for she was cheerful and affectionate with everyone and especially with her suitor, and seemed perfectly happy and content with her choice. The pair were soon summoned into M. Zubin's study, and the betrothal took place there before a few witnesses. While the priest read the prayers, the old man shed tears; when the rite was over, he told the bridegroom to kiss the bride and embraced them both himself with a great effort; then he gazed earnestly at Alexei Stepanich and said, 'Love her always as you do now; God is giving you such a treasure . . .' and then he broke down. The engaged couple and the witnesses returned to the drawing-room, where all the men embraced the bridegroom and kissed the bride's hand, while all the ladies embraced the bride and had their hands kissed by the bridegroom. When this fuss was over, the pair were made to sit on a sofa side by side, and exchange kisses again; and then the company, holding glasses in their hands, repeated their congratulations and good wishes. Anichkov acted as host, and Mme Alakaev as hostess. Alexei Stepanich, who had never in his life drunk anything but water, was forced to take a glass of wine, and the unfamiliar stimulant had a strong effect upon him, weakened as he was by recent illness and prolonged agitation. He became uncommonly lively, laughed and cried, and talked a great deal, to the amusement of the company and the mortification of the bride. The guests soon grew merry: glass followed glass, and a fine supper was served. All ate and drank heartily, and at last the party broke up amid noise and merriment. The bridegroom's head was beginning to ache; and Mme Alakaev took him home in her carriage.

M. Zubin felt that he was in great danger and therefore wished to have the wedding as soon as possible; but as he also wished his daughter's outfit to be rich and splendid, it was necessary to postpone the ceremony for some months. Her mother's diamonds and emeralds had to be sent to Moscow, to be reset and restrung in the newest fashion; silver had to be ordered from Moscow, and some dresses and presents; the other dresses, curtains for the state bed, and a sumptuous black-brown fur cloak which cost 500 roubles then and could not be bought now for 5,000—all these were made in Kazan; a quantity of table-linen and holland sheets were also provided. Ten thousand roubles, the amount fixed for the dowry, was a great sum in those days; and, as many valuable things were provided as well, the inventory of the bride's outfit assumed such splendid proportions, that when I read it now I can hardly believe in the simple life of our ancestors at the end of last century.

The first business after the formal betrothal was to send complimentary letters to all relations on both sides. One of Sofya Nikolaevna's gifts was her remarkable skill in letter-writing; and her letter to her future husband's parents was such that Stepan Mikhailovich, though no letter-writer himself, set a high value on it. First he listened to it with great attention: then he took it out of Tanyusha's hand, praised the distinct handwriting, and read it through twice himself. 'Well, she's a clever girl,' he said, 'and I make sure she has a warm heart.' This enraged the family, but they had the sense to keep silent. Alexandra alone could not restrain herself: her gooseberry eyes flashed with rage as she said: 'She can write a fine letter, father, I admit; but all is not gold that glitters.' The old man scowled at her and said in his dangerous voice: 'How do you know? You're snarling at her already, and you've never even seen her! Take care! Keep your tongue from wagging, and don't stir up the rest! All sat as silent as mice, and of course hated Sofya Nikolaevna worse than ever. Meanwhile Stepan Mikhailovich under the influence of that warm and affectionate letter, took the pen himself and wrote as follows, in defiance of all established etiquette:

My dear, precious, sensible Daughter-in-Law to be,

If you, without seeing us, have learnt to love and respect us old people, we feel the same for you. And when, by God's blessing, we meet, we shall love you still better; and you will be to us as our own daughter, and we shall rejoice in the happiness of our son Alexei.

On her side, Sofya Nikolaevna valued the old man's simple words as they deserved; from what she had heard, she had already taken a fancy to him. As she had no relations living, the bridegroom had no letters to write; but she asked Alexei Stepanich to write a letter of intimation to M. Anichkov, the friend at Moscow whom she had never seen and who had taken her brothers under his care. The bridegroom of course gladly consented. Not having much confidence in his power to express himself on paper, she asked to see the letter before it was sent. When she read it, she was horrified! Alexei Stepanich, who had heard a great deal of M. Anichkov as a wit, took it into his head to adopt an elaborate style. Therefore he had recourse to some novel of the day, and filled two sides with phrases which, in other circumstances, would have made Sofya Nikolaevna laugh outright; as it was, the blood rushed to her face, and then the tears poured from her eyes. When she grew calmer, she wondered how she was to get out of such an awkward situation. She did not wonder long however. She wrote a rough draft of a letter herself, and then said to her betrothed that, not being in the habit of writing to strangers, he had written in a way that might not please M. Anichkov; and therefore she had written a rough draft, which she asked him to copy out and send off. She felt shame and pain, and was hurt on his account; her voice shook, and she nearly broke down. But he welcomed her suggestion with enthusiasm; when she read him the letter, he was charmed with it, praised her wonderful skill, and covered her hands with kisses. This was the first step in disrespect for her future husband, the first step towards realizing her dream of complete domination over him; and she did not find it easy to take.

Knowing that his parents had little money and were forced to be chary in spending any, Alexei Stepanich wrote to ask for a very moderate sum; and to strengthen his request, he asked Mme Alakayeff to write to his father, to assure him that the request was reasonable and that some expense was inevitable in view of the marriage. He asked only 800 roubles, but Mme Alakaev stated the necessary sum at 1,500. The old people replied that they had not got such a sum; they sent him all they had—300 roubles, and suggested that, if the other 500 were necessary, he should borrow them; but they promised to send him a team of four horses with a coachman and postilion, and provisions of all kinds. They did not even answer Mme Alakaev: so indignant were they with her for demanding such a huge sum. It could not be helped: Alexei Stepanich thanked them for their kindness and borrowed 500 roubles; when even this proved insufficient, Mme Alakaev gave him 500 more, without the knowledge of his parents.

Meantime, as the engaged couple met more often and were together longer, they became more intimate. Sofya Nikolaevna for the first time saw her lover as he really was, and realized for the first time what a heavy task lay before her. She had made no mistake in thinking that he possessed natural intelligence, a very kind heart, strict principles of honour, and perfect integrity in official life; but otherwise she found such a limitation of ideas, such a pettiness of interests, such an absence of self-esteem and independence, that her courage and firmness in the execution of her purpose were more than once severely shaken. More than once, in despair, she took the engagement ring off her finger, laid it before the ikon of Our Lady of Smolensk, and prayed with tears that her feeble intelligence might be enlightened by divine wisdom. As we know already, she was accustomed to act thus at each crisis in her life. When she had prayed, she felt braver and calmer. Interpreting this feeling as heavenly guidance, she would put her ring on again and go back, composed and cheerful, to join her lover in the drawing-room. Her father felt that he was losing strength daily; and she was able to assure him that she was constantly discovering fresh merits in her lover, that she was quite content and looked forward to happiness in her marriage. By this time disease had dulled M. Zubin's perspicacity: he not only believed that she was sincere, but was convinced himself that his daughter would be happy. 'Thank God!' he used to say; 'now I can die happy.'

And now the wedding-day drew near. The bride's outfit was all ready. The bridegroom too made his preparations, being guided by the advice of Mme Alakaev, who assumed the entire management of him. The old lady, in spite of her shrewdness, was surprised at his profound ignorance of the customs of polite society. But for her, he would have been guilty of many blunders which would have made his bride blush for shame. Thus he intended to give her as a birthday present a kind of cloth for a dress which would have only been suitable as a present to her maid; and he thought of driving to the church in an old carriage without springs, which would have made all the town laugh; and so on. The things were not of importance in themselves; but it would have tried Sofya Nikolaevna too hard to see her bridegroom the laughing-stock of Ufa society. All such things were put right by Mme Alakaev, or rather by the bride herself, for the two women discussed every point together. Sofya Nikolaevna told her lover in time that he must not think of giving her a present for her birthday, because she loathed birthday presents in general. For the wedding, she made him get a new English carriage which had lately been ordered from Petersburg by a local landowner, whose name was Murzakhanov* and who had managed to run through his fortune in a few months. The price paid for the carriage was

* The Russianized form of an oriental name, Mirza Khan.

350 roubles; Sofya Nikolaevna bought it herself as a present from her father to the bridegroom, and begged him not to trouble the dying man by thanking him. And the other difficulties were got over in the same fashion.

Then the bride and bridegroom wrote, for themselves and M. Zubin, to Stepan Mikhailovich and Arina Vasilevna, pressing them to honour the wedding by their presence; but the old people, as a matter of course, declined the invitation. They had lived so long in their country solitude that town society seemed to them something strange and formidable. None of the daughters wished to go either; but Stepan Mikhailovich thought this awkward, and desired Elizabeth and Alexandra to attend the wedding. The latter was accompanied by her husband, Karataev; but Erlykin was detained by his duties at Orenburg.

The presence of these uninvited and unexpected guests was the cause of much annoyance to Sofya Nikolaevna. Her future sisters-in-law were clever and cunning women: they were determined to dislike her, and their behaviour to her was cold, unfriendly, and even rude. Though Sofya Nikolaevna knew very well the sort of attitude they were likely to adopt, yet she thought it her duty to be friendly and even cordial to them at first; but when she saw that all her efforts were vain, and that the better she treated them the worse they treated her, she retired behind a wall of cold civility. But this did not protect her from those mean hints and innuendoes which it is impossible not to understand and not to resent, though it is awkward to do either, because you lay yourself open to the retort— 'If the cap fits, wear it!' This odious form of attack, now banished to the servants' hall by the advance of refinement, was formidable in those days, and much used in the houses of rural landowners, many of whom differed little from their own servants in their manners and customs. But is it true that it has really been banished? Does it not still live on among us, concealed under more decent and artistic forms?

The good people of Ufa made fun, as might be expected, of the country clothes and manners of the two ladies. As to Karataev, who had now adopted all the Bashkir habits and began drinking Bashkir decoctions at eight in the morning, when he was first introduced to Sofya Nikolaevna he kissed her hand with a sounding smack three times over, and cried out with real Bashkir enthusiasm, 'My word! what a dazzler brother Alexei has hooked!' The coarse jests and compliments of the man were as distressing as the malicious sallies of the women; and both forced Sofya Nikolaevna to swallow many tears. But worse than all was the blindness of Alexei Stepanich: he seemed perfectly satisfied with the relations between his sisters and his bride, and this was not only a mortification for the present but also a peril for the future. These venomous creatures, who were staying with their brother, began at once to drop their poison into his simple soul, and did it so artfully that he did not suspect their manœuvres. Allusions to the young lady's pride, to the poverty which she hid under jewels and fine clothes, to her caprices and his meek submission to them, were dinned into his ears all day long. Much passed unnoticed, but much also went straight to the mark and made him thoughtful and vaguely uneasy. All their attacks, whether secret or open, were accompanied by a pretence of sympathy and sisterly affection. 'What makes you look so worn, my dear boy?' Elizabeth would ask; 'Sofya Nikolaevna wears you out with all her commissions. You've just got back from the other end of the town, tired and hungry, and off you run again, without eating a morsel, to dance attendance on her. As your sisters, we can't help being sorry for you'; and then sham tears, or at least some play with the pocket-handkerchief, completed the crafty sentence. Then Alexandra would make a furious entry into the conversation. 'No, my dear, I really cannot stand it! I know you will be angry, and perhaps you will cease to love us; but I can't help it. I must tell you the truth. You are quite changed: you're ashamed of us and have forgotten us altogether; your one wish is to slobber over that girl's hand; your one fear, to get into her black books. You have become her lackey, her slave! Then it cuts us to the heart to see that old witch, Mme Alakaev, ordering you about like a servant and making you fetch and carry for her; and she's not content with that, but finds fault with you and urges you to greater activity.' Alexei Stepanich could think of no answer to all this, except that he loved his sisters and would continue to do so, and—it was time to go and see Sofya Nikolaevna; whereupon he took his hat and hurried off. 'Oh, go by all means!' Alexandra called after him, 'and go quickly; or else she will be angry and perhaps withhold her hand from your lips!' Scenes like this took place again and again and undoubtedly left their impression.

Sofya Nikolaevna could not help noticing that his sisters' visit had brought about a certain change in her lover. He seemed depressed, was less exact in keeping his engagements, and spent less time with her. The reason for this she herself understood very well; and Mme Alakaev, who had become a very intimate friend and also knew all that went on in the Bagrovs' lodgings, did not fail to provide her with detailed information. Her impulsive nature made her unwilling to let things drag on. She reasoned justly, that she ought not to give time for the sisters' influence to take root at leisure, that she must open her lover's eyes and put the strength of his character and affection to a decisive test. If they proved too weak, it was better to part before marriage than to unite her fate to such a feeble creature, who was, to use her own expression, 'neither a shield from the sun nor a cloak to keep out the rain'. She summoned him early one morning and ordered that no visitors should be admitted to the drawing-room where they were sitting. Then she turned to Alexei Stepanich, who was looking pale and frightened, and addressed him as follows:

'I wish to have a frank explanation with you and to make a clean breast of what I am feeling; and I ask you to do the same. Your sisters detest me and did their best to rouse your parents against me. That I know from yourself. But your love overcame all obstacles: your parents gave you their approval, and I resolved to accept you and brave the hatred of all your family. I hoped to find protection in your love for me and in my endeavour to prove to your parents that I don't deserve their displeasure. But now I see that I was mistaken. You saw yourself how I received your sisters, how friendly I was and how hard I tried to please them; and though their rudeness made me draw back, yet I never once failed in politeness to them. And what has been the result? It is only a week since they came, and you treat me differently already: you make me promises and then forget to keep them; you spend less time with me; you are depressed and anxious, and even less affectionate to me than you used to be. Don't defend yourself, or deny it; that would not be honourable on your part. I know that you love me still, but you are afraid to show it: you fear your sisters, and that is why you are depressed and even avoid opportunities of being alone with me. You know yourself that all this is quite true. Well then, tell me, how can I hope that your love will stand firm? It is a strange kind of love that turns coward and hides, because your sisters disapprove of your bride, as you knew they did long ago. Suppose your parents disapprove of me and turn up their noses at me? What then? Then you will really cease to love me. No, Alexei Stepanich, honourable men do not behave so to the woman they love. The knowledge that your sisters disliked me should have made you twice as attentive and twice as devoted in their presence; and then they would not have dared to utter a syllable; but you have suffered them to use insulting language in your presence. I know just how they speak to you. From all this I conclude that your love is not love at all, but love-making, that I cannot rely on you, and that we had better part now than be unhappy for life. Consider carefully what I have said; I shall give you two days to think it over. Come to the house as usual, but I shall not see you alone and shall not refer to this interview. After two days, I shall ask for an honest answer to these questions: "Have you sufficient firmness to be my defender against your relations and anyone else who chooses to insult me? Can you shut your sisters' mouths and prevent them from uttering in your presence a single insulting word or allusion against me?" To break her engagement a week before her marriage is a great misfortune for any girl; but it is better to bear it once for all than to suffer all one's life. You know that I am not in love with you, but I was beginning to love you; and I believe my love would have been stronger and more constant than yours. Now, goodbye! For today and tomorrow we are strangers.'

Long before she ended, Alexei Stepanich had been in tears, and he tried several times to interrupt; but before he could open his mouth, she had left the room and shut the door behind her. It was some time before he recovered from this tremendous blow. But at last the terrible thought of losing his adored Sofya Nikolaevna presented itself to him with appalling reality, and summoned up that energy and vigour of which the mildest and gentlest of men are capable, though they cannot keep it up for long. He hurried home; and when his sisters, with no pity for his evident disturbance and distress, greeted him with the usual malicious jests, he flew into such a rage and attacked them with such fury that they were frightened. The wrath of a gentle patient man is a formidable thing. Among other things, he told his sisters that if they ventured to say another insulting word about his bride or about himself, he would instantly move to other lodgings, from which, as well as from M. Zubin's house, they would be excluded; and he would write to his father and tell him the whole story. That was enough. Alexandra had a clear recollection of her father's warning—'Keep your tongue quiet, and don't stir up the rest of the family!' She knew very well what a thunder-cloud her brother's complaint would call up, and what alarming consequences she might expect. Both the sisters fell on their brother's neck and begged forgiveness with tears; they solemnly declared that it should never happen again; they were really very fond of Sofya Nikolaevna, and it was only out of pity for his health and fear that he was doing too much that they had ventured on those foolish jests. They called on Sofya Nikolaevna that same day and paid court to her with the utmost servility. The meaning of all this was not lost upon her, and she felt she had prevailed.

The position of her lover really deserved pity. His feelings, which had been calmed and composed to some extent by frequent interviews with Sofya Nikolaevna, her simple friendly behaviour to him, and the near prospect of the marriage, had then been rather alarmed and abashed by the sneers of his sisters; and now they flamed up so fiercely, that at the present moment he was capable of any self-sacrifice or any desperate action, a true knight-errant! His state of mind was clearly reflected on his handsome young face during those two endless days. The lovers met several times, and Sofya Nikolaevna could not look on his face without pain; but she had the firmness to support the test she had imposed. The agitation and pity which she felt was a surprise to herself. She felt that she did really love this simple, modest young man, who was absolutely devoted to her and would not have hesitated to put an end to his existence if she made up her mind to refuse him. At last the two long days were over. Early on the third day, Alexei Stepanich sat in the drawing-room, waiting for Sofya Nikolaevna to appear. The door opened softly, and in she came, more beautiful, more charming than ever. She was smiling, and her eyes expressed such tenderness that when he looked at her and saw her kind hand stretched out towards him, the excess of his emotion deprived him for an instant of the power of speech. He soon recovered, and then, instead of taking her hand, fell at her feet and poured forth a torrent of burning heartfelt eloquence. She interrupted him and raised him to his feet. Then she said: 'I see and feel your love, and I share it; I believe all your promises; I put my fate in your hands without fear.' She had never been so affectionate to him before, and she used words of tenderness which he had never before heard from her lips.

Only five days remained before the marriage. All their preparations were complete, and the lovers were free to spend most of their time together. For five whole months Sofya Nikolaevna had been true to her intention of educating her future husband over again. She never lost a suitable moment, but did her best to impart those ideals which he did not possess, to clear up and develop feelings of which he was dimly conscious, and to root out the notions which he had derived from his early surroundings. She even made him read, and discussed with him the books he had read, explaining what puzzled him, filling up gaps in his memory, and illustrating fiction from real life. But it is probable that she got on faster with her task during these five days than in the course of five long months; for the recent incident which I have described had raised her lover's mind to a higher level of refinement, and he was in an unusually receptive and impressionable mood. How far the teacher succeeded on the whole in impressing her ideas upon the pupil, I cannot venture to decide. It is hard to know how much weight to attach to the opinions of the two persons concerned; but it is certain that in later years they both maintained —and they appealed to the evidence of disinterested persons in confirmation of the statement—that a great change took place in Alexei Stepanich, and even a complete transformation. I am very willing to believe it; but I have a proof that his proficiency in social etiquette left something to be desired. I know that he made his bride very angry the day before the marriage, and that her vehemence left a strong and painful impression on his mind. It happened in the following way. Two ladies were calling on Sofya Nikolaevna when a servant brought in a paper parcel and handed it to his mistress, with the explanation that Alexei Stepanich had sent it by his coachman and wished her at once to make a cap for his sister Alexandra. Her lover had left her half an hour before without saying one word about this commission, and Sofya Nikolaevna was exceedingly annoyed. The ladies, who were of some importance, had supposed at first that the parcel contained a present from the bridegroom; and now they did not try to conceal their amusement. Sofya Nikolaevna lost patience: she ordered the parcel to be returned, with a message that Alexei Stepanich had better apply to a milliner; it was no doubt a mistake to have brought the thing to her. The explanation was quite simple. On going home, he had found his sister in a great difficulty, because the milliner who had engaged to make her a cap for the wedding had fallen ill and returned the materials. As he had seen with his own eyes the skill with which Sofya Nikolaevna could trim hats and caps, he offered to help his sister out of her trouble, and told his servant to carry the parcel to his bride, with a humble request that she would trim a cap for Alexandra. But the servant was busy, and instead of going himself, sent the coachman; and the humble request became in the coachman's mouth an imperious demand. Alexei Stepanich hastened back to explain matters, and carried with him the same unlucky parcel. Sofya Nikolaevna had not yet cooled down, when she saw him coming into the room with the odious parcel under his arm; and she flared up worse than ever, and said many violent and unkind things which she had better have left unspoken. The culprit, utterly dumbfounded, tried to defend himself, but did it very badly; he was seriously hurt by this onslaught. She sent the materials for the cap to some milliner she knew of; and then, repenting of her violence, she tried to put matters right. But to her surprise Alexei Stepanich could not get over it: he felt that he had been unjustly treated, and she had frightened him. He became very depressed, and her efforts to calm and cheer him were unsuccessful.

The wedding day, the 10th of May 1788, arrived, and the bridegroom paid an early visit to his bride. After her excitement of the previous day, she was distressed to see that Alexei Stepanich still wore the same pained expression. She felt hurt; for she had always supposed that he would be in an ecstasy of joy on the day when he led her to the altar; and here he was, looking grave and even depressed! She expressed her feelings, and that made matters worse. Of course, he assured her that he considered himself the happiest man in the world, and so on; but the pompous and trivial phrases, which he had repeated many a time before and she had heard with satisfaction, were now distasteful to her ear, because they lacked the fire of inward conviction. They soon parted, to meet next in church, where the bridegroom was to be in waiting for her at six in the evening.

Sofya Nikolaevna was assailed by a terrible misgiving—would she be happy in her marriage? A host of dark forebodings passed before her heated imagination. She blamed herself for her hot temper and violent language; she recognized that the offence was trifling, and that she must expect many slips of the kind on her lover's part, and must take them calmly. They had happened often enough before; but on this occasion, the unlucky combination of circumstances and the presence of the two unfriendly visitors had pricked her vanity and irritated her natural impetuosity. Conscious that she had frightened her lover, she repented of her fault; but at the same time she was aware in the depth of her heart that she was quite capable of committing the same fault again. And now she realized afresh all the difficulty of the tremendous task she had undertaken—the reformation and regeneration of a man of twenty-seven. Her whole life—and it might be long—must be spent with a husband whom she loved indeed but could not entirely respect; there would be constant collision between utterly different ideas and opposite qualities, and they would often misunderstand one another. Doubts of success, doubts of her own strength, doubts of her power to command the qualities of firmness and calmness so foreign to her nature—these rose before her for the first time in their appalling truth, and she shrank back in terror. But what could she do? If she broke off the marriage at the eleventh hour, what would be the consequences? It would be a terrible blow to her dying father, who took comfort in the conviction that his daughter would be happy in the care of a kind husband; her rivals in society and enemies would mock at her; she would be the talk of the town and the laughing-stock of the district, perhaps even a mark for calumny; and, above all, she would kill, literally kill, her devoted lover. And all for what? Merely because she was afraid she might lack firmness to carry out a purpose which she had deliberately formed and which was beginning to take shape with triumphant success. 'No! that shall never be! God will help me; Our Lady of Smolensk will be my intercessor and will give me strength to conquer my impetuous nature.' Thus Sofya Nikolaevna thought, and thus she decided. She wept and prayed and regained her stability.

The Church of the Assumption was quite close to the Zubins' house, and there was then an empty space round it. Long before six o'clock, it was surrounded by a crowd of curious spectators. The high steps projecting from the house into the street were blocked by the carriages of the privileged persons who had been invited to escort the bride. The bride was dressed, and her little brother, Nikolenka, whose birth had cost his mother her life three years before, put on the stockings and shoes, according to established custom, though of course the maids lent their assistance. By six the bride was ready; she received her father's blessing and came into the drawing-room. The rich bridal dress lent an added lustre to her beauty. The bridegroom on his way to church had to pass right under the drawing-room windows, and Sofya Nikolaevna saw him drive past in the English carriage drawn by the four fine horses bred at Bagrovo; he had his head out and was looking up at the open windows; she smiled and nodded. Next came the bridegroom's sisters with Mme Alakaev, and all the men who were escorting him to church. She did not wish to keep him waiting, and insisted, in spite of various hindrances, that they should start at once. Sofya Nikolaevna was calm and composed when she entered the church; she gave her arm cheerfully and smilingly to the bridegroom; but she was vexed to see that his face still wore the same sad expression; and it was generally remarked that they both looked depressed during the ceremony. The church was brilliantly lighted and full of people; the cathedral choir did not spare their voices. Altogether, it was a dignified and splendid ceremony. When the rite was over, the young couple were escorted to the Zubins' house by the bridegroom's sisters, the whole train of friends and relations on both sides, and all the important people of Ufa. Dancing began at once and went on till an early but sumptuous supper was served. Privileged guests paid a visit to M. Zubin in his study and congratulated him on his daughter's marriage. The usual festivities took place on the next and following days— balls, dinners, and calls, in fact the regular routine which we see nowadays even in Moscow and Petersburg.

The shade of sadness soon vanished from the faces of the young couple. They were perfectly happy. Kind people could not look at them without pleasure; and everyone said, 'What a handsome couple!' A week later, they prepared for a visit to Bagrovo; the bridegroom's sisters had gone back there three days after the wedding, and Sofya Nikolaevna had sent by them an affectionate letter to the old people.

Startled by their brother's explosion, Elizabeth and Alexandra had been cautious of late. They refrained from all hints and sneers and grimaces in his presence, and were even polite to Sofya Nikolaevna. She, of course, was not taken in by this;

but their brother entirely believed in the sincerity of their devotion to his bride. At the wedding and the festivities which followed, they were, naturally, somewhat out of place, and therefore hastened their departure. On arriving at Bagrovo, they determined to do nothing rash and to hide their hostility towards Sofya Nikolaevna from their father; but to their mother and two sisters they described the marriage and events at Ufa in such a way as to fill their minds with a strong prejudice against the bride; and they did not forget to mention their brother's threats and his fury excited by their attacks upon Sofya Nikolaevna. It was agreed to treat her kindly in the presence of Stepan Mikhailovich, and to say nothing bad about her directly; at the same time they were to use every opportunity to excite by indirect means his displeasure against their enemy. It was a highly delicate operation; and Elizabeth and Alexandra could not trust it in any hands but their own.

My grandfather questioned them minutely about the wedding, the people they had seen there, the health of M. Zubin, and so on. They praised everything, but the poison under their praises could be smelt and tasted, and they failed to deceive their father. By way of a joke, and perhaps also for the sake of comparison, he turned to Karataev and said: 'Well now, friend Ivan, what say you of the daughter-in-law? As a man, you are a better judge of the point than the women are.' Karataev, disregarding a signal from his wife, burst out with enthusiasm: 'I do assure you, *batyushka*, that such another dazzler'—he always used this phrase of a beautiful woman— 'as brother Alexei has bagged is not to be found in the whole world. A look from her is as good as a shilling. And her cleverness! it's past all telling. But there's one thing, *batyushka*: she's proud: she can't stand a joke. When you try to have a little fun with her, she gives you a look that makes you bite off the end of your tongue.' 'I see, my friend, that she made short work with your nonsense,' said the old man with an amused look; then he laughed and added, 'Not much amiss there, so far.' In fact, Stepan Mikhailovich, from what he had heard and the bride's letters and Karataev's description, had formed in his own mind a highly favourable opinion of Sofya Nikolaevna.

The expected visit of the young couple produced bustle and confusion in the quiet or, one might say, stagnant waters of life at Bagrovo. They had to bestir themselves, to clean things up, and bring out their best clothes. The bride was a fine town lady, poor perhaps, but accustomed to live in luxury; she would be critical and contemptuous—so they all thought, and so they all said, except the master of the house. As there were no separate rooms in the house unoccupied, Tanyusha had to turn out of her bedroom, one corner of which overlooked the garden and the clear waters of the Buguruslan with its green bushes and loud nightingales. Tanyusha was very unwilling to move to the bath-house, but there was no other place; all her sisters were put up in the house, and Karataev and Erlykin slept in the hayloft. The day before the visitors' arrival brought their state-bed and bed-hangings and curtains for the windows, and with them a man who knew how to put everything up properly. Tanyusha's room was completely furnished in a few hours. Stepan Mikhailovich came to see it and expressed his admiration, but the women bit their lips with envy. At last a messenger galloped up and announced that the couple had stopped at the village of Noikino, eight versts from Bagrovo; they were to change their dress there and would arrive in two hours. This caused a general stir. The priest had been summoned hours before; but as he had not yet arrived, Stepan Mikhailovich sent a mounted messenger to hasten his steps.

Meantime the following scene was taking place in the Mordvinian village of Noikino. The travellers were making their way along side roads and had always to send a man ahead to arrange about fresh horses. The people of Noikino had all known Alexei Stepanich from childhood, and had a great regard and respect for his father. Every one of the six hundred inhabitants of the village, men and women, old and young, gathered before the cottage where the young people were to make their halt. Sofya Nikolaevna had probably never seen people of this tribe close at hand; and therefore the dress of the women and the uncommonly tall stout girls—their white shifts embroidered with red wool, their black woollen girdles, and the silver coins and little bells which hung from their heads over their breasts and backs—was very interesting to her. But when she heard them all break out into joyful greetings and compliments and good wishes, childish enough and expressed in bad Russian, but coming from the heart, then she both laughed and cried. 'What a fine wife God has given you, Alesha! How glad our father Stepan Mikhailovich will be! Good luck! Good luck!' But when the bride, arrayed in her fine city clothes, came out to take her seat in the carriage, there was such a roar of enthusiastic applause that the horses actually shied. The travellers made a present of ten roubles, to be spent on whisky, to the whole village, and went on their way.

The stackyard at Bagrovo was at the top of the hill, and now the high carriage was seen emerging from behind it. The cry, 'They're coming! They're coming!' flew from room to room, and house-servants and labourers soon gathered in the large courtyard, while the young people and children ran to meet the carriage. The master and mistress, attended by all their family, came out upon the steps. Arina Vasilevna wore a silk jacket and skirt and a silk handkerchief adorned with gold sprigs upon her head; Stepan Mikhailovich was clean-shaved and wore an old-fashioned frock-coat and a stock round his neck. Husband and wife stood on the top step; and he held in his hands an ikon representing the Presentation of the Virgin, while she carried a loaf of bread and a silver salt-cellar. Their daughters and two sons-in-law were grouped round them. The carriage drove up to the steps. The young couple got out, knelt down before the old people, and received their blessing; then they exchanged embraces with each member of the family. Hardly had the bride completed this ceremony and turned again towards her father-in-law, when he caught her by the hand and looked keenly at her eyes from which the tears were falling. His own eyes grew wet; he clasped her in a tight embrace, kissed her, and said, 'I thank God. Let us go and thank Him together!' He took her by the hand and led her through the crowd of people into the parlour. There he made

her sit near him; and the priest, who was waiting for them
with his robes on, pronounced the solemn words:

'We praise thee, O God: we acknowledge thee to be the
Lord.'

FRAGMENT IV

THE YOUNG COUPLE AT BAGROVO

STEPAN MIKHAILOVICH joined fervently in the prayers, and so did his daughter-in-law. When the service was over, all kissed the cross, and the priest sprinkled the young pair and the rest of the company with holy water. Then the kissing and embracing began over again, with the phrases customary on such occasions—'We beg that you will look on us as relations and love us', and so on—said of course by those to whom the bride was still a stranger. Stepan Mikhailovich said nothing: he only looked affectionately at the tearful eyes and flaming cheeks of Sofya Nikolaevna, listened attentively to every word she spoke, and noted her every movement. Then he took her by the hand and led her to the drawing-room, where he sat down on the sofa and made the pair sit near him. Arina Vasilevna seated herself next her son at the other end of the sofa, while her daughters with their husbands sat round the central group. It should be said that Stepan Mikhailovich never sat in the drawing-room: he entered it very seldom and never stayed long. There were only two parts of the house which he used—his own room, and the outside stoop, a very simple contrivance of beams and boards; there he was thoroughly at home, but in the drawing-room he was never quite at his ease. For once he put constraint upon himself and carried on a friendly conversation with his daughter-in-law. He began by asking about her father's health, and expressed sincere regret on hearing that he grew weaker daily: 'In that case, my dear,' he said, 'I must not keep you too long at Bagrovo.' It need not be said that the bride was at no loss for words: she was not merely polite, but cordial and eager to make a good impression. Arina Vasilevna, naturally a very simple woman, took her tone from her husband, as far as her intelligence and her dread of disobeying her daughters would let her. She was friendly to her son's wife and had taken a real liking to her at first sight; but the others were silent, and it was not hard to guess their feelings from their faces. After half an hour the bride whispered to her husband, who rose at once and went to the bedroom which had been specially prepared for them near the drawing-room. Stepan Mikhailovich looked on with surprise; but the bride's lively talk engaged his attention, and he was so much interested by it that he was startled when presently the folding doors of the bedroom opened and his son came in, holding a large silver salver, so loaded with presents for the family that it actually bent under their weight. Sofya Nikolaevna sprang to her feet; she took from the salver and presented to her father-in-law a piece of fine English broadcloth, and a waistcoat of watered silk, richly laced with gold thread and embroidered all over with spangles; and she told him quite truly that she had worked it all with her own hands. Stepan Mikhailovich looked uneasily at his son standing with the salver in his arms, but he accepted the presents graciously and kissed his daughter-in-law. Next, Arina Vasilevna was presented with a silk handkerchief covered with gold embroidery, to wear over her head, and a complete length of excellent China silk, which even then was considered a rarity; each sister-in-law received a piece of costly silk, and each of their husbands a piece of English broadcloth; but these presents were naturally rather less valuable. All got up, kissed the hands of the donor, and bowed their thanks. Meanwhile the door leading to the parlour was cracking with the pressure of curious spectators of both sexes, and the well-oiled heads of the maids kept peeping timidly out of the bedroom door, which they had to themselves, because none of the outdoor servants dared to enter the elegant apartment of the young couple. In the parlour there was a great noise; for the men-servants were prevented by the intruders from laying the table, and were unable to turn them out. Stepan Mikhailovich guessed what was going on; he got up and glanced through the door; one look and one quiet word was enough: 'Off', he said, and the parlour was empty in a moment.

The dinner passed off in the usual fashion. The young pair sat side by side between the old couple; there were a great many courses, one richer and more indigestible than another; the cook, Stepan, had been lavish with his spice, cloves, and pepper, and especially with his butter. The bride ate the dainties pressed upon her by Stepan Mikhailovich, and prayed that she might not die in the night. There was little talking, partly because every mouth was otherwise occupied, and also because the party were not good at conversation. Indeed they were all uncomfortable in their own ways. Erlykin in his sober intervals drank nothing but water, and hardly spoke at all at such times, which gained him a reputation for exceptional intelligence; and Karataev dared not open his mouth in the presence of Stepan Mikhailovich except to answer a question, and went no farther than repeating the last words of other people's remarks. If they said: 'the hay crop will be good, if we get no rain', or 'the rye made a good start till that sudden frost came'—Karataev came in like an echo, 'if we get no rain', 'till the frost came'; and his repetitions were sometimes ill-timed. As the hosts had not thought of procuring sparkling wine from Ufa, the health of the bride and bridegroom was drunk in strawberry wine, three years old and as thick as oil, which diffused about the room the delicious perfume of the wild strawberry. Mazan, with long boots smelling of tar on his feet, and wearing a long coat which made him look like a bear dressed up in sacking, handed round the loving-cup; it was ornamented with a white pattern and had a dark-blue spiral inside its glass stalk. When the young pair had to return thanks, Sofya Nikolaevna was not much pleased to drink from the cup which had just left Karataev's greasy lips; but she made no wry faces. Indeed she was intending to drain the cup, when her father-in-law stopped her: 'Don't drink it all, my dear,' he said; 'the liquor is good and sweet but strong; you are not accustomed to it, and your little head would ache.' She declared that such a noble drink could not hurt her, and begged to be allowed a little more, till Stepan Mikhailovich allowed her one sip from the cup which he held in his hands.

It was clear to all the family that the old man was pleased
with his daughter-in-law and liked all that she said. And she
could see this herself, though she had been surprised twice over
by a shadow of displeasure passing over his face. But more
than once during the meal she had encountered his expressive
look, as his eyes rested with satisfaction on her. At last the
long and solemn dinner came to an end. Sofya Nikolaevna,
unlike the rest, had found this rustic feast very wearisome, but
she had done her best to enliven it by cheerful conversation.
When they rose from table, his son and daughters kissed their
father's hand, and Sofya Nikolaevna tried to do so too, but the
old man embraced and kissed her instead. It was the second
time this had happened, and Sofya Nikolaevna, with her
natural impulsiveness, asked him in a lively affectionate tone:
'Why do you not give me your hand, *batyushka*? I am your
daughter too, and I wish to kiss your hand out of love and
respect, like the rest.' The old man looked at her keenly and
attentively; then he said in a kind voice: 'I love you, my dear,
but I am not a priest, and no one kisses my hand except my
own children.'

The party went back to the drawing-room and sat down
where they were before. The maid Aksyutka brought in coffee,
which was only served on very solemn occasions; the old man
did not drink it; but all his family were very fond of it; they
always called it 'coff', never 'coffee'. When it was swallowed,
Stepan Mikhailovich rose and said: 'Now it is time to have a
good sleep, and the young people too would be none the
worse for a rest after their journey'; then he went off to his
own room, escorted by his son and daughter-in-law. 'This is
my den, my dear,' said the old man cheerfully; 'sit down and
be my guest. As your husband knows, it was an exception for
me to sit in the drawing-room with you all, with this bearing-
rein on as well,' and he pointed to his stock: 'and in future,
if anyone wants my society, I shall welcome them here.' Then
he kissed her, gave his hand to his son to kiss, and let them
go. When alone, he undressed and lay down to rest from the
unusual bodily exertions and mental excitement of the day.
He was soon sound asleep; and his powerful snoring echoed

through the house and swayed to and fro the curtains which Mazan had drawn round his old master.

His example was followed by the rest. Erlykin and Karataev went off to the stable to lie down on the hay-mow; both their faces showed that they had done well at dinner, and Karataev had also drunk too much. The daughters assembled in their mother's room which was separate from their father's; and now began such a debate and discussion, carried on in whispers, that not one of the party even lay down to sleep that afternoon. Poor Sofya Nikolaevna was their theme, and her sisters-in-law simply tore her to pieces; they were enraged beyond all bounds by their father's evident partiality for her. But there was one kind heart there—Aksinya, the eldest sister, who was now a widow for the second time; she stood up for Sofya Nikolaevna and brought down their wrath on her own head: they turned her out of the room and banished her for the future from their family councils; and to her old nickname of 'Miss Simplicity', they now added another offensive title which she still bore in advanced old age. Yet, for all the persecution of her sisters, her kind heart never swerved from its devotion to her sister-in-law.

Meanwhile the young pair went off to their own fine bed-room. With the help of her own maid Parasha, a brisk black-eyed girl, Sofya Nikolaevna unpacked the large number of boxes and trunks which the English coach had brought from Ufa. Parasha was able already to run through a list of outdoor servants and old people among the peasants who deserved special notice; and her mistress, who had brought with her a goodly store of trifles, fixed the present to be given to each, taking account of their age and services and the respect which their owners had for them. The husband and wife were not tired and did not think it necessary to rest. Sofya Nikolaevna changed into a simpler dress, and left Parasha to finish the unpacking and arrangement of the bedroom, while she went out with her young husband, who was very anxious, in spite of the heat, to show her all his favourite haunts—the beech-wood, the island with its lime-trees just coming into leaf, and the transparent waters of the river where it made a bend round the island. And how delightful it was there at that season, when the freshness of spring combines with the warmth of summer! Alexei Stepanich was passionately in love with his adored wife, and time had not yet blunted the edge of his happiness; but he was disconcerted to find that she was not charmed either by wood or island, and indeed took little notice of either. She sat down in the shade on the bank of the rapid river, and began at once to speak to her husband of his relations. She discussed their reception. 'I like your father so much,' she went on, 'and I could see at the first glance that he liked me; perhaps your mother liked me, but she seemed afraid to show it. Aksinya seems the kindest of them, but she is afraid of something too. Oh, I understand it all perfectly; I know in what quarter the damp wood is smouldering. I did not miss a single word or a single glance; I know what I am bound to expect. God will judge your sisters, Elizabeth and Alexandra!' But Alexei Stepanich was hardly listening to her words. The fresh shade, the green of the boughs bending over the stream, the low ripple of the running water, the fish jumping, his adored wife sitting beside him with one arm round his waist —in such surroundings how was it possible to find fault or make objections or express discontent? How was it possible even to take in what was said? And in fact Alexei Stepanich did not take in what his young wife was saying to him: he was so happy that nothing but silence and oblivion of the world around him could serve as a full expression of his intoxicating bliss. But Sofya Nikolaevna went on: she said a great deal, with warmth and feeling; and then she noticed that her husband was not listening and was nearly asleep. She sprang up at once, and then followed a scene of conflict and mutual misunderstanding, more pronounced than any they had ever had before, though there had been premonitory symptoms once or twice already. Sofya Nikolaevna kept nothing back this time: the tears rushed from her eyes as she poured forth a torrent of reproaches for his indifference and inattention. Alexei Stepanich was puzzled and distressed: he felt as if he had fallen from the skies or awakened from a delightful dream. Thinking to calm his wife, he assured her with perfect sincerity, that there was nothing wrong at all, that it was all her imagination, and that all the family loved her; how could anyone help loving her, he asked. That he was honestly convinced of this was clear as day; and his eyes and face and voice all expressed his devoted love for his wife; yet Sofya Nikolaevna, for all her cleverness and lively sensibility, did not understand her husband, and found in his words only a fresh proof of the same indifference and inattention. Statements and explanations went on with increasing heat, and I do not know how far they would have gone; but suddenly Alexei Stepanich caught sight of his sister Tatyana's maid crossing the high gangway and hastening towards them. He guessed that they were being searched for because his father had got up, and told his wife at once what he feared. She regained her self-control in a moment, caught his arm, and hastened home with him; but he was not in good spirits as he walked beside her.

Preparations had been made beforehand at Bagrovo to celebrate the day of the young people's arrival by an entertainment given to the outdoor servants and all the serfs on the estate; and if serfs from neighbouring estates chose to come on foot or on wheels they were welcome too. A quantity of beer had been brewed, and some twenty buckets of strong home-made spirits distilled; and drinking vessels of all kinds were ready. Before he lay down after dinner, Stepan Mikhailovich had asked whether many had come from the neighbouring villages. When he was told that the whole population, from the old men and women to the babies, had assembled, he smiled and said, 'Well, we shall not stint them; tell the housekeeper and steward to have everything ready.' He did not sleep long, but he woke in even better spirits than when he lay down. 'Is all ready?' he asked at once, and was told that all was ready long ago. The old man dressed quickly; instead of his ceremonial frock-coat, he put on his familiar dressing-gown of fine camel's hair, and went out to the stoop to superintend the entertainment in person. On the broad lawn, which was not fenced off from the road, tables had been put up on trestles, and the tables were laden with barrels of beer,

casks of whisky, and piles of buns to eat with the liquor; these
buns, made of wheat-flour, were cut in halves. The outdoor
servants stood in a group apart near the house; a great crowd
of serfs and their wives stood farther off, and beyond them a
still greater crowd of Mordvinians of both sexes. Stepan
Mikhailovich threw a hasty glance over the scene, saw that
all was in order, and went back to his stoop. The family had
collected round him, and he was just going to ask where the
young couple were, when they appeared together. He greeted
his daughter-in-law even more affectionately than before, and
treated her with no more formality than if she had been his
own daughter. 'Now then, Alesha,' he said, 'take your wife's
arm and lead her round to greet the people; they are all
anxious to see her and kiss the hand of their young mistress.
Let us start!' He went in front himself; then came Alexei
Stepanich, leading his wife, and last, at a little distance, Arina
Vasilevna with her daughters and their husbands. The sisters-
in-law, except Aksinya, found it hard to restrain their wrath.
The signs of growing affection on their father's part, his
mention of Sofya Nikolaevna as 'the young mistress', the
triumph of this hated intruder, her beauty and pretty clothes,
her ready easy tongue, her charming respect and affection for
her father-in-law—all these things rankled in their jealous
bosoms. They felt at once that they had sunk in importance.
'It matters less to us,' whispered Alexandra: 'we are severed
branches; but I can't look at Tanyusha without crying. She is
nothing now in the household but Sofya Nikolaevna's maid.
And you, mother—no one will respect you any more; the
servants will all look to her for orders.' Her voice shook, and
the tears gathered in her round rolling eyes. Meanwhile Stepan
Mikhailovich had got to the outdoor servants and was calling
the peasants to come nearer: 'Why don't you all stand together?
You all belong to the same family. Well,' he went on, 'here
you see your young mistress; the young master you know
already. When the time comes, serve them as faithfully and
zealously as you have served me and Arina Vasilevna, and
you will earn their love and favour.' All the people bowed to
the ground. The bride, unaccustomed to such demonstrations,

felt disconcerted, not knowing where to go or what to do. Noticing this, her father-in-law said: 'Don't be frightened! Their heads may bend, but they won't come off. Well, my friends, first kiss your young mistress's hand, and then drink to her health.' The people all got up and came near Sofya Nikolaevna. She looked round and signed to her man Theodore and handy Parasha, who were standing on one side, holding the presents. In a moment they handed her a large parcel and a well-filled box. It felt strange to her to stretch out her hand to be kissed while standing motionless as a statue; and she began to kiss them all herself. This ceremony was repeated, as each received a gift from her hands. But Stepan Mikhailovich interfered at this point: he saw that at that rate he would not get his tea till supper-time. 'My dear,' he said, 'you can't possibly kiss them all once, let alone twice! There are too many. The old people are a different matter; but it will be enough if they kiss your hand.' This simplified and shortened the rather tiresome ceremony, but even so it lasted a long time. Stepan Mikhailovich sometimes spun it out himself, because he could not refrain from naming some of the people and praising them to her. Many of the old people spoke some simple words of love and devotion, some shed tears, and all looked at the bride with pleasure and cordiality. Sofya Nikolaevna was much moved. 'These good people are ready to love me, and some love me already,' she thought: 'how have I deserved it?' At last, when young and old had kissed her hand and she had kissed some of them, and when all had received handsome presents, Stepan Mikhailovich took her hand and led her to the crowd of Mordvinians. 'I am glad to see you, neighbours,' he cried in a hearty cheerful voice; 'and thank you for coming. I ask your goodwill for this young lady who is coming to live near you. You are welcome to eat and drink what God has given us.' The Mordvinians showed their pleasure by shouting, 'Many thanks, Stepan Mikhailovich! Thank God for giving such a wife to your son! You deserve such luck for your goodness, Stepan Mikhailovich.'

When the drinking began, Stepan Mikhailovich, surrounded by his family, hastened back to his beloved stoop. He was conscious that his tea-time was long past: it was now past seven, and tea was invariably served at six. The long shadow of the house was sloping towards the south, and its edges touched the storehouse and stable; the samovar had long been hissing on a large table close to the stoop, and Aksyutka was in attendance. While the rest sat down round the table, Stepan Mikhailovich stuck to his favourite place: he first spread out his invariable woollen mat to sit on, and then sat down on the stoop. Tatyana, assisted by Aksyutka, poured out tea. Then Sofya Nikolaevna asked leave of her father-in-law to sit beside him, and he consented with obvious satisfaction. She sprang up from the table, carried her half-finished cup of tea to the stoop, and sat down beside the old man. He caressed her and ordered a mat to be put down for her, that she might not spoil her dress. Then they began a lively cheerful talk; but at the tea-table angry looks and even whispers were exchanged, in spite of the presence of the young husband. He could not help noticing this, and his spirits, which had not been high before, fell yet lower. Suddenly the old man's loud voice rang out: 'Come and join us, Alesha; it's livelier over here.' Alesha started; but the change of place seemed to improve his spirits. When tea was over, they remained where they were and went on talking till supper, which was served at nine—an hour later than usual. All the time the loud singing and hearty laughter of the revellers rang out far and wide as the darkness slowly gathered round; but they all departed to their own homes as soon as the family had finished supper. On saying goodnight, Sofya Nikolaevna asked her father-in-law to give her his blessing, and the old man at once signed her with the cross and kissed her with a father's tenderness.

The young couple were escorted to their room by the lady of the house and her eldest daughter, who sat there a few minutes; and then it was the turn of Alexei Stepanich to escort his mother and sister to rest. Sofya Nikolaevna hastily dismissed her maid and sat down by one of the open windows fronting the river, which was fringed at that point by a thick border of osier and alder. It was a lovely night: the freshness from the river and the scent of the young leaves came through

the open windows, together with the trills and calls of the
nightingales. But Sofya Nikolaevna had something else to
think of. As a clever woman who knew in advance what
awaited her in her husband's family, she had naturally formed
a plan of action beforehand. She had always lived in a town
and had no conception of the sort of life led by landowners of
moderate means on their scattered estates in that vast country.
She had not expected much, but the reality was far worse
than she had imagined. Nothing was to her taste, neither house,
nor garden, nor wood, nor island. In the neighbourhood of
Ufa she had been accustomed to admire noble views from the
mountainous bank of the river Belaya; and this little village
in a hollow, the time-stained and weather-beaten wooden
house, the pond surrounded by swamps, and the unending
clack of the mill—all this seemed to her actually repulsive.
And the people were no better: from her husband's family
to the peasants' children, she could love none of them. But
there was one exception, and that was Stepan Mikhailovich.
But for him, she would have been in despair. She had formed
a favourable opinion of him from the beginning; then, when
she first saw him, she was frightened by his rough exterior;
but she soon read in his intelligent eyes and kindly smile, and
heard in his voice, that this old man had a tender heart which
beat kindly to her, that he was ready to love her and would
love her. Knowing from the first that all her hopes depended
upon him, she had firmly resolved to gain his love by all
means; but now she had learnt to love him herself, and her
deliberate plan coincided with the impulse of her heart.
In this respect Sofya Nikolaevna was satisfied with herself:
she saw that she had reached her goal at once. But she was
distressed by the thought that by her impetuosity she had
hurt her kind husband. She waited impatiently for him, but
as if to spite her, he did not return. Had she known where
he was, she would have hurried off in search of him long ago.
She longed to throw herself into his arms and beg his forgiveness with tears, and to remove the last trace of dissatisfaction
from his mind by a torrent of loving words and caresses. But
Alexei Stepanich still did not return; and the happy moment,

when she was penitent and loving and filled with a passionate desire to atone for her faults, went by to no purpose. An impulse soon passes, and Sofya Nikolaevna first grew alarmed and then angry at her husband's long absence. When he came in at last, looking rather upset and distressed, instead of rushing into his arms and begging to be forgiven, his wife called out to him in an excited and somewhat irritated voice, as soon as he crossed the threshold: 'Where on earth have you been? Why did you leave me alone? I am quite worn out with waiting for you two whole hours!' 'I sat a quarter of an hour or so with my mother and sisters,' he answered. 'And that was time enough for them to complain of me and invent calumnies against me, and you believed them! Why are you so depressed and sad?' Sofya Nikolaevna's face expressed strong emotion, and her beautiful eyes filled with tears. The young husband was startled and even alarmed; he was beginning to dread her tears. 'Sonechka,' he said, 'calm yourself; no one complained of you; why should they, when you have injured no one?' This was not quite a true statement. If nobody had complained openly or attacked her in plain terms they had implied by hints and allusions that his wife was singling out her father-in-law to pay court to, with the object of trampling on the rest of the family; but they saw through her tricks, and so would her husband some day when he found himself under her feet! Alexei Stepanich did not believe these innuendos; but the feeling of sadness, which had never left him since the scene on the island, became heavier and lay like lead on his kind heart. He only said, 'It is no use talking like that,' and left the room. But instead of returning at once to his bedroom, he spent some time in walking alone up and down the parlour which was now dark and empty. Through the seven open windows he looked at the Jackdaw Wood sleeping in darkness, and at the dark line of trees by the river, the scene of his childhood's amusements and occupations; and he listened to the sound of the mill, the whistles of the nightingales, and the screeching of the owls. Feeling somewhat relieved, he went off to the bedroom, entirely unconscious of the reception he was to meet there.

But Sofya Nikolaevna soon grew calmer: the voice of penitence began to speak again in her heart, though not with the same force as before; she changed her tone and turned to her husband with a genuine feeling of love and pity; she caressed him and begged his forgiveness. She spoke with unfeigned warmth of her happiness in finding that she loved his father, and begged him to be perfectly frank with her: frankness, she said, was essential between them. Her husband was soothed and comforted; and in the fullness of his heart he told her all he had determined to keep secret at all costs, lest he should make a quarrel between his wife and his sisters. He lay down and went to sleep at once, but Sofya Nikolaevna lay awake for long, and her brain worked busily. At last she remembered that she had to get up early, because she intended to join her father-in-law on the stoop at sunrise, long before the family assembled; she wished to cheer the old man by her presence and to speak her mind to him at leisure. At last, with a strong effort, she fell asleep.

Sofya Nikolaevna woke with the first rays of the sun. Though she had not slept long, she rose fresh and vigorous. She dressed quickly, kissed her husband and told him she was going to his father, and he might sleep on another hour or so, and then hurried off. Stepan Mikhailovich, after sleeping longer than usual, had just washed himself and gone out to the stoop. It was a lovely May morning, with all the charm of late spring, fresh and yet deliciously warm; all living things sang together for joy, and the long morning shadows still hid the coolness and moisture from the conquering rays of the sun. The feeling of the morning took hold of Sofya Nikolaevna and breathed life into her, though she was not accustomed to be moved by natural beauty or the charms of the country. Her father-in-law was surprised and pleased to see her. Her fresh face and shining eyes, her neat hair and pretty dress, made it impossible to guess that she had sprung out of bed after little sleep and had spent but little time over her toilet before she hurried out. Stepan Mikhailovich liked people to be lively and quick and clever: and all these requirements he was pleased to find in Sofya Nikolaevna. He kissed her and said good-humouredly: 'What made you get up so early? You can't have had your sleep out. I'm sure you're not accustomed to rise so early; you will have a headache.' 'No, *batyushka*,' she replied, embracing the old man with genuine tenderness; 'I am used to early rising. From childhood I have had much to do and many cares, with a sick father and a whole family to look after. Of late I have been spoilt and have lain in bed longer. But I woke early this morning, and Alexei told me'—here the old man frowned—'that you were up already; so I came out here, hoping that you would not drive me away but allow me to give you your tea.' The words were ordinary enough, but they came from the heart and were spoken so earnestly that the old man was touched. He kissed her forehead and said: 'Well, in that case, thank you, my dear child. You shall give me my tea, and we will have a leisurely talk together.' Aksyutka had already set the samovar on the table. Stepan Mikhailovich gave orders that no one else should be called, and Sofya Nikolaevna began to arrange about the tea. All her actions were as quick and neat as if she had done nothing else all her life. The old man was pleased, as he watched that young and pretty figure, so unlike what he was accustomed to, and those busy active fingers. The tea was made strong, and served exactly as he liked it: that is, the teapot, covered with a napkin, was placed on the top of the samovar; his cup was filled close up to the brim; Sofya Nikolaevna handed it without spilling a single drop in the saucer; and the fragrant beverage was so hot that it burnt his lips. The old man took his cup and tasted the tea. With surprise and pleasure he said: 'I declare you are a witch: you know all my tastes and fancies. Well, if you make yourself as pleasant to your husband, he will be a happy man.' He generally drank his tea alone, and the family did not begin theirs till he had finished; but this morning, when he had got his second cup, he told his daughter-in-law to pour one out for herself and drink it sitting beside him. 'I never drink more than two, but I will take a third cup today; the tea tastes better somehow,' he said in the kindest of tones. And indeed, the pleasure which Sofya Nikolaevna felt in her occupation was so visible on her expressive face that it could not but communicate itself to the susceptible nature of Stepan Mikhailovich; and his spirits rose unusually high. He made her take a second cup and eat a scone, of the kind for which the ovens at Bagrovo were long famous. The tea was cleared away, and a conversation began, most lively and animated, most frank and affectionate. Sofya Nikolaevna gave free course to her eager feelings; she talked easily and charmingly; her conquest of the old man was complete. In the middle of their talk he suddenly asked, 'What of your husband? Is he asleep?' 'Alexei was waking when I left him,' she said quickly; 'but I told him to sleep on.' The old man frowned severely and was silent. After a moment's reflection, he spoke, not angrily but seriously. 'Listen to me, my dear little daughter-in-law; you are so clever that I can tell you the truth without beating about the bush. I don't like to keep a thing on my mind. If you take my advice—well and good; if you don't—well, you are not my daughter and can please yourself. I don't like your calling your husband "Alexei", as his parents might; he has got another name;* "Alexei" is a name you might address to a servant. A wife must treat her husband with respect, if she wishes other people to respect him. There was another thing yesterday I did not like: you sent him to fetch the presents and he stood there holding the tray like a footman. Then again just now, you said you had "told" him to go to sleep. A wife ought not to give orders to her husband; if she does, mischief comes of it. That may be the fashion with you in the town, but according to our old-fashioned country notions, all that is a great mistake.' Sofya Nikolaevna listened respectfully, and then she spoke, so frankly and feelingly, that every word made its way to the old man's heart: 'I thank you, *batyushka*, for not keeping back from me what displeased you. I shall gladly do what you wish, and I begin to see myself that I was wrong. I am still young, *batyushka*, and I have had no one to guide me: my own father has not left his bed for six years. I caught up that way of addressing my husband from others; but it shall never happen again, either in your presence or

* i.e. Stepanich, son of Stephen, which should be used in public by the wife.

behind your back. *Batyushka,*' she went on, and the large tears welled from her eyes, 'I have come to love you like a father; treat me always as a daughter: stop me, scold me, whenever I do wrong, but forgive me and do not keep displeasure in your heart against me. I am young and hasty, and I may go wrong at every step. Remember that I am a stranger in this house, where nobody knows me and I know nobody. Do not you fail me.' Then she fell on his neck and embraced him like a daughter, kissing his breast and even his hands; and the old man's own eyes filled with tears. He let her keep hold of his hands and said, 'Well, that is all right.' As we know already, Stepan Mikhailovich had a natural sagacity which divined the presence of evil and was attracted by goodness; and he never made a mistake in either case. He had taken a fancy to his daughter-in-law at first sight; and now that he understood her and appreciated her, he loved her for better and for worse. That love was exposed to many trials in later years, and any other man might have wavered, but he never wavered in his love for her to his last breath.

Alexei Stepanich soon appeared, and was followed by all the family. Her daughters had urged Arina Vasilevna to go out long before, but she did not dare to appear, because, when Stepan Mikhailovich gave orders 'that no one should be called', it was taken to mean that he did not wish to see anyone. She only came out now because her husband had told Mazan to summon all the family. There was no trace of tears on Sofya Nikolaevna's face; and she greeted the newcomers with more than usual cordiality. Nor could one tell from Stepan Mikhailovich that anything unusual had happened; but the bride could not conceal her high spirits, and the two sisters-in-law noticed this at once and guessed the alarming truth pretty accurately.

Stepan Mikhailovich had settled that the young couple were to visit their relations in order of seniority; and it was therefore arranged that they should go to Aksinya's house next day. Aksinya herself went home that afternoon, accompanied by her sister Elizabeth, who was to help her in entertaining the guests. The distance was only fifty versts, and the strong Bagrovo horses could go all the way without baiting. The start was fixed for six o'clock next morning.

Stepan Mikhailovich did not in the least conceal his feeling towards his daughter-in-law. He kept her beside him and talked with her repeatedly, asking questions about her family affairs, or making her speak of her life at Ufa; and he listened to her with attentive interest, now and then giving his opinion in some pithy phrase. She eagerly caught up his pertinent remarks; but it was clear that she was moved, not by obsequious concurrence with the old man's ways of thinking, but by a full comprehension of his words and a conviction of their truth. Then in his turn he initiated her into the past and present history of her new relations; and his whole description was so simple and true, so frank and lifelike, that she realized it as few could have done, and was charmed by it. Never in her life had she met his equal. Her own father was intelligent and kind, emotional and unselfish; but at the same time he was weak, falling in with the prevailing tone of his surroundings, and bearing the stamp of the evasive time-serving official who had worked his way up from a clerk's stool to the position of Governor's Deputy. Here she saw before her an old man of little education and uncouth exterior, and report said of him that he was ruthless when angry; and yet he was sensible and kind, honest and inflexible in his clear judgement of right and wrong—a man who was upright in all his actions and truthful in every word he spoke. Her quick intellect conceived a noble type of manly worth, which set aside her old ideas and opened up new possibilities. And what happiness that this man was her husband's father! On him depended her peace of mind in her husband's family, and perhaps even the happiness of her marriage!

Dinner was a much more lively and cheerful affair than on the previous day. The bride set as before between her husband and her father-in-law; but Arina Vasilevna now took her usual place opposite Stepan Mikhailovich. Immediately after dinner, Aksinya left, accompanied by her sister Elizabeth. As the old man was lying down to rest as usual, he said, 'Well, Arisha, I think God has given us a splendid daughter-in-law; it would be a sin not to take her to our hearts.' 'True indeed, Stepan Mikhailovich,' she answered; 'if you approve of Sofya Niko- laevna, of course I do.' The old man made a wry face but said nothing; and she hurried away, fearing to make a slip of the tongue, and anxious to report to her daughters the remarkable words of Stepan Mikhailovich, which must be accepted as law and obeyed, in appearance at least, to the letter.

Though she had slept little at night, Sofya Nikolaevna could not sleep after dinner. She went out with her husband, and they walked, by his wish, to the old beech-wood where the jack- daws built, and down the course of the river. There was no repetition of the old disagreements. She had been charmed and captivated by her father-in-law, and she now tried to convey to her husband the feelings of her own eager impressionable mind. As all people of her temperament are apt to do, she transferred to her handsome young husband some part of the merits she had found in his father, and loved him more than ever. He listened with surprise and pleasure to the enthusiasm of his beautiful wife, and said to himself, 'Thank God that my father and she have become such friends! There will be no further trouble.' He kissed her hands, and said that he was the happiest man on all the earth, and she a peerless goddess before whom all should bow down. He did not quite understand his wife nor appreciate her estimate of his father, so acute and profound; he only felt, as he had always felt, perfectly con- vinced that Stepan Mikhailovich was the kind of man whom all must respect and even fear. This time Sofya Nikolaevna found no faults: his feelings were her feelings and his language hers: she praised the deep river and the beech-wood with all its uneven stumps; even of her sisters-in-law she spoke kindly.

When he woke up in the afternoon, Stepan Mikhailovich at once summoned all the family. It was a long time since he had been seen in such a bright and gentle mood: whether it was due to a good sleep or to happy feelings, it was clear to everyone that the old master was satisfied and cheerful beyond his wont. After their father's pronouncement, Alexandra and Elizabeth were on their guard, while Tanyusha (as she was always called) and her mother were very willing to be more friendly and conversational. At a sign from his wife Karataev began with more boldness to echo what was said, even when he was not addressed; but his brother-in-law, the General, persisted in his gloomy silence and frowned significantly. The conversation became unusually brisk and animated. The old man expressed a wish to have his tea early, in the shade near the stoop, of course; and the privilege of pouring it out was conferred on Sofya Nikolaevna exclusively. Tanyusha was quite willing to hand over the office. After tea Stepan Mikhailovich ordered two cars to be brought round, took his daughter-in-law in one, and drove off with all his family to the mill. It should be said that a mill was a special hobby of my grandfather's, and that he understood the working of it thoroughly. The mill itself was not much to look at, and the weed grew round it in an untidy way; but the stones did their work thoroughly well. He liked to show off his mill, and now displayed it in detail to his daughter-in-law, taking pleasure in her utter ignorance and astonishment, which sometimes turned to fear, when he suddenly turned on a strong current of water upon all the four wheels, till the machinery began to move and swing and rattle, the stones to whirl round, creaking and whizzing, and the building, filled with flour-dust, to quiver and shake under foot. All this was an entire novelty to Sofya Nikolaevna, and she did not like it at all, though out of politeness she asked many questions and expressed surprise and admiration at everything. He was much pleased, and kept her there a long time. When the pair went out upon the dam, where Alexei Stepanich and his sisters were fishing, they were hailed with laughter by the anglers: they were both covered with flour. Stepan Mikhailovich was accustomed to this; besides he had given a shake and a brush to his clothes on leaving the mill; but Sofya Nikolaevna had no suspicion that she was so completely and artistically powdered. When he looked at her, her father-in-law himself laughed heartily; and she laughed more than anyone, and was very merry, regretting only that she had no looking-glass to consult, to find out if her ball-dress became her. Seeing the anglers intent upon their sport, Stepan Mikhailovich next drove his companion round the pond and over the bridge; and after visiting the stream higher up, he came back along the dam to the place where the anglers were engaged, while Arina Vasilevna, who was very stout, sat on the ground and watched them. The whole course of their drive was over bog and swamp; it was hardly safe to cross the crazy little bridge, and difficult to make way over the dam which was made of manure and sank under the wheels. Though Sofya Nikolaevna found all this distasteful, it was impossible for Stepan Mikhailovich to detect it. He saw neither mire nor swamp, and he was impervious to the unpleasant smell from the stagnant water and the material of the dam. He had planned and constructed it all himself, and he enjoyed it all. It grew damp at sunset, and all set off for home in good spirits. The anglers carried their spoil with them, perch and other kinds. The bailiff was waiting for his master by the stoop; and orders were given about work on the land, while the bride put her dress in order. Meanwhile the fish was boiled or fried in sour cream, while the largest perch were baked in their skins and scales; and all these were pronounced very good at supper.

So the second day passed, and the party broke up soon, because the young couple had to make an early start next morning for their visit. When alone with her mother and youngest sister, Alexandra threw off the mask with relief and gave full play to her infernal temper and cruel tongue. She saw perfectly that all was lost and all her forebodings realized: that her father was taken in the toils and infatuated with the adventuress, and there was nothing to be done now except to dismiss the pair to Ufa as soon as possible and devise some scheme in their absence. She abused her mother and sister for being too affectionate. 'But for me', she said, 'you would have been taken in too by that dressed-up doll, that pauper with a Cossack for her grandfather.'

At six exactly next morning the young couple started in their English coach drawn by six of the fine horses bred at Bagrovo. Sofya Nikolaevna was up in time to give his tea to her father-in-law; and he embraced her at starting, and even signed her with the cross, because she was to be absent for the night. They drove down the river and across it, and then uphill to the little town of Buguruslan. Without a halt our travellers crossed the river Great Kinel, and the horses trotted at the rate of ten versts an hour along the rutty road on the flat side of the river, where the grass grew tall and thick and there was no sign of habitation. It was long since Alexei Stepanich had been across the Kinel; and he was delighted by the greenness and fragrance of the steppe. Bustards constantly rose off the road, and solitary snipe kept up with the carriage, wheeling over it and flying on ahead, or perching on the guide-posts and filling the air with their notes. Alexei Stepanich was very sorry that he had not taken his gun. In those days the steppe was alive with birds of every kind, and the sound of their myriad voices was so attractive to him, and indeed absorbed his attention so completely, that his ears were generally deaf to the lively and clever conversation of his wife. She soon noticed this and became thoughtful; her high spirits gave place to displeasure, and she began to talk to her maid Parasha, who was with them in the coach. After crossing a district of high level land, they arrived at their destination exactly at noon. The little wooden house, an even greater contrast than Bagrovo to the house of Ufa, stood on the flat bank of the Little Kinel, divided from it only by a kitchen-garden containing a few sunflowers and young vegetables and rows of peeled pea-stakes. I still recall with pleasure this unpretending spot, which I first saw ten years after this time; and I understand why my father liked it and my mother was bound to dislike it. It was a bare empty place, quite flat and fully exposed to the sun, without a bush or a tree; the level steppe with its marmot-burrows lay all around; and the quiet river flowed by, deep in places and overgrown with reeds. It had nothing striking or picturesque to attract anyone; yet Alexei Stepanich preferred it even to Bagrovo. I don't agree with him, but I had a strong liking for that quiet little house on the riverbank, the clear stream, the weed swaying in the current, the wide stretch of grassy steppe, and the ferry which started from close to the door and took you across to a yet wilder steppe, where the prairie-grass stretched southwards to what seemed an illimitable distance.

The hostess, with her two little boys and a daughter of two

years old, met her guests at the door; her sister Elizabeth and
her husband were there also. In spite of the unpromising aspect
of the simple rooms, everything was very clean and nice, much
more so indeed than at Bagrovo. Though 'Miss Simplicity', as
her sisters called her, was a widow with small children, there
was a neatness and order in the place which showed that it was
managed entirely by a female hand. I have said already that
Aksinya was a kind woman and had taken a fancy to her
sister-in-law; it was therefore very natural that she should do
honour to her guests and receive them with cordiality in her
own house. This had been foreseen at Bagrovo, and Elizabeth
had been sent on purpose to restrain the excessive friendliness
of her sister by means of her superior intelligence and higher
position in society, due to her husband's rank. But that simple
soul held out against her clever cunning sister: to all her urgent
admonitions her answer was short and plain: 'Do as you
please at Bagrovo; you may hate and abuse Sofya Nikolaevna,
but I like her; she has always been polite and kind to me, and
therefore I intend to make her and my brother happy in my
house.' And she carried out her purpose with sincere affection
and satisfaction, showing every attention to her sister-in-law
and pressing her good things on both guests. But the proud
Elizabeth and even her husband—though he drank so much
towards evening that he had to be shut up in an empty bath-
house—were much colder and more distant in their behaviour
than at Bagrovo. Sofya Nikolaevna took no notice of them,
and was charming to her hostess and the children. After dinner
the party rested for a little and then went out for a walk by the
river; they crossed by a ferry to the far bank and drank tea
there. Sofya Nikolaevna was asked to fish, but she declined,
saying that she hated fishing and was quite happy sitting with
her sisters-in-law. But Alexei Stepanich, much pleased to see
how well his wife got on with his eldest sister, eagerly accepted
the proposal and sat till supper-time on the bank, hidden in
the thick reeds; he landed several of the large bream which
abounded in the quiet waters of the Kinel. The servants used
constantly to fish, for their own amusement and for that of
their young masters. The guests determined to start next

morning at six, and were half inclined to depart even earlier, so as not to keep Stepan Mikhailovich waiting for his dinner. Their hostess and her sister were to wait till the evening, spending a night at Buguruslan to rest the horses, and reaching Bagrovo the following day.

Sofya Nikolaevna was still a little vexed with her husband. For all her intelligence she could not understand how a man who loved her dearly could also love his damp Bagrovo, with its stump-strewn woods, unsavoury dam, and stagnant pools; how he could gaze with delight at the tiresome steppe with its stupid snipe; and, above all, how he could desert his wife for hours for the sake of a fishing-rod and those bream which smelt so damp and disgusting! So she felt almost offended when Alexei Stepanich tried to communicate to her his delight in nature and in sport. She was wise enough, however, not to start upon explanations or reproofs this time; the scene on the island was still fresh in her memory.

The young couple passed a peaceful night in Aksinya's own bedroom which she had given up to them; and she had done it up for them to the best of her ability, undeterred by the caustic remarks of her sister. They left the house half an hour earlier than the time originally fixed; and nothing particular happened on their way back, except that Alexei Stepanich was not quite so much absorbed by the steppe and the snipe, and did not call out quite so loud when bustards rose off the road, so that he could listen with more attention to his wife and look at her more tenderly. They reached Bagrovo before they were expected. But preparations were being made for dinner, and Alexandra had had time to say: 'Poor papa will have to wait for dinner today; but how can you expect town people to get up so early several days running?' The old man saw through this perfectly. He astonished them all by saying very good-humouredly, 'Well, never mind; we can wait for our guests.' This caused a sensation, because Stepan Mikhailovich had never in his life sat down to dinner later than twelve o'clock, though sometimes, when he felt hungry, he had it earlier, and the slightest delay or unpunctuality made him exceedingly angry. 'You see what Sofya Nikolaevna can do,' whispered

Alexandra to her mother and youngest sister; 'if *she* keeps him waiting, there is no complaint; but if you had come back from Neklyudovo late for dinner, you would never have heard the end of it, nor should we.' The malicious whisper was hardly ended when the carriage dashed up to the steps; while the tired horses snorted, the old man kissed his daughter-in-law and praised her for being in time; then his voice rang through the house, 'Mazan, Tanaichenok, dinner at once!'

The day passed off as before. After tea Stepan Mikhailovich, whose affection for his daughter-in-law seemed to grow with every hour, ordered the drove of horses to be driven in from the steppe. He wished to show it to Sofya Nikolaevna, who happened to say that she had never seen such a thing and would like to see it. When the animals were driven into the yard, the old man took his daughter-in-law round himself, pointing out the best brood-mares, the yearlings and two-year-olds and young geldings, all fat and healthy from the steppe where they grazed together all summer. He gave her two fine mares with foals at foot, and hoped she would have good fortune with their stock. Sofya Nikolaevna was much pleased by the foals, and liked to watch them as they started and bounded and then nuzzled against their mothers; and she expressed much gratitude for the gift. Then Stepan Mikhailovich gave strict orders to his head groom, Spirka: 'See', he said, 'that extra care is taken of Sofya Nikolaevna's mares; and we shall put a special mark on the foals by splitting one ear rather lower; and later we must make a brand with the young mistress's name on it.' Then he turned to her: 'I wish you were a lover of horses, my dear,' he went on; 'Alexei does not care for them in the least.' The old man was very fond of them himself; and though he was not rich, by endless trouble he had got together a large stud and owned a breed which was the admiration of fanciers and good judges. He was pleased by her interest in his stud; though her only motive was to please him, he believed that she meant what she said, and carried her off to see how the carriage-horses, his own and those of his guests, were fed; of the latter there were often a large number in the stables at Bagrovo.

I am afraid of wearying the reader by such a minute description of the young couple's visit, and shall only say that the next
day, which was the fifth, was spent just like the preceding day.
According to the order of seniority the next formal visit should
have been to the Erlykins; but as their estate was 170 versts
from Bagrovo and much nearer Ufa, it was settled to take them
on the return journey to the town. There was this other reason,
that General Erlykin, Elizabeth's silent gloomy husband, having
broken out at Aksinya's house, had started on one of his regular
drinking bouts, which generally lasted at least a week, so that
his wife had been forced to leave him with some friends at
Buguruslan, and give out that he was ill. Alexandra was therefore to receive the next visit, and started off home with her
husband on the previous day; with her father's consent, she
invited the oldest and youngest of the sisters for the occasion,
while Elizabeth remained behind, ostensibly to be near her sick
husband, though her real object was to bring her influence to
bear on her parents. The Karataevs lived about fifty versts
from Bagrovo; the distance was the same as to Aksinya's house,
but the road ran in the opposite direction, due north, and
passed through woods and hills in the second half of the
journey. The visitors started after an early lunch. As the road
was little used and heavy for the horses, they halted half-way
for two hours in the open field, and reached Karataevka about
tea-time. The house was infinitely worse than Aksinya's: the
small dark windows caught the eye at once; the floors were
uneven, riddled with rat holes, and so dirty as to defy soap
and water. Sofya Nikolaevna felt fear and disgust as she entered
this inhospitable and repulsive dwelling. Alexandra was haughty
in her reception of them; she was profuse in sarcastic apologies
of this kind: 'We are glad to see our guests and bid them
welcome; my brother, I know, will not be critical, but I doubt
if Sofya Nikolaevna will deign to enter our poor house after
her father's grand mansion at Ufa. Of course *we* are poor
people, with no official rank; living on our own property, *we*
have no lucrative salaries to maintain us.' But Sofya Nikolaevna
gave as good as she got: she replied that the way people lived
depended as much on their tastes as on their money, and that

it was all one to her where her husband's relations lived and how they lived. When supper was over, the young couple were shown to their bedroom, which was the so-called drawing-room. As soon as the candle was out, a great disturbance began in the room; the pattering and noise increased, and swarms of rats soon assailed them with such boldness that the poor bride lay awake all night, shaking with fear and disgust. Alexei Stepanich was forced to light a candle and arm himself with a window prop for the defence of the bed, on which the rats kept jumping up as long as it was dark. He felt neither fear nor disgust; it was no novelty to him; at first he was rather amused by the ceaseless activity and bold springs of the repul-sive creatures, and then he fell asleep, lying across the bed and still holding the window-prop. But his wife woke him again and again and only fell asleep herself at sunrise, when the enemy sought the concealment of his trenches. She got up with a headache, but her hostess only laughed at the fright the rats had given her, and added that they only attacked strangers, and the people of the house were used to them. Tanyusha was afraid of rats herself; and she and Aksinya could not look unmoved at the signs of suffering on their sister-in-law's face. They expressed sympathy with her, and Aksinya even scolded Alexandra for not taking the ordinary precautions by placing the bed in the centre of the room, attaching curtains to it, and tucking the ends under the mattress; but the hostess said with an angry laugh, 'It is a pity they did not bite off her nose.' 'You had better look out!' said her sister; 'if this gets to our father's ears, you will catch it.'

Karataevka was situated on the slope of a hill, above a little spring-fed stream which was dammed up at the end of the village and turned a small mill. The position was not bad, but the owners and all their ways were so objectionable that the place had no attractions for anyone. M. Karataev, who was afraid of Stepan Mikhailovich at Bagrovo and of his wife at home, would have liked to pay some attentions to Sofya Nikolaevna when his wife was out of the room; but he only found courage to ask leave from time to time to kiss her hand, and generally added that she was the most beautiful creature in the world. When he repeated his request, it was refused. His was a strange existence. Most of his summer was spent in visiting wandering Bashkir tribes, and drinking kumiss every day till he was intoxicated; he spoke the Bashkir language like a native; he rode on horseback whole days without dismounting, and had become as bow-legged as a Bashkir; he had their skill with the bow and could smash an egg at long range with the best of them. All the rest of the year he spent in a kind of lumber-room warmed by a stove, near the house-door; he wore a skin coat, and kept the little window always open even in the hardest frosts; and there he remained all day with his head stuck out of the window, humming Bashkir songs and taking a sip now and then of Bashkir mead or some decoction of herbs. Why Karataev looked out of his window over the empty yard with a rough path running across it, what he saw and noted there, what thoughts passed through the brain at the top of that big body—these are problems which no ingenuity can solve. Sometimes, it is true, his philosophic meditations were disturbed: when some plump woman or girl appeared from the servants' quarters and walked mincingly along the path towards the cattle-shed, then a pantomime of nods and signals took place between the window and the yard; but soon the fair vision turned out of sight and vanished like a ghost, and Karataev was left staring into empty void.

Sofya Nikolaevna was eager to escape from this horrible place: after an early dinner, during which the horses were already standing at the door, they said goodbye at once and started. The hostess kissed her sister-in-law on both cheeks and on the shoulders, and thanked her significantly for her kind visit; and Sofya Nikolaevna just as significantly thanked the lady for her kind hospitality.

When alone with her husband in the carriage, Soyfa Nikolaevna gave vent to her anger. Aksinya in her simplicity had let out accidentally that the hostess had purposely taken no precautions against the rats; and the bride, though she had refrained from an outburst in her enemy's house, was unable any longer to control her excitable nature. Forgetting that Alexandra was her husband's sister, and that Parasha was in the carriage with them, she was lavish in her terms of abuse. Alexei Stepanich, a straightforward and kindly man himself, could not believe that there was any intention on the part of his sister: attributing what had happened to mere carelessness, he was hurt by his wife's violent language, which was really inexcusable under any provocation. The young husband was angry for the first time with his young wife: saying that she should be ashamed to speak so, he turned from her and was silent. Such was their state of mind when they arrived at Mertovshchina, where Mme Mertvavo, a remarkably intelligent old lady, was then living with her daughter Katherine, who had lately been married to Peter Chichagov. Sofya Nikolaevna was warmly attached to both the Chichagovs. She did not in the least expect to find them there, and soon forgot all her displeasure in this agreeable surprise; she became very lively and cheerful, but no one could fail to notice that Alexei Stepanich remained silent and sad.

Chichagov's history, and especially his second marriage, is quite a romance; and I shall tell it as briefly as I can, because we shall often come across this family in future, and especially because the life of the young Bagrovs was a good deal influenced by this pair. Peter Chichagov was a man of exceptional ability or, I should rather say, exceptional acuteness, and had received what was for those days an advanced education in many subjects: he knew several languages, could draw and understood architecture, and wrote both in prose and verse. In his hot youth he fell in love at Moscow with a young lady of the Rimsky-Korsakov family, and went so far as to misrepresent his position in order to win her hand. This was discovered after the marriage, and he was banished to Ufa. His wife soon died. Within a year he consoled himself and fell in love with Katherine Mertvavo, who was attracted by his gay and amiable temper, his intelligence and acquirements; his face was so very plain that it could exercise no attraction. She was no longer a girl and had too strong a character to be controlled by her mother and brothers: they let her marry Chichagov, and he was pardoned soon afterwards but not allowed to leave the province of Ufa. Sofya Nikolaevna liked him for two reasons; because he was the husband of her dearest friend, and perhaps still more for his own cleverness and wide information. Mme Mertvavo had just settled to leave Ufa and live in the country, and the Chichagovs had come on purpose to help her in building a house and a church. After a week's experience of her husband's relations, this meeting was a spring in the desert to Sofya Nikolaevna; it was like a breath of fresh air in which her heart and quick intelligence expanded; she talked on with her friends till near midnight. But Alexei Stepanich would have sat there in silence and solitude, had not the old lady grasped the situation and entertained him by her pleasant talk. After supper, however, he said goodnight, and went off to the bedroom allotted to the visitors; when Sofya Nikolaevna came she found him fast asleep. They started for Bagrovo early next day without disturbing their hosts.

During their drive Alexei Stepanich was still sullen and silent. In reply to direct questions from his wife, his answers were so cold and short that she gave up speaking to him. Her lively and impatient temper resented this treatment, but she did not care to clear up matters in Parasha's presence, preferring to wait till the after-dinner rest when she would be alone with her husband. For the present she started a conversation with her maid about their life at Ufa, while Alexei Stepanich squeezed into a corner of the carriage and either fell asleep or pretended to. They reached Bagrovo two hours before dinner. Stepan Mikhailovich was obviously pleased to see his daughter-in-law again, and even said that he had missed her. 'My dear,' he added, 'you really must not stay here too long, or I shan't be able to let you go; as it is, I shall miss you, likely enough.' He made her give him a minute account of their expedition. He praised Mme Mertvavo whom he knew well, and said that he would send her an invitation next day to come with her daughter and son-in-law and dine at Bagrovo; he fixed on the following Sunday, which was four days ahead, for the entertainment. 'You must visit the Kalpinskys and Lupenevskys the day after tomorrow,' he said; 'and then you can invite them too for Sunday; and then, three days later, you had better be off home to Ufa. Your father has never been parted from you before, and must miss you terribly; and I am sure, my dear, that you are even more anxious to see him, poor suffering old man!'

Stepan Mikhailovich was not long in finding out that something disagreeable had happened on this expedition. In the course of conversation, he said, 'Well, were the Karataevs glad to see you?' The answer was of course in the affirmative; but Sofya Nikolaevna happened to mention that she had been kept awake all night by rats. This surprised the old man: he had only been there once long ago, and had heard of nothing of the kind. But here Arina Vasilevna unsuspiciously joined in, in spite of the warning signs of her daughter Elizabeth; she suffered for it afterwards, poor lady, at the hands of her daughters. 'Oh yes, yes, *batyushka* Stepan Mikhailovich!' she cried; 'the rats there are perfectly awful! Without bed-curtains, it's impossible to get a wink of sleep.' 'Had you no curtains to your bed, then?' asked the old man, and there was an ominous change in his voice as he spoke. 'No' was the only possible answer. 'An excellent hostess!' he said, and looked at his wife and daughter in such a way that a cold shiver ran down their backs.

The Karataev party had not yet returned, but were expected by tea-time. Dinner was not a cheerful meal: all were out of spirits, and each had his or her reasons. Arina Vasilevna and Elizabeth were conscious of the approaching storm, and feared that the thunderbolt might smite them also. It was long since Stepan Mikhailovich had been in a rage, and the prospect was more alarming to them because they had become unused to such outbreaks. Sofya Nikolaevna noted the frown on her father-in-law's face; she did not object to his giving a good fright to his daughter, whom she detested as her avowed enemy; but she feared she might somehow get involved herself. She had no unkind intention in speaking about the rats: she never supposed that her father-in-law would take any special notice of this circumstance or attach serious importance to it. Nevertheless, a stone lay on her heart also: she could not determine how to act towards her husband. He had been angry with her for the first time when she used insulting language about his sister: was it best to wait till he appealed to her voluntarily, or to put an end to the uncomfortable situation by begging him to forgive her? Her love and her tender caress might then cause him to forget her regrettable impulsiveness. And she certainly would have chosen this course; for she was passionately in love with her kind young husband. She blamed herself severely: she ought to have foreseen everything and been prepared for everything. She knew that Alexei Stepanich would not hesitate to die for her, but she knew also that she ought not to demand of him what he could not give —a tender and constant observation, and a full comprehension of all the trifling occurrences that might give her pain. And this was hard for her, with her hot blood and sensitive nerves, her eager excitable brain and impressionable nature. Such were the poor woman's thoughts and feelings as she walked up and down her room waiting for her husband; his mother had stopped him on the way there after dinner and asked him to come to her bedroom. The minutes seemed to her like hours. The thought that he was loitering on purpose, fearing a scene and unwilling to be alone with her; the thought that without relieving her heart of its many troubles and without a reconciliation with her husband, she would see him again in the presence of her enemies and must play a part the whole evening—this thought oppressed her heart and threw her into a fever. Suddenly the door opened, and Alexei Stepanich walked in. There was no hesitation in his movements; he was no longer timid and sad, but fearless and even displeased. He began at once to reproach her for complaining to his father and getting Alexandra into trouble. 'They are all trembling and crying now, and God only knows what will come of it,' he said, primed with all that his mother and sister had been impressing upon him. 'It is wrong and a sin on your part to cause trouble and quarrels in your husband's family. I told you what my father is like when he is angry; and you, knowing this and seeing his love for you, took advantage of it!' Sofya Nikolaevna's patience snapped instantly, and she fired up at once; love was silent, and of pity and contrition not a trace was left; and her poor husband discovered that Stepan Mikhailovich was not the only person who could fly into a passion. An irresistible flood of complaints, accusations, and reproaches poured down upon him. He was utterly crushed and confounded; he could make no defence, and was all but a monster in his own eyes. Soon he was kneeling at her feet and begging forgiveness with tears. It was not surprising that Alexei Stepanich was powerless before that volcanic eruption of feeling and intelligence, that heartfelt conviction and wonderful power of eloquence. A man entirely in the right, a man much more resolute than Alexei Stepanich, would have pleaded guilty before the youth and beauty of a woman whom he loved. And Alexei Stepanich was certainly not in the right.

When the storm had calmed down in the bedroom of the young couple, it was still brewing at the other end of the house, in the smallish room which belonged to Stepan Mikhailovich. Sleep had not brought peace to him or smoothed the frown from his high forehead. He sat for some time across his bed in gloomy silence, and then called out, 'Mazan!' Mazan had long been lying outside the door, breathing heavily according to his wont, and looking in through a chink; he had been placed there as a sentry, while the family were sitting in the parlour full of gloomy apprehensions. He called out at the top of his voice, 'What is your pleasure, sir?'—and hurried into the room. 'Has my daughter Alexandra arrived? Yes? then bring her here.' Alexandra entered on his heels, for on such occasions delay was more dangerous than anything. 'How dared you, Madam,' began the old man in the voice she knew and dreaded—'how dared you set rats on your brother and his wife?' 'I am sorry, father,' humbly answered Alexandra, while her knees trembled beneath her, and fear kept down her own infernal temper. 'I put my guests on purpose in the drawing-room, and I never thought of putting curtains to their bed. I was so busy and so glad to see them that it slipped my memory.' 'You were so glad to see them! Do you expect me to believe *that*? How did you dare to act so to your brother and to me? How did you dare to bring shame on your father in his old age?' The affair would perhaps have gone no farther than angry words and loud threats and possibly a rap from his fist; but Alexandra, stung by the thought that she was suffering on account of Sofya Nikolaevna, and hoping that the storm would still blow over, forgot that any sort of answer was a new offence. She could not resist saying, 'I am punished for nothing on her account.' A fresh and terrible fit of rage seized Stepan Mikhailovich, that rage which invariably ended in painful and shocking violence. Words of fury were on the point of rushing from his lips, when Arina Vasilevna, with her daughters, Aksinya and Tanyusha, ran into the room, and fell at the old man's feet with tears and cries; they had been standing outside the door and had seen what was coming. Karataev had been standing there with them; but he ran out of the house and into the wood, where he slashed furiously at the innocent birch branches with his stick, punishing them for the wrong done to his wife. Elizabeth did not venture to enter the room, knowing that her own conscience was not clear, and that her father was quite aware of the part she had played. 'Batyushka Stepan Mikhailovich!' cried Arina Vasilevna, 'your will is law, you are our master, do what pleases you! Only do not shame us and disgrace your family in the sight of your daughter-in-law! You will frighten her out of her life; all this is new to her.' The words seemed to have some effect on the old man. He was silent for a moment; then he pushed Alexandra from him with his foot, crying, 'Begone, and don't venture to show yourself till I send for you!' No one waited for any further orders: in a moment the room was cleared, and all was silence round Stepan Mikhailovich; but his blue eyes long remained dark and clouded, and his chest rose and fell with his heavy breathing, as he restrained the passionate anger which had been aroused and not satisfied.

The samovar had long been hissing on the drawing-room table, not in the shade of the stoop, because heavy rain had just ceased falling and it was damp out of doors. Nature seemed to sympathize with what was passing in the house of Bagrovo. Soon after dinner two clouds of intense blackness had met in the zenith and long remained there motionless, emitting from time to time flashes of lightning and shaking the air with peals of thunder. At last the rain came down in torrents, the clouds shifted to the east, and the setting sun shone out. Fields and woods smelt sweeter, refreshed by the rain, and the birds began to sing louder; but alas! the storms of human passion are not followed by such a calm.

Alexandra pretended illness, but the other daughters came with their mother to the drawing-room: Karataev also was there, but Erlykin was still absent from the house, on the pretext of ill-health. Stepan Mikhailovich had tea in his room and gave orders that he was not to be disturbed. The door of the young couple's room was locked; after a short delay, tapping was tried and brought them out at once. Sofya Nikolaevna looked cheerful and her husband really was more cheerful than before; but it was easy to guess from their faces that something unusual had been happening in their room. Of what had passed in the bedroom of Stepan Mikhailovich, they knew nothing. As for Arina Vasilevna and her daughters, they looked like people who had just been pulled out of the water or snatched from the fire. It is a pity that there was no one to observe the scene; for it is certain that the different expressions on the faces of the company would have afforded an entertaining spectacle. All attempts to keep up a conversation were unsuccessful. The absence of the father and of one daughter puzzled Sofya Nikolaevna beyond endurance: she invented some pretext for going to her own room, where she summoned Parasha and got to the bottom of the mystery. They knew all about it in the maids' room: not only had Mazan and Tanaichenok been listening all the time, but the old lady and her daughter were in the habit of keeping nothing back from their waiting-women. Thus Parasha was able to give her mistress an exact and detailed report. Sofya Nikolaevna was much disturbed. She had never expected such alarming consequences; she heartily regretted having told her father-in-law about those wretched rats; and she was sincerely sorry for Alexandra. She went back to the drawing-room and asked leave to visit the invalid, but was told she was asleep. During her absence, Alexei Stepanich had heard the whole story. After a hasty supper they separated to their rooms at ten o'clock. When alone with her husband, Sofya Nikolaevna, with much agitation and many tears, fell on his neck, and again asked his forgiveness with heartfelt penitence, blaming herself much more than she really deserved. But he did not understand the delicacy of feeling which prompted her genuine grief and drew tears from her. He was only sorry to see her distress herself about trifles; and he tried to console her by saying that all's well that ends well, that the family were accustomed to such scenes, that his father would wake in a good temper tomorrow and forgive Alexandra, and all would go on as well as before. Only he begged her not to have any explanations with any of the family, and not to ask pardon, as she wished to do, for her unintentional slip; and he advised her not to visit his father in the morning but to wait till he sent for her. Sofya Nikolaevna understood her husband's character better than she had ever done before; and the knowledge hurt her deeply. While he slept peacefully all night, she never closed an eye.

Stepan Mikhailovich was the worse for his fit of anger and also disliked the thought that his daughter-in-law might have heard of it. His honest nature resented every underhand action and deliberate unkindness; and also he saw, in what his daughter had done, disregard to his own authority and position. He was on the brink of an illness; he ate no supper, stayed indoors instead of going to sit on the stoop, and when he should have seen his bailiff, sent his orders by a servant. But the benign darkness of night which gives light to the eye of our mind, the stillness, and then sleep, which calms the passions of men and rains down blessing upon them—all these did their kindly office. Early next day he summoned Arina Vasilevna and gave her his instructions to convey to his daughters—they were intended mainly for Alexandra, but in part also for Elizabeth—that Sofya Nikolaevna was not to know of any unpleasantness, and they were to behave accordingly. In a short time the samovar was placed on the table, and all the family summoned. Arina Vasilevna fortunately had time to send a message by her son to Sofya Nikolaevna, begging her to do her best to cheer up the master of the house: 'He is not quite well,' she said, 'and in low spirits for some reason.' In spite of her sleepless night and the aching of her own heart, Sofya

Nikolaevna carried out this request to admiration; all the party, and she herself more than any, were anxious it should be done.

Sofya Nikolaevna was an astonishing woman! Lively, impressionable, and excitable, she could be carried away in a moment by impulses of the head or heart, and was capable of very sudden and complete transformations of behaviour. In later years stupid people accused her of insincerity on this ground, but no one else did. It was really a kind of artistic power, which enabled her to adapt herself instantly to a new atmosphere and a new position, and to act absolutely in accordance with her immediate purpose; and this purpose, being entirely sincere, acted like a spell on others. In this case she laid herself out to calm the agitation of her father-in-law, for whom she had conceived a warm affection, and who had championed her cause at the cost of his peace of mind and at the risk of his health; and she wished to relieve her husband and his family, who had been terrified and assailed owing to her slip of the tongue. Her imagination and feelings were so completely mastered by this purpose, that she exercised a kind of magical power over the party and soon subdued them all by the irresistible spell of her personality. She poured out tea herself and handed the cups herself, first to her father-in-law and then to the rest; she talked to everyone so easily and pleasantly and brightly that the old man, quite convinced that she had caught no glimpse of the skeleton in the cupboard, soon relaxed his features. Of him also it was true that his cheerfulness was infectious; and before an hour had passed, all traces of the storm of yesterday had disappeared.

Immediately after dinner the young couple started off to pay two ceremonial visits—to Ilarion Kalpinsky and his wife Catherine at Neklyudovo, and to our old acquaintance Mme Lupenevsky, who lived within two versts of the Kalpinskys. Kalpinsky was in his own way a remarkable man: though he had received no regular education, he was very intelligent and well-read; his origin was obscure—it was said that he was of Mordvinian descent—but he had risen to a considerable rank in the public service, and had made a marriage of interest with the daughter of a country gentleman of good family. His present pursuit was farming, and his object to save money. He set up for a free-thinker; and his few neighbours who had heard of Voltaire called him a Voltairean. He lived at home without taking any part in the life of the family, and reserved to himself complete freedom in the gratification of his somewhat epicurean tastes and habits. Though she had heard of him, Sofya Nikolaevna had never seen him, because he had only recently removed to Orenburg from his public office at Petersburg. She was surprised to find in him a man possessed of intelligence and culture according to the standards of the time, and dressed like a gentleman living in the capital. She was pleased with him at first, but he soon began to show off before such an attractive visitor, and then his profanity and the shameless immorality of his family life made her feel a disgust for him which she never afterwards got over. His wife was far more intelligent than her sister, Mme Lupenevsky, but not her superior in any other respect. The visit lasted for an hour, and was followed by a visit to Mme Lupenevsky. In both houses tea was given to the guests and home-made jam, and the meal was seasoned with a kind of conversation which horrified Sofya Nikolaevna. Both families were invited to dine at Bagrovo on the following Sunday. By one of those striking inconsistencies in human nature which it is impossible to explain, Mme Lupenevsky fell in love at first sight with Sofya Nikolaevna, and used such language to her at parting that her guest must needs either blush or laugh aloud; nevertheless her words were the expression of sincere and even enthusiastic attachment.

The pair reached home an hour before supper-time, and were welcomed with unusual cordiality and pleasure by Stepan Mikhailovich, whom they found sitting on the familiar stoop. He was much amused when he was told that Mme Lupenevsky had conceived such a passion for his daughter-in-law, kissing her repeatedly, claiming that they were kindred spirits, and lavishing terms of affection upon her. Contrary to custom, the whole family went out again to the stoop after supper, and spent a long time there in cheerful conversation with the master of the household, in the cool of the night and under the starry sky. Stepan Mikhailovich, though he could not have explained why, was fond of the faint colourless light that follows the glow of sunset.

The solemn feast on the Sunday was to be something beyond what had ever been seen at Bagrovo, but nothing special happened on either of the intervening days. Erlykin came back from Buguruslan looking yellow and ill, as he always did after a drinking bout. Stepan Mikhailovich knew of his son-in-law's unfortunate weakness or disease, and tried to cure him by dosing him with unpalatable drinks, but without success. When sober, Erlykin had a loathing for alcohol and could not raise a glass of wine to his lips without a shudder; but he was seized four times a year with a sudden and irresistible craving for spirits. If the attempt was made to keep drink from him, he became a most pitiable and wretched object, talking constantly and weeping and begging abjectly for the poison; and if it was still refused he became frantic and even capable of attempts at suicide. Sofya Nikolaevna, who had heard the whole story, was exceedingly sorry for him. She spoke kindly to him and tried to make him talk to her. But it was no good: the General persisted in his sullen silence and gloomy pride. Instead of being grateful to her sister-in-law, Elizabeth resented these advances to her husband, and expressed her resentment in bitter terms. But Stepan Mikhailovich noticed this and addressed a stern reproof to his clever daughter, who did not love her sister-in-law any the better in consequence.

Stepan Mikhailovich twice took his daughter-in-law out to see his crops of rye and spring-sown wheat, and drove with her to all his favourite water-springs in the hills, and the 'Sacred Wood' where the trees had been protected from the axe by a religious service. The old man believed that all these sights were interesting and agreeable to her; but in fact she positively disliked them all. Her sole support was in the thought that she would soon leave Bagrovo and would do her best never to set eyes on it again. If anyone had told her that she would spend most of her life there, grow old there, and even die there, she would not have believed it: she would have said that death was preferable, and would have meant what she said. But whatever God decrees, to that man can become accustomed, and that he can endure.

Sunday came and the guests began to assemble. Mme Mertvavo came, and the Kalpinskys and Lupenevskys, and two old bachelors, the judge and the mayor of Buguruslan. Another guest was Afrosinya Andreevna (her surname, which was never used, I forget), a spare little old lady and a great talker; she had a small estate near Bagrovo. She was famous for her powers of invention, and Stepan Mikhailovich liked at times to listen to her, as a grown man sometimes listens with pleasure to a fairy tale intended for children.

But Afrosinya Andreevna deserves that the reader should have at least a bowing acquaintance with her. At one time in her life she had spent ten years in Petersburg to watch a lawsuit; when she won it, she came back to her little estate in the country. She brought back with her from Petersburg a store of anecdotes whose extravagance made Stepan Mikhailovich laugh till he cried. For instance, she used to represent herself as a bosom friend of the Empress Catherine, adding by way of explanation that two people could not live ten years in the same town without being thrown together. 'I was in church one day'—she talked this way when she was in the vein— 'the people were going out, and the Empress walked past me, and I made a low curtsey and ventured to congratulate her on the festival; and then Her Majesty was so very kind and condescending as to say: "How are you, Afrosinya Andreevna? How is your suit going? Why don't you come to see me of an evening and bring your knitting with you? We could chat together and pass the time pleasantly." Of course I never missed an evening after that. I got to know the people about the court, and everyone in the palace without a single exception knew me and liked me. Suppose a royal footman was sent anywhere, to buy something it might be, he never failed to look in at my house and tell me all about it. As a matter of course, I always offered him a glass of something good; I kept a bottle of whisky in the cupboard on purpose. I was sitting by my window one evening when I saw a royal footman in red uniform, with a coat of arms on it, ride past at a gallop; he was soon followed by a second and a third. That was too much for me: I threw up the window and called out, "Philip Petrovich! Philip Petrovich! what are you galloping for, and why don't you pay me a visit?" "No time, Afrosinya Andreevna!" was his answer; "a terrible thing has happened: candles will soon be wanted at the palace, and we've run out of them!" "Stop!" I cried out; "I have five pounds of candles laid in; you can come in and take them." Philip Petrovich was delighted; I carried out the candles with my own hands and relieved the people from their difficulty. So you see, *batyushka* Stepan Mikhailovich, they simply couldn't help being fond of me.'

Stephan Mikhailovich had many traits of character peculiar to himself; and this was one—though he was a sworn foe to deliberate lying of every kind, and detested the most trifling deception and even the kind of evasion which is sometimes quite excusable, yet he liked listening to the harmless fabrications and fictions of simple people, who were innocently carried away by the vividness of their imagination till they actually came to believe in their own incredible romancing. He liked talking to Afrosinya Andreevna, not only at a merry party, but also when they were alone together, if he was in the right mood for it; and she spent whole hours in pouring out for his benefit the story of her life in Petersburg, which consisted entirely of such incidents as that which I have already quoted.

But it is time to go back to the guests arriving at Bagrovo. The mayor's kaftan and the judge's uniform were equally remarkable; but the best sight of all was Kalpinsky: on each side of him stood a female scarecrow in the person of his wife and of her sister, while he himself wore an embroidered coat of French cut, a pair of watch-chains, a number of rings, silk stockings, and shoes with gold buckles. All the family wore their best bib and tucker, and even Stepan Mikhailovich was forced to smarten himself up. M. Chichagov, who had a critical satirical turn of mind, made fun with much effect of the motley assembly and especially of his friend Kalpinsky; he was talking all the time to his wife and to her inseparable companion, Sofya Nikolaevna, who sat together and apart from the rest. Sofya Nikolaevna had hard work to keep from laughing: she tried not to listen, and begged Chichagov either to hold his tongue or to start a conversation with Stepan Mikhailovich, whom he would find worthy of respect. He did so, and soon took a great fancy to the old man; and his feeling was reciprocated. But Stepan Mikhailovich disliked Kalpinsky, both as an upstart and also as an unbeliever and loose-liver.

The splendour of the banquet may be imagined. Stepan Mikhailovich for once resigned all his favourite dishes—haggis, roast ribs of pork, and porridge made of green rye. A chef had been procured, of special skill in the culinary art. Materials of all sorts were provided in abundance—a six-weeks-old calf, a pig fed to monstrous proportions, fat sheep, and poultry of all kinds. It was the custom then to place all the courses at once on the cloth; and the table at Bagrovo could hardly hold them all or support their weight. Cold dishes came first—smoked hams seasoned with garlic; next came green cabbage soup and crayfish soup, with forcemeat balls and rolls of different kinds; then fish salad on ice, sturgeon kippered and sturgeon dried, and a dish heaped mountain high with crayfish tails. Of entrées there were only two: salted quails *aux choux*, and stuffed ducks with a red sauce containing raisins, plums, peaches, and apricots. These entrées were a concession to modern fashion; Stepan Mikhailovich did not like them and called them 'kickshaws'. They were followed by a turkey of enormous size and fatness, and a hindquarter of veal; the accessories were preserved melons and gourds, apple chips, and pickled mushrooms. The dinner ended up with round jam tarts and raised apple pies served with thick cream. All this was washed down with home-made liquors, home-brewed March beer, iced kvass, and foaming mead.

Such were the meals which our heroic grandfathers and grandmothers consumed without leaving out a single course, and even managed to digest satisfactorily! But they took their time over it, and the meal went on for hours. The dishes were solid substantial affairs, as we have seen, and there were plenty of them; and the servants also, both those of the house and those whom the guests brought with them, had no idea of waiting: they bustled about and collided with one another and seemed likely at every moment to spill the sauce or the gravy over some lady's dress.

The dinner was a cheerful meal. The master of the house had Mme Mertvavo on his right, and on his left Chichagov, who steadily rose in his host's good graces and was quite capable, unaided, of enlivening the dullest of parties. The young couple were near the head of the table, with Mme Chichagov and Kalpinsky; the latter, while paying constant attentions to the two young women and exchanging an occasional jest with Alexei Stepanich, ate for two all the time, to make up for the voluntary abstinence which he practised at home in his eagerness to save money. Erlykin sat next to Chichagov; unlike the rest of the party, he ate little and drank nothing but cold water; he never spoke, but looked gloomy and profound. The lady of the house had her daughters and nieces with other guests near her at table. The party next adjourned to the drawing-room, where there were two tables set out with sweetmeats. On one stood a round cabinet of Chinese porcelain, resting on a round metal stand which was gilt and painted in bright colours. The cabinet contained a number of closely fitting trays, each of which held a different sort of preserved fruit—raspberries, strawberries, cherries, gooseberries, and blackberries; and there were crystallized rose petals in a small round receptacle at the top. This cabinet, which would be considered very rare and precious nowadays, was a present sent by the bride's father to Stepan Mikhailovich. Small plates were set out on the other table, filled with black and white currants, apricots, peaches, dates, raisins, nuts of many kinds, and almonds in the shell.

Stepan Mikhailovich rose from table in such good spirits that he did not even wish to lie down and rest. All could see—and indeed he wished it to be seen—his pride in his daughter-in-law and his affection for her; and her love and respect for him were as plain to see. During dinner he often turned towards her and asked her to do him some trifling service—to hand something, or pour out something. 'Please help me

yourself,' he would say, 'for you and I agree in our tastes'—
or, 'Just remind me of what I said to you the other day'—
or, 'Do repeat what you told me yesterday; I seem to have
forgotten it.' After dinner it was the same: he often asked her
to give some order, or to hand him something, and so on. The
form of his address was always plain and unpretentious, sometimes even unceremonious; but the tone of affection in which
these appeals were expressed left no doubt in the mind of any
spectator that he was entirely captivated by his daughter-in-
law. And she, I need hardly say, replied with love and gratitude to every token of the stern old man's love for her—tokens
often so slight that many would have missed them. Stepan
Mikhailovich, who was thoroughly enjoying himself, tried to
make Mme Lupenevsky talk: pretending ignorance, he asked
in a loud voice, 'Well, Flena, what say you of my daughter-
in-law?' The lady's enthusiasm had been raised to a higher
pitch by the ale and strong waters she had been drinking. She
declared most positively and solemnly that she had fallen in
love at first sight with Sofya Nikolaevna, and rather preferred
her to her own daughter, Lizanka; and that Alexei Stepanich
was the most fortunate of men. 'It used to be quite another
story,' said the old man significantly; 'don't change back again,
my dear!' But now Sofya Nikolaevna, perhaps from a dislike
for this topic, strongly urged her father-in-law to go and lie
down, if only for a short time. He consented, and she went
with him and drew his curtains with her own hand; he asked
her to see to the entertainment of the party, and she hurried
back, pleased and flattered by this commission. While some
lay down to rest, the others crossed to the island and sat on
the river bank in the shade of the trees. Sofya Nikolaevna was
reminded of the scene that had taken place there so recently—
her unreasonable excitement and the unjust reproaches which
had rankled in the mind of her husband. Her heart was full;
and though she saw him now, in perfect content and happiness,
laughing loudly at a story which Kalpinsky was telling, she
drew him aside, threw her arms round him, and said with
tears in her eyes, 'Forgive me, my dear, and bury in oblivion
all that happened here on the day we came!' Alexei Stepanich

had a strong objection to tears; but he kissed both her hands and said good-humouredly, 'How can you recall such a trifle, my darling? You are quite wrong to trouble yourself.' Then he hurried back to hear the end of the story, which was very amusing as Kalpinsky told it. Though there was really no cause for distress, Sofya Nikolaevna felt a momentary heartache.

The master of the house soon woke and summoned all the party to join him by the stoop. Tables and chairs were placed in the broad thick shadow cast by the house; and the samovar was soon hissing. Tea was poured out by Sofya Nikolaevna; there were rolls and scones and cream so thick that it had a golden tinge on it; and for all this some at least of the guests still found room. The Kalpinskys and Mme Lupenevsky went off after tea: there was positively no room for them to sleep at Bagrovo, and they had not far to go, only fifteen versts. The guests from Buguruslan also took their leave.

Mme Mertvavo and her party left early next morning, and the Erlykins after dinner, to prepare for a visit from the young couple on their way back to Ufa. The same evening Stepan Mikhailovich announced quite frankly that the time had come for the rest of the party to disperse: he wished to spend the last days alone with his son and daughter-in-law, and to enjoy their society without interruption. As a matter of course, his wishes were carried out. Alexandra said goodbye to her sister-in-law as graciously as she could, and the sister-in-law said goodbye to her with unfeigned satisfaction. Her secret wish to spend some days without the hateful presence of Elizabeth and Alexandra had been divined by Stepan Mikhailovich; and she blessed him in her thoughts for his power of intuition. Aksinya was quite different; and Sofya Nikolaevna parted from her with feelings of gratitude and real affection. None of this escaped the old man's keen eyes. Tanyusha and her mother caused no constraint, partly because they were more good-tempered and friendly to their guest, and also because they often withdrew and left the others to their own devices.

The three remaining days were spent at Bagrovo in perfect peace of mind, untroubled by malevolent observation or pretences of affection or venomous innuendoes. The strain on

Sofya Nikolaevna's nerves was relaxed, and she was able to take her bearings with less prejudice and study the peculiarities of the little world in which she found herself. In spite of their complete unlikeness to herself, she could now understand her mother-in-law and Tanyusha better, and make allowances for them; she could form a cooler judgement of Stepan Mikhail-ovich, and could understand how her husband came to be what he was. To some extent she realized that Alexei could not be entirely changed, and that the time was distant—perhaps it would never come—when misunderstandings between them would cease. But this last thought passed too lightly through her mind; and the old dream, that she could educate her husband over again and make a new man of him, took fresh hold of her eager imagination. What happens to most young wives in the course of life was happening now to Sofya Nikolaevna: she found in her husband a certain inferiority, certain limitations of feeling and perception; and though her love for him was none the less passionate on that account, she was beginning to feel vaguely dissatisfied with his love for her, because he found room in his heart for other things—the pond and the island, the steppe and its population of snipe, the river and those horrid fish! A feeling of jealousy, though directed to no definite object as yet, was lurking at her heart; and she felt a dim presentiment of coming disaster.

Stepan Mikhailovich also had been somewhat taken up hitherto by constant observation of the feelings and actions of his daughters; but now he was more at leisure to attend to his daughter-in-law and his son also. For all his want of education and rough-and-ready way of expressing himself, his natural sagacity and power of intuition revealed to him the whole difference of character between the two; and he found here matter for serious reflection. Their present love for one another was a pleasant sight to him and he felt happy when he saw Sofya Nikolaevna's eyes constantly fixed on her husband and her eager desire to please him; but his happiness had a shade of fear and of disbelief in the solidity and permanence of a state of things in itself so charming. He would have liked to speak his mind on the subject, to give them some hints or some useful advice; but whenever he began, he could not find the right words for thoughts and feelings which he could not make clear even to himself; and he went no farther than those trivial commonplaces, which, for all their triviality, have been bequeathed to us by the practical wisdom of past generations and are verified by our own experience. His failure troubled him, and he said so frankly to his daughter-in-law. She was a clever woman, yet she failed to understand the thoughts which the old man was turning over in his brain, and the feeling hidden in his heart. To his son he said: 'Your wife is very clever and very excitable. Her tongue will probably run away with her at times; if so, don't be weak with her: stop her at once, and make her see her mistake. Scold her, but forgive her at once; if she displeases you, don't be sullen or keep up resentment; have it all out with her at once. But trust her absolutely; she is as true as steel.' Again, when he was alone with Sofya Nikolaevna, he said to her: 'My dear daughter-in-law, God has given you many good gifts. I have only one thing to say to you: don't give the rein to your impetuous temper. Your husband is honest and kind; his temper is mild, and he will never willingly hurt your feelings; don't you hurt his. Honour him and treat him with respect. If you cease to respect your husband, things will go wrong. Suppose he says or does something you don't like, then say nothing; don't be too exacting, and don't expect perfection. I can see through and through you, and I love you dearly. For God's sake, don't fill the cup till it runs over: anything can be overdone, even the affection between husband and wife.'

The advice was received as always by his son with profound respect, and by Sofya Nikolaevna with the ardent gratitude of a daughter. There was much talk on other subjects—their future life at Ufa, the husband's prospects in his profession, and the means of defraying their expenditure. Definite arrangements were made on all points, and all parties were satisfied.

And now the day came for their departure. The silk curtains in the bedroom were taken down; the muslin and satin pillow-cases with broad lace edging were taken off the pillows; and all this finery was packed up and dispatched to Ufa. Pies of different kinds were baked for the travellers. Father Vasili was summoned once more, and the prayers for those 'travelling by land or by water' were said. Fresh horses were to be in readiness at Korovino, forty versts away; to that point they were to be taken by the Bagrovo horses, the same fine team of six which had conveyed the pair on their ceremonial visits. They dined together for the last time; and for the last time Stepan Mikhailovich pressed his favourite dishes on his daughter-in-law. The carriage was already standing at the steps. When the party rose from table, they went to the drawing-room and sat there in silence for some minutes. Then Stepan Mikhailovich crossed himself and rose to his feet; the rest followed his example, said a prayer,* and began their goodbyes. All shed tears except Stepan Mikhailovich, and even he had hard work to refrain. He embraced his daughter-in-law and gave her his blessing; then he whispered in her ear, 'Mind, I look forward to a little grandson.' She blushed up to the ears and kissed his hands without speaking; and now he did not resist her doing so. All the outdoor servants and most of the peasants were standing by the steps. Some of them had half a mind to come forward and say farewell to their young master and mistress; but Stepan Mikhailovich, who hated good-byes and parting scenes, called out, 'What are you up to there? Make your bow, and that will be enough!' Sofya Nikolaevna had only time to exchange greetings with one or two of the people. They took their seats quickly, and the strong horses started off with the carriage as if it had been a mere feather.

Stepan Mikhailovich shaded his eyes from the sun with his hand; for some minutes he tried to make out the moving carriage in the cloud of dust which followed it; and when it had reached the stackyard at the top of the hill, he went back to his own room and lay down to sleep.

* In prayers of this kind, nothing is said aloud: the worshipper turns towards the ikons on the wall and crosses himself.

FRAGMENT V

LIFE AT UFA

DURING the first few minutes Sofya Nikolaevna felt sorry for her father-in-law and sad to part with him. The image of the old man who had learnt to love her and was suffering now from the separation, came vividly before her. But before long the easy motion of the carriage, with the fleeting glimpses of fields and coppices and the outline of the hills along which they were driving, had a soothing effect upon her mind; and she began to feel heartily glad that she had left Bagrovo. Her joy was too great to be concealed, though she realized that her husband would not like it. He, she thought, was sadder than he had any business to be. Some explanations might possibly have followed, but were fortunately prevented by the presence of Parasha. The carriage rolled quickly through the village of Noikino, where it was saluted by hearty shouts from the Mordvinians, and then crossed the river Nasyagai by a crazy bridge. They crossed the same river again and passed through the village of Polibino, and came at last to Korovino, where a fresh team was waiting for their arrival; their own horses were to rest there for some hours and return to Bagrovo in the evening.

Sofya Nikolaevna had provided herself with writing materials, and now she wrote a warm letter of thanks to her husband's parents. It was intended especially for Stepan Mikhailovich; and he understood this perfectly and hid the letter in the secret drawer of the modest writing-desk which satisfied his needs; and there Sofya Nikolaevna came upon her own letter unexpectedly eight years afterwards, when the old man was in his grave. The horses were put to, goodbyes were said to the coachman and postilion—long-legged Tanaichenok was acting as position on this occasion—and the pair resumed their journey. Fortune was kind at this point to Sofya Nikolaevna: it proved impossible to get to the Erlykins' house, and thus she was saved from a most tiresome and oppressive visit. A deep river had to be crossed on the way, and the bridge had rotted and collapsed. As it would take a long time to mend it, the young couple could keep straight on towards Ufa. As they got near the town, Sofya Nikolaevna could think of nothing but her sick father, who had not seen her for more than a fortnight; he had been left in the care of servants and must be feeling lonely and eager for his daughter's return. The travellers took a full hour to cross the river Belaya in a crazy ferry-boat; and the ascent of the steep hill on the other side took time. Before it was over, Sofya Nikolaevna was very impatient and in great agitation. At last she got to the house. In a fever of excitement she hurried to her father's room and softly opened the door. He was lying in his usual position; and near him, in the very armchair which was usually occupied by Sofya Nikolaevna herself, his servant Nikolai was sitting.

This man was a Kalmuck, and I must say something of his history. In those distant times it was a common practice in the district of Ufa to buy native boys and girls, either Kalmucks or Kirghizes, from their parents or relations, and to make use of them later as serfs. Forty years before the date of my story, M. Zubin had bought two Kalmuck boys. He had them baptized, became fond of them, and made pets of them. He had them taught to read and write; and when they grew up, they became his personal servants. Both of them were intelligent and neat-handed and appeared to be very devoted; but when Pugachev* raised the standard of revolt, they both ran off and joined the rebels. One of them soon lost his life; but the other, who had been his master's favourite and was called Nikolai, now became the favourite of one Chika, who was prominent among the rebels and stood high in the favour of Pugachev himself. It is well known that one band of the revolters was encamped for a long time near Ufa, on the opposite bank of the river Belaya. Nikolai was in this camp and had by this time been promoted to a position of

* See note to p. 67.

some authority. It was said that he was fiercer than any of
them and breathed fire and slaughter against no one so much
as his old master who had brought him up. Tradition tells
that whenever the rebels were preparing to cross the river and
fall upon the defenceless town, they saw a great army march
out to defend the heights on the opposite bank, and an ancient
warrior at their head, riding on a snow-white horse and holding
a spear in one hand and a cross in the other. The cowardly
band of outlaws were terrified by this vision and desisted from
all their attempts; and they had done nothing when the news
came that Pugachev was defeated. Of course they scattered at
once. The revolt came to an end, and the scattered rabble were
seized and brought to trial. Nikolai, who was one of these,
was condemned to the gallows. I cannot vouch for the truth
of this; but I have been assured that after his trial at Ufa the
noose was actually round his neck, when M. Zubin claimed
the privilege which he possessed as a landholder, pardoned his
old favourite, and took him home, undertaking to be responsible himself for the criminal's behaviour. Nikolai seemed
penitent and tried by zeal and devotion to atone for his crime.
By degrees he contrived to get back into his master's confidence;
and when Sofya Nikolaevna, after her stepmother's death, took
over the management of the household, she found Nikolai
established as butler; he had been a favourite with her stepmother, and this now became a passport to her father's goodwill. Nikolai had been guilty of much insolence to his young
mistress during her time of humiliation; but he was a very
cunning fellow and quite realized his present position. He
played the part of the repentant sinner, throwing all the guilt
on the stepmother, and blaming himself for the slavish spirit
in which he had carried out her orders. It would have been
quite easy for Sofya Nikolaevna to get rid of him for good and
all; but her youth and generous nature made her believe that
his repentance was genuine. She pardoned him, and actually
begged her father to leave him in his old position. As time
went on, she was sometimes vexed by the way in which he
settled things without consulting her, and she felt doubts
about his honesty. She noticed also that his intimacy with

her father, though concealed from her, was closer than she liked. But he was very zealous in his attendance upon his sick master, sleeping always in the same room, and also found time to do his work as butler exceedingly well. She was therefore content with mild reproofs, and the man was left free to take root at leisure in his double office. When she became engaged, she had to see herself to the buying of her wedding clothes and to spend much time with her future husband; and so she was less with her father and gave less attention to household affairs. Nikolai took full advantage of this opportunity, and his power over the old invalid increased daily. Hoping soon to get rid of his mistress and to become master of the house himself, he grew more insolent and less careful to conceal his power. Sofya Nikolaevna sometimes snubbed him sharply; she was grieved to see her father's increasing dependence on this man and abdication of his own authority.

Nikolai had made full use of the few days that preceded and followed the marriage, and of her absence for a fortnight at Bagrovo: his master, now at death's door, was completely under his control. Sofya Nikolaevna guessed the true state of affairs as soon as she saw the man lying asleep in the armchair; never before had he ventured on such a liberty. She gave him a look which sent him in some haste and confusion out of the room. Her father was by no means as pleased to see her as she expected; he made haste to tell her that Nikolai was not to blame: 'It is at my urgent wish', he said, 'that he sometimes takes a seat at my bedside.' 'It is a pity you do that, father,' she said; 'you will spoil him altogether and be forced to turn him off; I know him better than you do.' Then, without entering upon further explanations, she expressed her joy at having found him no worse. Alexei Stepanich soon came in; and then the old man, touched by his daughter's unfeigned tenderness, his son-in-law's attentive behaviour, and the love between husband and wife, listened with pleasure to their narrative and thanked God with tears for their happiness.

Sofya Nikolaevna began at once the business of instalment. She chose three rooms, quite separate from the rest, for their own occupation; and in a few days her arrangements were so complete that she could receive her own guests without any disturbance to her father. It was her intention to arrange as before about the management of the house and the attendance on her father, and to assign to Nikolai the subordinate part of carrying out her instructions; but the man had always hated her, and now felt himself strong enough to declare open war against his young mistress. While attending to the father more zealously than ever, he contrived with extraordinary cunning to insult the daughter at every turn; and to Alexei Stepanich he was so insolent that the young man lost patience, in spite of his easy and unexacting temper, and told his wife that he could not possibly put up with the position. For some time Sofya Nikolaevna did not trouble her father, hoping by her own influence to keep Nikolai within the bounds of reasonable politeness; she relied upon his intelligence, and also believed that he knew her determined character and would not venture to drive her to extremities. But the malicious Asiatic—this was the servants' name for him—was convinced beforehand that he would conquer, and tried to provoke Sofya Nikolaevna into some passionate outburst. Long ago he had been able to instil into his master the belief that the young lady could not endure her father's faithful servant and would certainly try to turn him out of the house. The invalid was horrified by this prospect, and solemnly declared that he would prefer death to such a deprivation. Sofya Nikolaevna tried to hint to her father in very gentle and affectionate terms that Nikolai forgot himself in his behaviour to her husband, and neglected to carry out her orders: it seemed to be his intention to provoke her to anger. But her father became agitated and refused to listen: he said that he was perfectly satisfied with Nikolai, and begged her not to trouble the butler but to give her orders to some other servant. Young and impulsive, and accustomed to undisputed authority in her father's house, Sofya Nikolaevna found it hard to endure the insulting behaviour of an unworthy menial; yet her love for her father, and her desire to nurse and comfort him and alleviate his sufferings as far as possible, kept her for long from the idea of leaving him in that dying state to depend entirely upon such a wretch as

Nikolai and other servants. She controlled her impulsiveness
and injured pride; she gave her household orders through one
of the other servants, knowing all the time that all her instructions were altered by her enemy at his will and pleasure. She
induced her father to order that Nikolai should not enter the
sick-room while she was sitting there. But this arrangement
soon broke down: under various pretexts, the man constantly
came into the room; and indeed the invalid himself constantly
asked for him. This painful situation continued for several
months.

Sofya Nikolaevna arranged her engagements in the town
in accordance with her own wishes. The people whom she
liked she often met, either in their houses or her own; the rest
she seldom saw, and was content to exchange formal calls
with them. Her husband was acquainted already with everybody in the town; but his wife's intimate friends now became
intimate with him. He became popular with them and got
on very well in his new position—I mean, in the select society
that gathered round his wife.

Meanwhile, soon after her return to Ufa, Sofya Nikolaevna
began to feel unpleasant symptoms of a peculiar kind, which
gave great satisfaction to Stepan Mikhailovich when he heard
of them. The continuation of his ancient line, the descendants
of the great Shimon, was a constant theme of the old man's
thoughts and wishes; it troubled his peace of mind and stuck
in his head like a nail. On receiving the good news from his
son, Stepan Mikhailovich was full of happy hopes and convinced that the child would infallibly be a boy. His family
always said that his spirits were unusually high at this time.
He had prayers said in church for his daughter-in-law's health,
forgave certain sums owed him by neighbours or dependants,
asked everyone to congratulate him, and made them drink
till they were dizzy.

In his excitement and joy, it occurred to him suddenly to
bestow a mark of his favour upon Aksyutka, the maid who
poured out tea and coffee, to whom he always showed an
unaccountable partiality. Aksyutka was a peasant's daughter
who had lost both parents and was brought to the house at

Bagrovo when she was seven years old, merely to save her from starvation. She was exceedingly ugly—red-haired and freckled, with eyes of no colour in particular; she was also bad-tempered and a horrible sloven. This does not sound attractive; but Stepan Mikhailovich took a great fancy to her, and never did dinner pass without his giving or sending to the child something taken from the dishes at table. When she grew up, he made her pour out his tea in the morning and talked to her for hours at a time. She was now a good deal over thirty. One morning, soon after the good news came from Ufa, Stepan Mikhailovich said to her: 'What makes you go about looking like a scarecrow? Be off, you stupid creature, and put on your best clothes that you wear on holidays. I mean to find you a husband.' Aksyutka grinned: she thought her master was not serious, and answered: 'Why, who would marry an orphan like me, except perhaps Kirsanka, the shepherd?' (Kirsanka, as everyone knew, was deformed and idiotic.) Stepan Mikhailovich seemed vexed; he went on, 'If I arrange the marriage, you can have your pick of the young men. Go and dress yourself, and come back at once.' Aksyutka went out surprised and delighted; and Stepan Mikhailovich summoned Little Ivan to his presence. We have heard something of this man already; he was now twenty-four years old, with a complexion of lilies and roses, a very fine young fellow, both tall and stout. At the time of Pugachev's revolt, when the master himself took refuge with his family at Astrakhan, Ivan's father had been left in charge of the serfs at Bagrovo; and it was generally supposed that his death was due to overwork and anxiety at that time. He left two sons, both called Ivan, and this one was known as Little Ivan, to distinguish him from his elder brother, who inherited his father's nickname of Weasel. Little Ivan appeared before his master, 'like a leaf before the grass'.* Stepan Mikhailovich looked at him with admiration, and then said in a voice so kind that

---

* i.e. 'instantly', though why the phrase means this I cannot discover. In Russian fairy tales, a witch regularly summons anyone she wants with the words, 'Stand thou before me, like a leaf before the grass!'

the lad's heart leaped for joy, 'Ivan, I mean to give you a wife.' 'Your will is law, *batyushka* Stepan Mikhailovich,' answered the man, devoted body and soul to his master. 'Well, go and dress yourself in your best, and come back to me in less than no time.' Ivan flew off to do his master's bidding. Aksyutka was the first to reappear; she had smoothed her red hair and greased it with oil, and put on her smartest jacket and skirt, and her bare feet were hidden in shoes; but alas! she was no more beautiful than before. She was much excited, and her mouth was constantly expanding into a broad grin, which she tried to hide with her hand, because she felt ashamed of it. Stepan Mikhailovich laughed: 'Oh, she's willing enough to take a husband,' he said. Back flew Ivan; but the sight of Aksyutka's ugly face and fine dress sent a cold shiver down his back. 'There is your bride,' said Stepan Mikhailovich; 'She is a good servant to me as your father was once. You may both count on my protection.' His wife now came in, and he turned to her and said: 'Arisha, the bride's clothes are all to be made out of our stuff; I shall give her a cow and provide everything to eat and drink at the wedding.' No one raised any objections, and the marriage took place. Aksyutka was charmed with her handsome husband, but he detested his repulsive wife, who was besides ten years older than he was. She was jealous of him all day long, and not without reason; and he beat her all day long, with some excuse on his side also; for nothing but the stick—and not even that for long— could shut her mouth and keep her wicked tongue from wagging. It was a pity, a great pity: Stepan Mikhailovich did a wrong thing when he made others sad because he was happy.

Of his happiness I judge partly by tradition but more from a letter which he wrote to Sofya Nikolaevna and which I have seen myself. We have seen that he was capable of strong and deep affection; yet it is hard to believe that a man with so little refinement of manner could give verbal expression to such tender and delicate solicitude as breathed through the whole of this letter. He begged her and commanded her to be careful of her health, and sent her much advice on the subject.

Unfortunately, I can only remember a few words of it: 'if you were living in my house'—this was one thing the old man said—'I would not suffer the wind to blow on you or a grain of dust to settle on your skin.'

Sofya Nikolaevna was able to appreciate this affection, though she understood that half of it was intended for the expected heir; and she promised to carry out scrupulously his wishes and instructions. But it was hard for her to keep this promise. She was one of those women who pay for the joy of motherhood by a constant discomfort which is more painful and distressing than any real illness; and she suffered in mind also, because her relations with her father became daily more humiliating and the insolence of Nikolai more unbearable. Alexei Stepanich, who saw no danger in his wife's constant sufferings, and was told that the symptoms were quite natural and would soon pass away, though he was sorry for his wife, was not excessively put out; and this was another cause of distress to Sofya Nikolaevna. He worked hard at his duties in the law-court, hoping soon to be promoted. He had become accustomed to living with his father-in-law; he avoided for the present all contact with Nikolai, and looked forward without impatience to a change in their position. His wife did not like this either. Things dragged on thus, as I have said already, for several months, and it was not a happy time for any of them.

But Nikolai was not satisfied with this state of things: he desired a final solution. Seeing that Sofya Nikolaevna was controlling her quick temper and righteous indignation, he determined to force her hand. It was necessary for his purpose that she should lose patience and complain to her father: and he warned the invalid more than once that he was constantly expecting Sofya Nikolaevna to complain of him and demand his instant dismissal. He did not wait for any pretext or opportunity. One day, in the presence of other servants, when his young mistress was standing close to him at the open door of the next room, he began, speaking loud and looking straight at her, to use such offensive language of herself and her husband that Sofya Nikolaevna was struck dumb for a moment by his insolence. But she recovered immediately, and without a word to him rushed to her father's room, where, choking with wrath and excitement, she repeated the insulting words which had been used almost to her face by his favourite. Nikolai came in at her heels and would not let her finish her story. Feigning tears and crossing himself, he solemnly swore, that it was mere slander, that he had never said anything of the sort, and that it was wicked of Sofya Nikolaevna to ruin an innocent man! 'You hear what he says, Sonechka,' said the invalid in a peevish voice. This was too much for Sofya Nikolaevna: stung to the quick, she forgot her magnanimous self-restraint and forgot also that she might kill her father with fright. She raised her voice with such effect that the favourite was forced to leave the room. Then she said to her father: 'After this insult I cannot live under the same roof with Nikolai; you must choose which of us is to go, he or I!'—and then she rushed wildly from the room. The old man had a seizure, and Nikolai hastened to his aid. The usual remedies were applied with success and then master and man had a long conversation, after which Sofya Nikolaevna was summoned to the room. 'Sonechka,' he said, with all the firmness and calmness he could muster, 'my weak and suffering state makes it impossible for me to part with Nikolai; my life depends on him. You must buy another house; here is the money for the purpose.' Sofya Nikolaevna fell fainting to the ground and was carried back to her own room.

To this had come the tender tie of affection between parent and child, a tie which should surely have been made doubly strong by the temporary coolness due to the stepmother, and then by the father's penitence and the daughter's devotion and forgetfulness of all her wrongs. And then, when she married, she had chosen her husband with this in view, and had stipulated that she should not be parted from her father! And now they were to part at a time when the doctors declared he would not live another month! But in this forecast the doctors were mistaken, just as they often are nowadays: he lived on for more than a year.

When Sofya Nikolaevna recovered from her swoon and her

eyes fell on the pale anxious face of Alexei Stepanich, she realized that there was one creature on earth who loved her: she threw her arms round her husband, and floods of tears gave relief to her heart. She told him all that had passed between her and her father. The narrative revived the smart of her wounded feelings, and brought out more clearly the difficulty of her position; and she would have despaired, but for the support of her kind husband. Though weaker in character and less far-sighted than she was, he never ran into extremes and never lost presence of mind and power of judgement in the trying hours of life. It may seem strange that Alexei Stepanich could give moral support to Sofya Nikolaevna; but, for all her exceptional intelligence and apparent strength of will, the effect of a sudden shock to her feelings was to make her lose courage and become utterly bewildered. As an honest chronicler of oral tradition, I am bound to add that she was too sensitive to the opinion of society and paid it too much deference, in spite of her own superiority to the people among whom she lived. What would be said by people at Ufa, and especially by the ladies who took the lead in society there? What would be thought by her husband's family? What, above all, would be said by Stepan Mikhailovich when he heard that she had left her father? As she asked herself these questions, the injury to her pride gave her as much pain as the wound to her feelings as a daughter. To her it seemed equally terrible that her father should be blamed for ingratitude to his daughter, and that she should be blamed for failing in affection to a dying father. One or other alternative was bound to be chosen; and either he or she was bound to be condemned.

Alexei Stepanich felt deep pity for her as he watched these sufferings, and he felt puzzled also. It was no easy task to administer consolation to Sofya Nikolaevna: her eager fancy painted appalling pictures of disaster, and her ready tongue gave them lively expression. She was prepared to brush aside every attempt to find an issue from the situation, and to trample on every suggestion of a settlement. But Alexei Stepanich had love to teach him, and also that sanity and simplicity of mind which was wanting in his wife. He waited

till the first irrepressible outburst was over, the first outcry of
the wounded heart; and then he began to speak. The words
were very ordinary, but they came from a kind simple heart;
and if they did not calm Sofya Nikolaevna, they did at least
by degrees make it possible for her to understand what was
said. He told her that she had always done her duty as a
loving daughter, and that she must continue to do it by
falling in with her father's wishes. It was probably no sudden
decision: her father might have wished for a long time that
they should live apart. For a sick and dying man it was
difficult or even impossible to part from the regular attendant
who nursed him so faithfully. Stepan Mikhailovich must be
told the whole truth; but to acquaintances it would be enough
to say that her father had always intended to set up the young
couple in a house of their own during his lifetime. She would
be able to visit her father twice a day and attend to him
almost as much as before. Of course people in the town would
find out in time the real reason of the separation—they had
probably some idea already of the facts—but they would only
pity her and abuse Nikolai. 'Besides,' he added, 'though your
father talked like that, when it comes to acting, he may
shrink from the separation. Talk it over with him, and lay all
your case before him.' Sofya Nikolaevna made no reply:
during a long silence her eyes rested with a curious puzzled
gaze on her husband. The truth of his simple words and his
plain way of looking at things—these breathed peace and
comfort into her heart. His plan seemed to her new and
ingenious, and she wondered she had never thought of it
herself. She embraced her husband with a heart full of love
and gratitude.

So it was settled that Sofya Nikolaevna should appeal to her
father to alter his decision and let them stay on in the house,
at all events until she had entirely recovered from her confinement; their household arrangements would be quite separate,
and all collisions with Nikolai would be avoided. In favour
of this suggestion, there was one very pressing argument—that,
while it was bad for Sofya Nikolaevna in her present condition
to be jolted over the ill-paved streets of the town, no risk to

herself would prevent her from paying a daily visit to her father. But the explanation with her father was unsuccessful. The old man told her calmly but firmly that his decision had been carefully considered and was no impulse of the moment. 'My dear Sonechka,' he said, 'I knew beforehand that after your marriage you could not live under the same roof as Nikolai. You are not able to judge him coolly, and I don't blame you for it: he sinned deeply against you in old days, and though you forgave him, you were unable to forget his conduct. I know that he does not behave properly to you even now; but you take an exaggerated view of it all.' At this point Sofya Nikolaevna tried to break in, but he stopped her and said: 'Wait and hear to the end what I have to say. Let us suppose that he is as guilty as you take him to be: that makes it all the more impossible for you to live in the same house with him; but I cannot face parting from him. Have pity on my helpless and suffering condition. I am no longer a man, but a lifeless corpse; you know that Nikolai has to move me in bed ten times a day; no one can take his place. All I ask is peace of mind. Death is hovering over me, and every moment I must prepare for the change to eternity. I was constantly made wretched by the thought that Nikolai was giving offence to you. Our parting is inevitable; go, my dear, and live in a house of your own. When you come to visit me, you shall not see the object of your dislike: he will be only too glad to keep out of the way. He has gained his object and got you out of the house, and now he will be able to rob me at his leisure. I know and see it all, but I forgive him everything for his unwearied nursing of me day and night. What he undergoes in his attendance on me is beyond the power of human endurance. Do not distress me, but take the money and buy a house for yourselves.'

I shall not describe all the phases through which Sofya Nikolaevna passed—her doubts and hesitations, her mental conflicts, her tears and sufferings, her ups and downs of feeling from day to day. It is enough to say that the money was accepted and the house bought, and husband and wife were settled there before a fortnight had passed. The little house was new and clean, and had never been occupied before. Sofya Nikolaevna began with her usual ardour to put her house in order and to settle the course of their daily life; but her health, much affected by her condition, and still more by all the agitation she had gone through, soon broke down altogether. She was confined to bed for a fortnight and did not see her father for a whole month. Their first interview was a touching and pitiful sight. He had grown much weaker; missing his daughter and blaming himself for her illness, he had suffered much by her absence. Their meeting gave happiness to both, but it cost them tears. He was especially grieved to see her so terribly thin and so altered in looks; but this was due not so much to grief and illness as to her condition. The features of some women look different and even ugly during pregnancy; and Sofya Nikolaevna was a case in point. In course of time things settled down and her relations with her father became easy; Nikolai never ventured to appear when she was present. There was just one person who could not reconcile himself to the thought that she had left a dying father to settle in a house of her own; and that was Stepan Mikhail-ovich. She quite anticipated this, and wrote him a very frank letter just before she was taken ill, in which she tried to explain her father's action and defend it as far as possible. She might have saved herself the trouble, for Stepan Mikhail-ovich blamed her and not her father, and said that it was her duty to bear without a sign of displeasure all the misconduct of 'that scoundrel' Nikolai. He wrote to his son to reprove him for allowing his wife to abandon her father to the hands of servants. But Stepan Mikhailovich did not realize either that the separation was necessary to preserve the peace of a dying man, or that a wife could act without the permission of her husband. In the present case, however, husband and wife were entirely of one mind.

To put the finishing touches to the new house and modest household arrangements, Sofya Nikolaevna called in the assist-ance of a widow whom she knew, who lived in a humble position at Ufa. This was Mme Cheprunov, a very simple and kind-hearted creature. She owned a little house in the suburbs, and a small but productive garden, which brought her in a trifle. She had other means of maintaining herself and her adored only child, a little one-eyed boy called Andryusha: she hawked about small wares of different kinds, and even sold cakes in the market. But her chief source of income was the sale of Bokhara muslin, which she went to Orenburg every year to buy. Sofya Nikolaevna was related through her mother to this woman; but she had the weakness to conceal the relationship, though everyone in the town knew it. Mme Cheprunov was devoted to her brilliant and distinguished kinswoman. She used to pay secret visits to Sofya Nikolaevna during the time when she was persecuted and humiliated by her stepmother; and Sofya Nikolaevna, when her time of triumph and influence came, became the avowed benefactress of Mme Cheprunov. When they were alone together, Sofya Nikolaevna lavished caresses upon her unselfish and devoted kinswoman; but when other people were present, the one was the great lady and the other the poor protégée who sold cakes in the streets. This treatment did not offend Mme Cheprunov: on the contrary, she insisted on it. She loved and admired her beautiful cousin with all her heart, and looked on her as a superior being, and would never have forgiven herself if she had thrown a shadow on the brilliant position of Sofya Nikolaevna. The secret was revealed, as it had to be, to Alexei Stepanich; and he, in spite of the ancient lineage which his sisters were always dinning into his ears, received this humble friend as his wife's worthy kinswoman, and treated her with affection and respect all his life; he even tried to kiss the work-worn hand of the cake-seller, but she would never allow it. He was only prevented by his wife's earnest entreaties from speaking of this relationship in his own family and in the circle of their acquaintance. This conduct earned him the love of the simple-minded woman; and whenever there were differences in the household in later years, she was his ardent champion and defender. She knew all the shops and was a great hand at a bargain; and so, with her help, Sofya Nikolaevna did her furnishing quickly and well.

When the young Bagrovs bought a house and started housekeeping by themselves, there was much talk and gossip in the town; and at first many exaggerations and inventions were current. But Alexei Stepanich had spoken the truth: the real reason came out before long. This was due chiefly to Nikolai, who boasted among his friends that he had ousted the pettish young lady, and took the opportunity to give a lively description of her character. So the talk and gossip soon quieted down.

Husband and wife had at last a house entirely to themselves. In the morning, Alexei Stepanich drove down to his work at the law-courts, dropping his wife at her father's house; and on his return he spent some time every day with his father-in-law, before taking his wife home. A modest dinner awaited them there. To sit alone together, at a meal of their own ordering, in their own house, was a charming sensation for a time; but nothing is a novelty for long, and this charm could not last for ever. In spite of her bad health and small means, Sofya Nikolaevna's clever hands made her little house as dainty as a toy. Taste and care are a substitute for money; and many of their visitors thought the furnishing splendid. The hardest problem was to arrange about their servants. Sofya Nikolaevna had brought two servants as part of her portion—a man named Theodore and a black-eyed maid called Parasha; these two were now married to one another; and at the same time Annushka, a young laundress belonging to Sofya Nikolaevna, was married to Efrem Evseich, a young servant who had been brought from Bagrovo. This man was honest and good-natured and much attached to his young mistress, which cannot be said of the other servants. She returned his affection, and he well deserved it: he was one in a thousand, and his devotion to her was proved by his whole life.

Evseich (as he was always called in the family) became later the attendant of her eldest son,* and watched over him like a father. I knew this worthy man well. Fifteen years ago I saw him for the last time: he was then blind and spending his last days in the province of Penza on an estate belonging to one

* i.e. the author.

of the grandsons of Stepan Mikhailovich. I spent a whole month there in the summer; and every morning I went to fish in a pool where the stream of Kakarma falls into the river Niza. The cottage where Evseich was living stood right on the bank of this pool; and every day as I came up I saw him leaning against the angle of the cottage and facing the rising sun. He was bent and decrepit, and his hair had turned perfectly white; pressing a long staff to his breast, he leaned upon it with the knotted fingers of both hands, and turned his sightless eyes towards the sun's rays. Though he could not see the light, he could feel its warmth, so pleasant in the fresh morning air, and his face expressed both pleasure and sadness. His ear was so quick that he heard my step at some distance, and he always hailed me as an old fisherman might hail a schoolboy, though I was then myself over fifty years old. 'Ah, it's you, my little falcon!'—he used to call me this when I was a child—'you're late this morning! God send you a full basket!' He died two years later in the arms of his son and daughter and his wife, who survived him several years.

Meantime life at Ufa took a very regular and unvarying course. Owing to her state of health and spirits, Sofya Niko-laevna paid few visits and only to intimate friends, whose small number was made smaller by the absence of the Chichagovs. Autumn was nearly over before those dearest of friends returned from the country with Mme Mertvavo. The disordered nerves and consequent low spirits of his wife were at first a source of great uneasiness to Alexei Stepanich. He was completely puzzled: he had never in his life met people who were ill without anything definite the matter, or sad with no cause for sadness; he could make nothing of illness due to some inexplicable grief, or grief due to some imaginary or imper-ceptible illness. But he saw that there was no serious danger, and his anxiety calmed down by degrees. He was convinced that it was all the effect of imagination, which had always been his way of accounting for his wife's moods of excitement and distress, whenever he found it impossible to arrive at any reason within his comprehension. If he ceased to be uneasy, he began to be rather bored at times; and this was very natural, in spite of his love for his wife and pity for her constant suffering. To listen for whole hours every day to constant complaints about her condition, which was not after all so very exceptional: to hear gloomy presentiments, or even prophecies, of the fatal results which were sure to follow (and Sofya Nikolaevna, thanks to her reading of medical works, was extraordinarily ingenious in discovering ominous symptoms); to endure her reproaches and constant demands for those trifling services which a man can seldom render—all this was wearisome enough. Sofya Nikolaevna saw what he felt, and was deeply hurt. If she had found him in general incapable of deep feeling and strong passion, she would have reconciled herself sooner to her situation. She used often to say herself, 'A man cannot give you what he has not got'; and she would have recognized the truth of the saying and submitted to her fate. But the misfortune was that she remembered the depth and ardour of her husband's passion in the days of his courtship, and believed that he might have continued to love her in the same fashion, had not something occurred to cool his feelings. This unlucky notion by degrees took hold of her imagination, and her ingenuity soon discovered many reasons to account for this coolness and much evidence of its truth. As to reasons —there was the hostile influence of his family, her own ill-health, and, worst of all, her loss of beauty; for her looking-glass forced upon her the sad change in her appearance. Her proofs were these—that her husband was not disquieted by her danger, took insufficient notice of her condition, did not try to cheer and interest her, and, above all, found more pleasure in talking to other women. And then a passion, which hitherto had lurked unrecognized, the torturing passion of jealousy as keen-sighted as it is blind, flashed up like gunpowder in her heart. Every day there were scenes—tears and reproaches, quarrels and reconciliations. And all the time Alexei Stepanich was entirely innocent. To the insinuations of his sisters he paid no attention at all; to his father's opinion he attached great importance, and that was so favourable to Sofya Nikolaevna that she had even risen in her husband's eyes in consequence. He was sincerely, if not deeply, distressed about her sufferings; and her loss of beauty he regarded as temporary, and looked forward with pleasure to the time when his young wife would get back her good looks. Though the sight of her suffering distressed him, he could not sympathize with all her presentiments and prognostications, which he believed to be quite imaginary. He was incapable, as most men would be, of paying her the sort of attention she expected. It was really a ticklish business to administer consolation to Sofya Nikolaevna in her present condition: you were quite likely to put your foot in it and make matters worse; it required much tact and dexterity, and these were qualities which her husband did not possess. If he found more pleasure in talking to other women, it was probably because he was not afraid that some casual remark might cause annoyance and irritation.

But Sofya Nikolaevna could not look at the matter in this light. Her view of it was dictated by her nature, whose fine qualities were apt to run to extremes. But what was to be done, if the nerves of one were tough and strong and those of the other sensitive and morbid, if hers were jarred by what had no effect upon his? The Chichagovs alone understood the causes of this uncomfortable situation; and though they received no confidences from either husband or wife, they took a warm interest in both and did much to calm Sofya Nikolaevna's excitement by their friendship, their frequent visits, and their rational and sensible conversation. Both husband and wife owed much to them at this period.

So things went on till the time that Sofya Nikolaevna became a mother. Though she was often troubled in mind, her health improved during the last two months, and she was safely delivered of a daughter. She herself, and her husband still more, would have preferred a son; but when the mother pressed the child to her heart, she thought no more of any distinction between boy and girl. A passion of maternal love filled her heart and mind and whole being. Alexei Stepanich thanked God for his wife's safety, rejoiced at her relief, and soon reconciled himself to the fact that his child was a girl.

But at Bagrovo it was quite another story! Stepan Mikhailovich was so confident that he was to have a grandson to carry on the line of the Bagrovs, that he would not believe at first in the birth of a granddaughter. When at last he read through his son's letter with his own eyes and was convinced that there was no doubt about it, he was seriously annoyed. He put off the entertainment planned for his labourers, and refused to write himself to the parents; he would only send a message of congratulation to the young mother, with instructions that the infant was to be christened Praskovya, in compliment to his cousin and favourite, Praskovya Ivanovna Kurolesova. His vexation over this disappointment was a touching and amusing sight. Even his womenfolk derived a little secret enjoyment from it. His good sense told him that he had no business to be angry with anyone, but for a few days he could not control his feelings—so hard was it for him to give up the hope, or rather the certainty, that a grandson would be born, to continue the famous line of Shimon. In the expectation of the happy news, he had kept his family tree on his bed, ready any day to enter his grandson's name; but now he ordered this document to be hidden out of sight. He would not allow his daughter Aksinya to travel to Ufa in order to stand godmother to the babe; he said impatiently, 'Take that journey for a girl's christening? Nonsense! If she brings a girl every year, you would have travelling enough!' Time did its work, however, and the frown, never a formidable frown this time, vanished from the brow of Stepan Mikhailovich, as he consoled himself with the thought that he might have a grandson before a year was out. Then he wrote a kind and playful letter to his daughter-in-law, pretending to scold her for her mistake and bidding her present him with a grandson within a twelve-month.

Sofya Nikolaevna was so entirely absorbed by the revelation of maternity and by devotion to her child, that she did not even notice the signs of the old man's displeasure, and was quite unaffected by Aksinya's absence from the christening. It proved difficult to keep her in bed for nine days after her confinement. She felt so well and strong that she could have danced on the fourth day. But she had no wish to dance; she wanted to be on her feet day and night, attending to her little

Parasha. The infant was feeble and sickly; the mother's constant distress of body and mind had probably affected the child. The doctor would not allow her to nurse the child herself. Andrei Avenarius was the name of this doctor; he was a very clever, cultivated, and amiable man, an intimate friend of the young people and a daily visitor at their house. As soon as possible Sofya Nikolaevna took her baby to her father's house, hoping that it would please the invalid to see this mite, and that he would find in it a resemblance to his first wife. This resemblance was probably imaginary; for in my opinion it is impossible for an infant to be like a grown-up person; but Sofya Nikolaevna never failed to assert that her first child was the very image of its grandmother. Old M. Zubin was approaching the end of his earthly career; both body and mind were breaking fast. He looked at the baby with little interest, and had hardly strength to sign it with the cross. All he said was, 'I congratulate you, Sonechka.' Sofya Nikolaevna was distressed by her father's critical condition—it was more than a month since she had seen him—and also by his indifference to her little angel, Parasha.

But soon the young mother forgot all the world around her, as she hung over her daughter's cradle. All other interests and attachments grew pale in comparison, and she surrendered herself with a kind of frenzy to this new sensation. No hands but hers might touch the child. She handed it herself to the foster-mother and held it at the breast, and it was pain to her to watch it drawing life not from its mother but from a stranger. It is hard to believe, but it is true, and Sofya Nikolaevna admitted it herself later, that if the child sucked too long, she used to take it away before it was satisfied, and rock it herself in her arms or in the cradle, and sing it to sleep. She saw nothing of her friends, not even of her dear Mme Chichagov. Naturally they all thought her eccentric or absurd, and her chief intimates were vexed by her conduct. She paid a hasty visit every day to her father, and returned every day with fear in her heart that she would find the child ill. She left her husband perfectly free to spend his time as he liked. For some days he stopped at home; but his wife never stirred from the cradle and took no notice of him except to turn him out of the little nursery, because she feared that twice-breathed air might hurt the baby. After this, he began to go out alone; till at last he went to some party every day; and he began to play cards to relieve his boredom. The Ufa ladies were amused at the sight of the deserted husband, and some of them flirted with him, saying that it was a charity to console the widower, and that Sofya Nikolaevna would thank them for it when she recovered from her maternal passion and reappeared in society. Sofya Nikolaevna did not hear of these good Samaritans till later; when she did, she was vexed. Mme Cheprunov, who came often to the house, watched Sofya Nikolaevna with astonishment, pity, and displeasure. She was a tender mother herself to her little boy with the one eye, but this devotion to one object and disregard of everything else seemed to her to border on insanity. With groans and sighs she struck her fists against her own body—this was a regular trick of hers—and said that such love was a mortal sin which God would punish. Sofya Nikolaevna resented this so much that she kept Mme Cheprunov out of the nursery in future. No one but Dr Avenarius was admitted there, and he came pretty often. The mother was constantly discovering symptoms of different diseases in the child; for these she began by consulting Buchan's *Domestic Medicine*, and then, when that did not answer, she called in Avenarius. He found it impossible to argue her out of her beliefs: all he could do was to prescribe harmless medicines. Yet the child was really feeble, and at times he was obliged to prescribe for it in real earnest.

It is difficult to say what would have been the upshot of all this; but by the inscrutable designs of Providence, a thunderbolt burst over the head of Sofya Nikolaevna: her adored child died suddenly. The cause of death was uncertain: it may have been too much care, or too much medicine, or too feeble a constitution; at any rate, the child succumbed, when four months old, to a very slight attack of a common childish ailment. Sofya Nikolaevna was sitting by the cradle when she saw the infant start and a spasm pass over the little face: she caught it up and found that it was dead.

She must have had a marvellous constitution to support this blow. For some days she knew no one and the doctors feared for her reason; there were three of them, Avenarius, Zanden, and Klauss; all three were much attached to their patient, and one of them was always with her. But, by God's blessing and thanks to her youth and strength, that terrible time passed by. The unhappy mother recovered her senses; and her love for her husband, whose own distress was great, asserted itself for the time and saved her. On the fourth day she became conscious of her surroundings: she recognized Alexei Stepanich, so changed by grief that he was hard to recognize, and her bosom friend, Mme Chichagov; a terrible cry burst from her lips, and a healing flood of tears gushed from the eyes which had been dry till then. Silently she embraced her husband and sobbed for long on his breast, while he sobbed like a child himself. The danger of insanity was past, but the exhaustion of her bodily strength was still alarming. For four days and nights she had neither eaten nor drunk, and now she could swallow no food nor medicine nor even water. Her condition was so critical that the doctors did not oppose her wish to make her confession and receive the sacraments. The performance of this Christian duty was beneficial to the patient: she slept for the first time, and, when she woke after two hours looking bright and happy, she told her husband that she had seen in her sleep a vision of Our Lady of Iberia, exactly as she was represented on the ikon of their parish church; and she believed, that if she could put her lips to this ikon, the Mother of God would surely have mercy on her. The picture was brought from the church, and the priest read the service for the Visitation of the Sick. When the choir sang, 'O mighty Mother of God, look down in mercy on my sore bodily suffering!'—all present fell on their knees and repeated the words of the prayer. Alexei Stepanich sobbed aloud; and the sufferer too shed tears throughout the service and pressed her lips to the image. When it was over, she felt so much relief that she was able to drink some water; and from that time she began to take food and medicine. Her two dear friends, Mme Chichagov and Mme Cheprunov, were with her constantly; she was soon pronounced out of danger, and her husband's troubled heart had rest. The doctors set to work with fresh zeal to restore her strength, and their great anxiety was in a way dangerous to their patient; for one of them found traces of consumption, another of marasmus, and the third was apprehensive of an aneurysm. But fortunately they were unanimous on one point: the patient should go at once to the country, to enjoy pure air and, preferably, forest air, and take a course of kumiss. At the beginning of June it was not too late to drink mare's milk, as the grass on the steppes was still fresh and in full growth.

Stepan Mikhailovich took the news of his granddaughter's death very coolly: he even said, 'No reason to tear one's hair over *that*! There will be plenty more girls.' But when he heard later of the dangerous illness of Sofya Nikolaevna, the old man was much disturbed. When a third message came, that she was out of immediate danger but very ill, and that the doctors were baffled and prescribed a course of kumiss, he was exceedingly angry with the doctors: 'Those bunglers who murder our bodies', said he, 'defile our souls also by making us swallow the drink of heathens. If a Russian is forbidden by his Church to eat horseflesh, then he has no business to drink the milk of the unclean animal.' Then he added with a heavy sigh and a gesture of disgust: 'I don't like it at all: her life may perhaps be saved, but she will never be right again, and there will be no children.' Stepan Mikhailovich was deeply grieved and remained for a long time in a state of depression.

Twenty-nine versts to the south-west of Ufa, on the road to Kazan where the Ufa falls into that noble river, the Dema, there lay in a rich valley a little Tartar village called by the Russians Alkino, surrounded by forests. The houses nestled in picturesque disorder at the foot of a hill called Bairam-Tau* which gave them shelter from the north; and another hill, Zein-Tau,† rose on the west. The little river Uza, fringed with bushes, flowed to the south-west; the forest glades were fragrant with grasses and flowers; and all round, oaks and limes and maples cleft the air and imparted to it an invigorating

* Hill of Feasting.   † Hill of Meeting.

virtue. To this charming spot Alexei Stepanich brought his wife, weak and pale and thin, a mere shadow of her old self; Avenarius, their friend and doctor, came with them, and they had some difficulty in getting the patient to the end of the journey. The owner of the village received them with cordial hospitality; he had a comfortable house, but Sofya Nikolaevna was unwilling to install herself there, and one of the out-buildings was cleared out for her occupation. The family were only too kind in their attentions to her, so that the doctor was obliged to forbid their visits for a time. They spoke Russian fairly well, though they professed the Mohammedan creed; and, though their dress and habits were then partly Russian and partly Tartar, kumiss was their invariable drink from morning till night. For Sofya Nikolaevna the health-giving beverage was prepared in a cleanly civilized manner; the mare's milk was fermented in a clean new wooden bucket and not in the usual bag of raw horse-hide. The natives declared that kumiss made in their fashion tasted better and was more effective; but Sofya Nikolaevna felt an unconquerable aversion to the horse-hide bag. When the doctor had laid down rules for the cure, he went back to Ufa, leaving Alexei Stepanich with Parasha and Annushka in charge of the invalid. The air and the kumiss, of which small doses were taken at first; the daily drives with Alexei Stepanich through the forest which sur-rounded the village—Evseich, who was now a favourite with Sofya Nikolaevna, acted as coachman; the woods, where the patient lay for whole hours in the cool shade on a leather mattress with pillows, breathing the fragrant air into her lungs, listening sometimes to an entertaining book, and often sinking into refreshing sleep—the whole life was so beneficial to Sofya Nikolaevna that in a fortnight she was able to get up and could walk about. When Avenarius came again, he was de-lighted by the effect of the kumiss, and increased the doses, but as the patient could not endure it in large quantities, he thought it necessary to prescribe vigorous exercise in the form of riding on horseback. For a Russian lady to ride was in those days a startling novelty: Alexei Stepanich did not like it, and Sofya Nikolaevna herself was shocked by the notion. Their host's daughters presented an instructive example, for they constantly rode far and wide over the country on their Bashkir ponies; but Sofya Nikolaevna for long turned a deaf ear to all persuasions, and even to the entreaties of her husband, whom the doctor had speedily and completely convinced of the necessity of the exercise. At last the Chichagovs came on a visit to Alkino, and Sofya Nikolaevna's resistance was overcome by a joint effort. What appealed to her most strongly was the example of Mme Chichagov, who, in the spirit of true friendship, sacrificed her own prejudices and began to ride, at first alone, and then with the patient. This hard exercise required a change of diet; and fat mutton, which Sofya Nikolaevna did not like either, was prescribed. Avenarius probably took a hint from the habits of the Bashkirs and Tartars, who, while moving from place to place throughout the summer, drink kumiss and eat hardly anything but fat mutton, not even bread; and they ride all day long over the broad steppes, until the prairie grass turns from green to grey and veils itself with a soft silvery down. The treatment answered admirably. They sometimes rode out in a large party with the sons and daughters of their host. There was a potash factory which they sometimes visited, about two versts from Alkino, situated in the depth of the forest and on the bank of a stream; and Sofya Nikolaevna looked with interest at the iron cauldrons full of burning wood-ash, the wooden troughs in which the dross was deposited, and the furnaces in which the product was refined and converted into porous white lumps of the vegetable salt called 'potash'. She admired the dexterity with which the work was carried on, and the activity of the Tartars; their skull-caps were a novelty to her, and also the long shirts which came down to their feet and yet left them free command of their limbs. In general her hosts were very kind, and tried to amuse their guest by making the natives sing and dance before her, or wrestle, or run races on horseback.

At first Alexei Stepanich was always present at these expeditions and entertainments; but when he ceased to feel anxious about his wife's health and saw her surrounded by troops of attentive friends, he began by degrees to find some time on his hands. Country life and country air, with the beauty of that landscape, roused in him a desire for his old amusements. He made fishing-lines and began to angle for the wily trout in the clear mountain streams round Alkino; and he went out sometimes to catch quails with a net. Theodore, Parasha's young husband, was a capital hand at this sport and could make pipes to decoy the birds. With sportsmen in general, netting for quails does not rank high; but really I do not know why they despise it. To lie on the fragrant meadow grass with your net hanging in front of you on the tall stalks; to hear the quails calling beside you and at a distance; to imitate their low sweet note on the pipe; to hear the excited birds reply and watch them run, or even fly, from all sides towards you; to watch their curious antics, and to get excited yourself over the success or failure of your strategy—all this gave me much pleasure at one time, and even now I cannot recall it with indifference. But it was impossible to make this pleasure intelligible to Sofya Nikolaevna.

In two months she was well on the way to recovery: her face filled out, and a bright colour began to play again upon her cheeks. When Avenarius paid a third visit, he was entirely satisfied; and he had a perfect right to triumph; for he had been the first to prescribe kumiss and had directed the treatment himself. He had always been attached to his patient; and now that he had succeeded in saving her life, he loved her like a daughter.

Alexei Stepanich sent a weekly bulletin to his father at Bagrovo. Stepan Mikhailovich was glad to hear that his daughter-in-law was getting better; but of course he disbelieved in the healing power of the kumiss, and was very angry about the riding, which they were rash enough to mention in writing to him. His wife and daughters made use of this opportunity, and the sneering remarks which they let fall on purpose in the course of conversation, worked him up to such a pitch that he wrote his son a rather offensive letter which gave pain to Sofya Nikolaevna. But when he was convinced that his daughter-in-law had quite recovered and had even grown stout, pleasing hopes began to stir again in his breast, and he grew reconciled in some degree to the kumiss and the riding.

The young Bagrovs returned to Ufa at the beginning of autumn. Old M. Zubin was very far gone by that time, and his daughter's wonderful recovery produced no sort of impression on him. All his earthly business was done, and all ties broken: every thread that held him to life was severed, and the soul could hardly find shelter in the disruption of the body.

The normal course of relations between the young couple had been, so to speak, arrested in its development by a number of events: first, by the birth of the child and the mother's extravagant devotion to it; then, by the child's death which nearly deprived the mother of her reason and her life; and, finally, by the long course of treatment and residence in the Tartar village. In the stormy season of her distress and sickness, Sofya Nikolaevna had ever before her eyes the genuine love and self-sacrifice of her husband. At that time there were none of those collisions which constantly occur at ordinary times between ill-matched characters; and even if there were occasions for such misunderstandings, they passed unnoticed. When gold is in circulation, small change is of little importance. In exceptional circumstances and critical moments, nothing but gold passes; but the daily expenditure of uneventful life is mainly carried on with small change. Now Alexei Stepanich, though he was not poor in gold, was often hard up for small change. When a man, if he sees distress and danger threatening the health and life of one whom he loves, himself suffers in every fibre of his being; when he forgets sleep and food and himself altogether; when the nerves are strung up and the moral nature uplifted—at such times there is no room for small exactions, no room for small services and attentions. But when the time of tragic events has gone by, everything quiets down again; the nerves are relaxed and the spirit contracts; the material life of flesh and blood asserts itself, in all its triviality; habits resume their lost power; and then comes the turn of those exactions and demands we spoke of, the turn of small services and polite attentions and all the other trifles which make up the web of actual ordinary life. Time will again apply the test and bring back the necessity of self-sacrifice; but meanwhile life runs on without a stop in the ordinary groove, and its peace and adornment and pleasure—what we call happiness, in fact—is made up entirely of trivial things, of small change.

For these reasons, when Sofya Nikolaevna began to recover and Alexei Stepanich ceased to fear for her life and health, there began by degrees to reappear, on one side, the old exacting temper, and on the other side, the old incapacity to satisfy its demands. Gentle reproaches and expostulations had become tiresome to the husband, and fierce explosions frightened him. Fear at once banished perfect frankness, and loss of frankness between husband and wife, especially in the less assertive and independent of the two, leads straight to the destruction of domestic happiness. After the return to Ufa, this evil would probably have grown worse in the trivial idle atmosphere of town life; but Sofya Nikolaevna's father was now actually dying, and his sad suffering condition banished all other anxieties and took up all his daughter's thoughts and feelings. Obedient to the law of her moral nature, she gave herself up without reserves to her duty as a daughter. Thus the process which was unveiling every corner of their domestic life, was again brought to a standstill. Sofya Nikolaevna spent her days and nights with her father. Nikolai, as before, waited on his sick master, nursing him with wonderful devotion and indefatigable care; and, as before, he kept out of sight of Sofya Nikolaevna, though he had now the right and the power to appear before her with impunity. Touched by his behaviour, she had sent for him; a reconciliation took place, and she gave him leave to be present with her in the sick-room. The dying man, in spite of his apparent insensibility to all around him, noticed this change: he pressed his daughter's hand in his feeble grasp, and said in a hardly audible whisper, 'I thank you.' Sofya Nikolaevna never left her father after this time.

I said that when Stepan Mikhailovich received the good news of his daughter-in-law's recovery, fond hopes awoke once more in his breast. They were not disappointed: before long

Sofya Nikolaevna wrote to him herself, that she hoped, if God was good to her, to give birth to a son, to be the comfort of his old age. At the instant Stepan Mikhailovich was overjoyed, but he soon controlled his feelings and hid his happiness from his womenfolk. Perhaps it occurred to him that this second child might be a daughter, that Sofya Nikolaevna and the doctors between them might kill it also with too much love and too much medicine, and that the mother might lose her health over again; or perhaps Stepan Mikhailovich was like many other people, who deliberately prophesy calamities with a secret hope that fortune will belie their prognostications. He pretended that he was not in the least glad, and said coolly: 'No, no! I'm too old a bird to look at *that* chaff. When the thing happens it will be time enough to believe it and rejoice over it.' His family were surprised to hear him speak so, and said nothing in reply. But, as a matter of fact, the old man for some unknown reason became convinced once more in his heart that he would have a grandson: he gave instructions again to Father Vasili to repeat in church the prayer for 'women labouring of child'; and he fished out the family tree once more from its hiding-place, and kept it always beside him.

Meanwhile M. Zubin's last hour on earth came quietly on. He had suffered much for many years; it seemed hardly natural that life should linger on in a body which had lost all force and motion; and the ending of such a bare and pitiful existence could distress no one. Even Sofya Nikolaevna had only one prayer—that her father's soul might depart in peace. And there *was* peace, and even happiness at the moment of death. The face of the dying man lit up suddenly, and this expression remained long upon the features, though the eyes were shut and the body had grown cold. The funeral was a solemn and splendid ceremony. M. Zubin had once been very popular; but he had become forgotten by degrees, and sympathy for his suffering had grown gradually weaker. But now, when the news of his death flew round the town, old memories revived and evoked a fresh feeling of love and pity for him. On the day of his funeral every house was empty, and all the population of Ufa lined the streets between the Church of the

Assumption and the cemetery. May he rest in peace! If he had the weakness of human nature, he had also its goodness.

After M. Zubin's death, guardians were appointed for the children of his two marriages; and Alexei Stepanich became guardian of his wife's two brothers, who, before finishing their education at the Moscow boarding-school, were summoned to Petersburg to enter the Guards. I forgot to mention that M. Zubin, shortly before his death, was successful in obtaining for Alexei Stepanich his promotion to a higher office at the law-courts.

Sofya Nikolaevna wept and prayed for a long time, and Alexei Stepanich wept and prayed at her side; but those tears and prayers were not painful or violent and had no ill effect on her recently restored health. Her husband's entreaties and the advice of her friends and doctors prevailed with her, and she began to take care of herself and to pay due attention to her condition. They convinced her that the health and even the life of the unborn child depended on the state of her own health and spirits. Their arguments were confirmed by bitter experience, and she resolutely submitted to all that was required of her. When her father-in-law wrote to her and expressed in simple words his sympathy with her loss and his fear that she might again injure her own health by excess of grief, she sent a very reassuring letter in reply; and she did in fact attend carefully to her bodily health and composure of mind. A regular but not monotonous plan of life was laid down. The two doctors, Klauss—who was becoming very intimate with the Bagrovs—and Avenarius, made her go out every day before dinner, and sometimes on foot; and each evening they had an unceremonious party of pleasant people at home, or went out themselves, generally to the Chichagovs' house. Mme Chichagov's brothers became great friends of the Bagrovs, especially the younger, Dmitri, who asked that when the time came he might stand godfather. Both brothers were well-bred men, and well educated according to the standards of the time; and they came often to the house and passed the time there with pleasure. In the Bagrovs' house, reading aloud was a favourite occupation. But, as no one can read or listen to reading without intervals, Sofya Nikolaevna was taught to play cards. Klauss took the chief part in initiating her into this science; and whenever the Bagrovs were alone of an evening, he never failed to make up their table. Avenarius could not take part in this pastime, because he never in his life knew the difference between the five and the ace.

Spring set in early that year, but in all its beauty. The ice on the Belaya broke up, and the blocks were carried down by the stream; the river broke its banks and spread till it was six versts across. The whole of this expanse could be clearly seen from the windows of the Bagrovs' little house; their orchard burst into leaf and flower, and the fragrance of bird-cherries and apple-blossom filled the air. They used this orchard as a drawing-room, and the warm weather did good to Sofya Nikolaevna and made her stronger.

At this time an event happened at Ufa which caused a great sensation there and was especially interesting to the young Bagrovs, because the hero of the story was an intimate friend of theirs, and, if I am not mistaken, distantly related to Alexei Stepanich. Sofya Nikolaevna, as one would expect from her character, took a lively interest in such a romantic affair. A young man, named Timashev, one of the most prominent and richest nobles of the district, fell in love with a Tartar girl, the daughter of a rich Tartar landowner. Her family, just like the Alkins, had altered their way of living to a certain extent in conformity with European customs, and they spoke Russian well; but they strictly observed the Muslim faith in all its purity. The beautiful Salmé returned the love of the handsome Russian officer, who was a captain in the regiment stationed near Ufa. As she could not be married to a Russian without changing her religion, it was perfectly certain that her parents and grown-up brothers would never give their consent to such a union. Salmé struggled long against her love, and love burns more fiercely in the hearts of women of Asia. At last, as is the rule in such cases, Mohammed was defeated, and Salmé made up her mind to elope with her lover, meaning to be baptized first and then married. The commander of Timashev's regiment was General Mansurov, a universal favourite

and the kindest of men, who gained distinction afterwards
when he crossed 'The Devil's Bridge' in the Alps with
Suvorov. He had lately married for love himself, and he knew
and sympathized with Timashev's enterprise, and promised to
take the lovers under his protection. One dark rainy night
Salmé sallied forth from her father's house, and found Timashev
waiting for her in a wood close by with a pair of saddle-horses;
they had to gallop about 100 versts to reach Ufa. Salmé was
a skilful rider; every ten or fifteen versts they found fresh
horses, guarded by soldiers of Timashev's regiment; he was
very popular with his men. Thus the fugitives flew along 'on
the wings of love', as a poet of that day would infallibly have
said. Meanwhile Salmé's absence was quickly noticed; her
passion for Timashev had long been suspected, and a strict
watch was kept over her movements. A band of armed Tartars
assembled instantly, and followed the enraged father* and
brothers in furious pursuit of the lovers, uttering fierce shouts
and threats of vengeance. They took the right track and would
probably have captured the fugitives—at any rate blood would
have been spilt, because a number of soldiers, eagerly interested
in the affair, were posted at different points along the road—
had not the pursuit been delayed by a stratagem. The bridge
over a deep and dangerous river was broken down behind the
lovers; and the Tartars were forced to swim across, and thus
lost some two hours. Even so, the boat which carried Timashev
and Salmé across the Belaya under the walls of Ufa had hardly
reached mid-stream, when the old Tartar galloped up to the
bank, attended by his sons and half of his faithful company;
the other half had stopped when their horses fell dead under
them. A whole regiment of Russian soldiers were in possession
of all the punts and ferry-boats, on the pretence of crossing
to the town. The unhappy father gnashed his teeth in fury,
cursed his daughter, and rode off home. Half dead with weariness and fear, Salmé was placed in a carriage and taken to the
house of Timashev's mother. The affair now assumed a legal
and official character: here was a Mohammedan woman asking

* Another version of the story tells that the mother led the pursuit
(*author's note*).

of her own free will to be received into the Christian Church, and the authorities of the town took her under their protection, informed the *mufti*, who lived at Ufa and was always called 'the Tartar bishop', of all that had passed, and called upon him to stop the injured family or any other Mohammedans from all attempts to recover by violence a person who had deliberately preferred the Christian faith. In a few days the clergy prepared the convert to receive the sacraments of baptism and unction. The rite was celebrated with great pomp in the cathedral: Salmé was christened Seraphima, and immediately afterwards, without leaving the church, the young lovers were married. All Ufa was interested in the affair. The young people and all the men naturally stood up for the beautiful Salmé; but the women, some of whom, perhaps, had personal reasons for disappointment, judged her conduct severely. Very few stretched out the hand of sincere friendship to the convert, whom her husband's station admitted to the inner circle of Ufa society. The young couple had no warmer sympathizers than Sofya Nikolaevna and Alexei Stepanich; and they were actively assisted by the wife of General Mansurov, an amiable young woman whose maiden name was Bulgakov. Before long the Timashevs had a firm footing in their new sphere. The bride's education was taken in hand; she had much natural ability, and soon became a success in society, where she aroused both sympathy and envy, due in some degree to her beauty and the peculiarity of her position. Sofya Nikolaevna kept up a steady friendship with Seraphima Timashev till death divided them. To the general regret, Mme Timashev died of consumption three years after her marriage; she left two sons. Her husband nearly went out of his mind with grief; he left the army, gave up his life to the care of his children, and never married again. It was currently reported, though I cannot vouch for the truth of the reports, that her illness and death were due to secret pining after the kinsfolk she had abandoned and remorse for her change of religion.

These events did nothing to arrest the quick flight of time. The day came when Sofya Nikolaevna was forbidden to go out to parties, or even to take drives in the country. In fine weather she walked up and down the garden for half an hour twice a day; if it was wet, she opened all the doors in the house and followed the same routine under cover. It is probable that all this seclusion and strict regimen did more harm than good; yet my opinion is contradicted by the facts, for Sofya Nikolaevna kept in perfect health. Alexei Stepanich found it necessary to let the doctors have their way; for he was constantly receiving instructions from his father to watch over his wife like the apple of his eye. Her friends also and especially the doctors who felt a strong personal attachment to her, kept such a close watch on Sofya Nikolaevna that she could neither take a step nor swallow a morsel or drink a drop without their permission. As Avenarius had to leave the town on some official business, it fell to Klauss, who was the other leading lady's doctor at Ufa, to undertake the personal supervision of her health. Klauss was a German, a very kind man, clever and well educated, but singularly grotesque in his appearance. Though he was still of middle age, he wore a bright yellow wig; and people asked where he could have got human hair of a colour never beheld on any human head; his eyebrows also were yellowish, and so were the whites of his small brown eyes; but his face, which was round and rather small, was as red as burning coal. His habits in society were very odd: though he liked kissing the hands of ladies, he would never allow himself to be kissed on the cheek, maintaining that it was a gross breach of manners on the part of a man to permit such a greeting. He had a great fondness for small children, which he showed in this way: he took the child on his knees, placed its hand on the palm of his own left hand and stroked it for hours at a time with his right hand. His special favourites he constantly addressed as 'Monster!' or 'Turk!'—and Sofya Nikolaevna naturally came in for her share of these endearments.*

Owing to his intimacy with the young Bagrovs, Klauss

* Klauss became lecturer on midwifery in the Foundling Hospital at Moscow in 1791, and died in 1821 after the conscientious discharge of his duties for thirty years. He never left off the yellow wig. He was an enthusiastic and well-known numismatist (*author's note*).

knew all about Stepan Mikhailovich—his eager desire for a grandson, and the impatience with which he was awaiting the event. As Klauss wrote Russian well, he wrote out a forecast, for whose accuracy he vouched, in a distinct handwriting for the old man's benefit; he foretold that Sofya Nikolaevna would give birth to a son between the 15th and 22nd of September. When the forecast was sent to Stepan Mikhailovich, 'German liar!' was his only comment; but in his heart he believed it; for his excitement and joy could be seen in his face and heard in every word he spoke. About this time, our old acquaintance Afrosinya Andreevna paid him a visit at Bagrovo. He let her see more than others of his main anxiety lest he might have another granddaughter; and she told him, that when passing through Moscow she had gone to Trinity Church there, to say her prayers to St Sergius; and there she heard that some well-known lady, the mother of several daughters, had taken a vow that if her next child was a boy, it should be christened Sergei; and she did give birth to a son before the year was out. Stepan Mikhailovich said nothing at the time; but he wrote a letter himself to his son and daughter-in-law by the next post, expressing his desire that they should say prayers in church to St Sergius the wonder-worker, and take a vow to call their child Sergei if it were a boy. In explanation of his wish he added: 'There has never yet been a Sergei in the Bagrov family.' These instructions were carried out to the letter. Sofya Nikolaevna spared no pains to provide everything that a careful mother could think for her expected child; above all, an admirable foster-mother was found at Kasimofka, one of the villages that had belonged to her father. Marya Vasilevna, a peasant woman, had every qualification for her office that one could wish for; and she was perfectly willing to undertake the duty, and moved to Ufa in good time, bringing her own infant with her.

The crisis was now approaching. By this time Sofya Nikolaevna was forbidden to walk. Catherine Chichagov was kept to her own house by ill-health and no other visitors were admitted. But Mme Cheprunov was constantly with her cousin, never leaving her except to see her own beloved little boy,

Andrusha. Klauss came to breakfast every morning, and again for tea, which he drank with rum in it, in the evening; then he played cards with husband and wife; and as the stakes were too small to buy cards with, the thrifty German procured some used packs which he brought with him. Reading sometimes took the place of cards, and Klauss was present on these occasions. Alexei Stepanich, who had gained some experience and skill in the art, was the regular reader; and sometimes Klauss brought a German book and translated it aloud, which gave pleasure to his hearers, especially to Sofya Nikolaevna, who wished to get some knowledge, if only a smattering, of German literature.

Sofya Nikolaevna had experienced already the absorbing and unlimited power of maternal affection, the strongest of all human feelings, and she was filled with awe by her present condition. She accepted it as a sacred duty to preserve mental composure, and so to ensure the health of her unborn infant and secure its existence, on which depended all her hopes, all her future, and all her life. We know Sofya Nikolaevna pretty well already; we know how apt she was to be carried away; and therefore we shall not be surprised to hear that she gave herself up wholly to her feeling for the child she bore. Every hour of the day and night was devoted to the task of taking care of herself in all possible ways. Her mind and her thoughts were so entirely concentrated upon this one object that she noticed nothing else and was, apparently, quite satisfied with her husband, though it is probable that things happened which might have made her dissatisfied. The more Alexei Stepanich got to know his wife, the more she surprised him. He was a man singularly unable to appreciate excessive display of feeling, or to sympathize with it, from whatever cause it arose. Thus his wife's power of passionate devotion frightened him; he dreaded it, just as he used to dread his father's furious fits of anger. Excessive feeling always produces an unpleasant impression upon quiet unemotional people: they cannot recognize such a state of mind to be natural, and regard it as a kind of morbid condition to which some persons are liable at times. They disbelieve in the permanence of a mental composure which may break down at any moment; and they are afraid of people with such a temperament. And fear is fatal to love, even to a child's love for his parents. In general I must say, that in point of mutual understanding and sympathy, the relations between Alexei Stepanich and his wife, instead of becoming closer, as might have been expected, grew less intimate. This may seem strange, but it often happens thus in life.

Just at this time Klauss was transferred to an official post at Moscow. He had already taken leave of his colleagues and all his acquaintance; and he waited on solely with a view to Sofya Nikolaevna's confinement, hoping to be of service to her in case of necessity. He calculated that he might be able to get away on the 17th or 18th of September, and hired horses for that date. Hiring was necessary, because he intended to break his journey to visit a German friend, who lived at some distance from the post-road, so that the coach would not serve his purpose. The 15th of September passed, but the expected event did not take place. Sofya Nikolaevna felt better and more enterprising than usual; and it was only the pedantry of the doctor, she said, that kept her to the sofa. When the 16th, 17th, and 18th had all gone by, the German, in spite of his love for Sofya Nikolaevna, got very angry, because he had to pay a rouble a day to the driver he had hired—a terribly high price, according to the ideas of those days; and the Bagrovs bantered him about this in a friendly way. The reading and card-playing went on every evening; and if the doctor won sixty kopecks from his hosts, he was much pleased, and said that his driver would not cost him much *that* day. The 19th passed off with no change. On the 20th, when Klauss came in the morning, Sofya Nikolaevna stood at her bedroom door and greeted him with a curtsey. He got very angry: 'Monster!' he said, 'you are treating me abominably'; but he kissed as usual the hand she held out to him. 'It is too bad, Alexei Stepanich,' he went on; 'your wife is ruining me. Her baby ought to have been born on the 15th, and here she is, dropping curtseys on the 20th!' 'Never mind, my dear fellow,' said Alexei Stepanich, patting him on the shoulder; 'you must rob us at cards tonight. But the packs are nearly worn out.'

Klauss promised to bring a new pack; he lunched there, and after sitting on till two o'clock, took his leave. He called again at six in the evening, punctual to the minute. Finding no one in the hall or parlour or drawing-room, he tried to get into the bedroom, but the door was locked; he knocked, and it was opened by Mme Cheprunov. The doctor went in and stood dumb with astonishment. The floor of the room was covered with rugs; green silk curtains hung by the windows, and a fine silk canopy over the double bed; a candle, shaded by a book, was burning in a corner; and in the bed, resting on embroidered pillows and wearing a dainty easy morning wrapper, lay Sofya Nikolaevna. Her face looked fresh, and her eyes were radiant with happiness. 'Congratulate me, my dear friend!' she said in a strong audible voice; 'I am the happy mother of a son!' The doctor, when he looked at her face and heard her voice, took the whole thing to be a mystification and a hoax. 'Monster! don't try to play tricks on so old a bird as I am!' he said. 'Better get up; I have brought a new pack of cards. It will be a present for the baby,' he added, coming up to the bed and shoving the cards under a pillow. 'My dear friend,' said Sofya Nikolaevna, 'I swear to you I have got a son! Look at him; there he is!' And there, resting on a large down pillow trimmed with lace, and wrapped in a pink velvet coverlet, he really saw a newborn infant, a strong boy; and Alena Maksimovna, the midwife, was standing near the bed.

The doctor flew into a furious rage. He sprang back from the bed as if he had burnt himself, and roared out, 'What! in my absence! after my staying on here for a week and losing money every day, you did not send for me!' His face turned from red to purple, his wig came half off, and his whole stumpy figure looked so ridiculous that the lady in the bed burst out laughing. Then the midwife tried to soothe him: '*Batyushka*,' she said, 'when God's gift came, we had no time to think of anything; when we had got things straight, we meant to send for your Honour, but Sofya Nikolaevna said you would be here at once.' The worthy man soon recovered from his vexation; tears of joy started to his eyes; he caught hold of the infant in his practised hands and began to examine it by the candlelight, turning it round and feeling it till it squalled loudly. Then he thrust a finger into its mouth, and when the infant began to suck lustily, the doctor was pleased and called out, 'How fine and healthy he is, the little Turk!' Sofya Nikolaevna was frightened when she saw her priceless treasure so freely handled; and the midwife tried to take it from him, fearing it would be 'overlooked'. But Klauss was inexorable: he ran about the room, holding the child, and called for a tub of warm water with a sponge and some soap, and a binder. Then he turned back his sleeves, tied on an apron, threw down his wig, and began to wash the babe, talking to it like this: 'Ah, my little Turk, that stops your crying; you like the feel of the warm water!'

Then Alexei Stepanich hurried into the room, almost beside himself with joy. He had been dispatching a special messenger to carry the good news to Stepan Mikhailovich, and writing letters to his parents; and there was a separate letter for his sister Aksinya, begging her to come as soon as possible and stand godmother to his son. Before the doctor had time to dry his hands, the happy father embraced him till he nearly choked him; he had already exchanged greetings with everyone in the house, and many tears of joy had been shed. And Sofya Nikolaevna—but what *she* felt, I dare not try to express in words: her bliss was such as few on earth ever feel and no one can feel for long.

The event produced extraordinary rejoicings within the house, and even the neighbours shared in it. The intoxication of joy was prolonged by liquor; and soon all the servants were singing and dancing in the court. Some who never drank at other times now took a drop too much; and one of these was Evseich. They found it impossible to control him: he was always begging to go to his mistress's bedroom to see the little son. At last his wife, with Parasha's help, tied him tightly to a heavy bench; and even then he went on kicking out his legs, cracking his fingers, and attempting to articulate the chorus of a song.

Tired out by his exertions and by joyful excitement, Klauss at last sat down in an armchair and much enjoyed a cup of tea. He was somewhat too liberal with the rum that evening, and felt a buzzing in his head after the third cup. So, after giving instructions that the baby was to have no milk but only syrup of rhubarb till the morning, he took leave of his happy host and hostess. He kissed the baby's hand, promised to call early the next morning, and went off to spend the night at his own house. As he passed through the court he saw the dancing, and the sound of singing came from every window of the kitchen and servants' quarter. He stood still; and though he was sorry to interfere with the good people's merriment, yet he advised them to stop their singing and dancing, because their mistress needed rest. To his surprise, they all took his hint and lay down at once, intending to sleep. As he passed out of the gate he muttered to himself: 'Well, he's a lucky child! How glad they all are to have him!'

And it is really true that this child was born under a happy star. His mother, who had suffered constantly before her former confinement, had perfect health before his birth; his parents lived in peace together during those halcyon days; a foster-mother was found for him who proved to be more devoted than most real mothers; he was the answer to prayers and the object of fond desires, and the joy over his coming into the world spread far beyond his parents. The very day of his birth, though the season was autumn, was warm as summer.

But what happened at Bagrovo, when the good news came that God had given a son and heir to Alexei Stepanich? This is what happened at Bagrovo. From the 15th of September, Stepan Mikhailovich counted the days and hours, and waited for the special messenger from Ufa. The man had been told to gallop day and night with relays of horses. This method of travelling was new, and Stepan Mikhailovich disapproved of it as a foolish waste of money and an unnecessary tax on the country people. He preferred to use his own horses; but the importance and solemnity of this occasion made him depart from his regular practice. Fortune did not keep him in suspense too long; on the 22nd of September, when he was sleeping after dinner, the messenger arrived, bearing letters and the good news. The old man woke from a sound sleep, and had hardly had time to stretch himself and clear his throat when Mazan rushed into the room and, stammering with joyful excitement, got out the words, 'A grandson, *batyushka* Stepan Mikhailovich! Hearty congratulations!'

The first movement of Stepan Mikhailovich was to cross himself. Then he sprang out of bed, went barefoot to his desk, snatched from it the family tree, took the pen from the ink-bottle, drew a line from the circle containing the name Alexei, traced a fresh circle at the end of the line, and wrote in the centre of the circle, 'SERGEI'.

Farewell, my figures, bright or dark, my people, good or bad—I should rather say, figures that have their bright and dark sides, and people who have both virtues and vices. You were not great heroes, not imposing personalities; you trod your path on earth in silence and obscurity, and it is long, very long, since you left it. But you were men and women, and your inward and outward life was not mere dull prose, but as interesting and instructive to us as we and our life in turn will be interesting and instructive to our descendants. You were actors in that mighty drama which mankind has played on this earth since time immemorial; you played your parts as conscientiously as others, and you deserve as well to be remembered. By the mighty power of the pen and of print, your descendants have now been made acquainted with you.* They have greeted you with sympathy and recognized you as brothers, whenever and however you lived, and whatever clothes you wore. May no harsh judgement and no flippant tongue ever wrong your memory!'

* This work first appeared in parts in a Moscow magazine. When they were collected in a book, this epilogue was added.

THE WORLD'S CLASSICS

DOSTOEVSKY: Crime and Punishment

Translated by Jessie Coulson, with an introduction by
John Jones

The first of the great novels of Dostoevsky's maturity is the
story of a murder committed on principle, of a killer who
wishes by his action to set himself outside and above
society. It is a work of fearful tension, physical and psychological, marked by the author's own harrowing experience
of interrogation and trial. Jessie Coulson's translation has
been described as 'the best in English, idiomatic and accu-
rate'; it preserves the character and spirit, the variety of
mood and the intellectual penetration of the original.

THE WORLD'S CLASSICS

HOMER: The Odyssey

A new translation by Walter Shewring

By its evocation of an heroic age, its contrasts of character and variety of adventure, above all by its sheer narrative power, *The Odyssey* has won and preserved its place among the greatest tales in the world. It recounts Odysseus' wanderings as he returns from the long war at Troy—the hazards he encounters, his visit to the underworld, and his arrival home, where he plots revenge on the insolent suitors who have for years besieged his wife, Penelope.

It is hard in any modern version of Homer to reconcile the easy flow of the story-telling with the poet's formal uncolloquial style. Walter Shewring's new attempt does this so successfully that it will surely be regarded as one of the few really outstanding translations of *The Odyssey*.

THE WORLDS' CLASSICS

ALEXANDER HERZEN

Childhood, Youth and Exile

Translated by J. D. Duff
With an introduction by Isaiah Berlin

Childhood, Youth and Exile comprises the first two parts of Herzen's autobiography, *My Past and Thoughts*, one of the greatest monuments of Russian literature, comparable to the major works of Tolstoy, Dostoevsky and Turgenev. Herzen begins with his nurse's account of Napoleon's occupation of Moscow in 1812. He tells of his solitary boyhood and his romantic friendship with his cousin Nick Ogarëv—how they stood together on the Sparrow Hills overlooking Moscow and swore to devote their lives to their struggle to better the lot of humanity. He goes to Moscow University, whose atmosphere at the time he captures exquisitely. He is sent to prison, and eventually into exile, for his socialist beliefs. His adventures in exile are extraordinarily vividly recounted, and indeed all stages of Herzen's story are studded with brilliant perceptiveness about himself and others and rich observation of detail.

'This autobiography is an amazing work of art; grand in the true sense of the word, and as noble a book as appeared in the 19th century . . . No man could have been more honest. He concealed nothing. His autobiography is ten times as truthful as Rousseau's . . .' Lord Lambton, *Spectator*

Also published by Oxford University Press

ALEXANDER HERZEN

From the Other Shore *and*
The Russian People and Socialism

With an introduction by Isaiah Berlin

Herzen wrote *From the Other Shore* as a memorial to his dis-
enchantment with the European revolutions of 1848 and
1849. It is a great polemical masterpiece, constituting his
profession of faith and his political testament. In *The Russian
People and Socialism* he expressed his Utopian hopes for the
communal organization of the uncorrupted Russian peasants. '*From the Other Shore* is a magnificent prose poem of
disillusionment, and Miss Moura Budberg's brilliant translation retains its passion and poetry . . . There is hardly a
page in this extraordinary book which does not stimulate
and excite. There is the additional pleasure of an introduction by Sir Isaiah Berlin, whose essays on 19th-century
Russia are the finest critical writing of this century . . . Now
that the Oxford University Press is producing these reason-
ably priced publications, our leading critics should escape
for once from their deep, worn ruts and encourage the
public to enjoy a writer, baffling, delightful, contradictory
whose brilliance will shine as long as books are read.' Lord
Lambton, *Spectator*

Oxford Paperbacks

A complete list of Oxford Paperbacks, including books in
The World's Classics, Past Masters, and OPUS series,
can be obtained from the General Publicity Department,
Oxford University Press, Walton Street, Oxford OX2 6DP.

A complete list of Oxford Paperbacks, including books in the World's Classics, Past Masters, and OPUS series, can be obtained from the General Publicity Department, Oxford University Press (JMB), Walton Street, Oxford OX2 6DP.